**Also available from Layla Reyne
and Carina Press
in the Agents Irish and Whiskey series**

Suggested reading order

*Single Malt
Cask Strength
Barrel Proof
Tequila Sunrise*

**Coming soon from Layla Reyne and Carina Press
in the Trouble Brewing series**

*Craft Brew
Noble Hops*

Also available from Layla Reyne

*Blended Whiskey
Relay
Medley*

To the federal agents and public servants
who dedicate their lives to keeping us safe

IMPERIAL STOUT

———

LAYLA REYNE

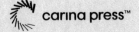
carina press™

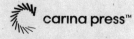
carina press™

ISBN-13: 978-1-335-08010-3

Recycling programs
for this product may
not exist in your area.

Imperial Stout

IMPERIAL
STOUT

Chapter One

One kiss.

One drunken, ill-advised kiss was going to ruin this entire fucking operation.

Because Nic was two seconds away from charging out of the surveillance van and telling the man he'd kissed to stand the fuck down. Nic's reputation as the calm, cool prosecutor would be shattered. Never mind that doing so would likely kill any chance of a second kiss. A second one would be even more ill-advised than the first. Didn't mean he wanted it any less.

He also didn't want Agent Cameron Byrne to die.

And if Nic's reputation went up in flames to save the Assistant Special Agent in Charge, then so be it. It was all going to hell these days anyway. Botching a takedown of one of the most wanted heist crews in operation would be icing on the cake.

But at least Cam would be alive.

Inside the surveillance van, Nic ripped off his suit coat, rolled up his shirtsleeves, and had his hand over his sidearm, ready to draw and move, when static crackled from the speakers in the wall of monitors.

Cam's Boston brogue followed. "Alpha team on the move."

Too late.

Fuck.

"Copy that, ASAC," replied Agent Lauren Hall, who was running Comm from inside the van with him. "Beta, Charlie, report."

"Beta team in position."

"Charlie team in position."

Beta team was on the roof of the luxury apartment building, right above the target penthouse, while Charlie team was a floor below. Cam and his assault team, kitted out in tactical gear, were moving up the interior stairwell, the camera attached to Cam's helmet giving Nic and Lauren a bird's-eye view of their ascent.

Nic should be with them, should be leading them. An ex-SEAL, he had the training, even if he had spent the past fifteen years in a courtroom. Not to mention this was his case—a joint task force between his US Attorney's office and the FBI's San Francisco field office. But Cam had pulled rank and sidelined him.

"Enough, Dominic!" Cam had shouted sometime around the tenth or so round of their argument over who would take lead. "I catch the criminals; you lock 'em up. End of fucking story." Technically, Cam had been right.

Didn't make Nic's suddenly parched mouth any easier to tolerate right now.

"Alpha team in position," Cam reported, voice quieter as they stood by the stairwell door outside the penthouse apartment.

"Alpha, Comm," Beta radioed. "Movement to the south."

"Hostiles?" Cam barked back.

Nic scanned the monitors. Where the fuck had they come from? The entire two-block radius around the building had been cordoned off and all the surrounding Financial District buildings cleared. Relatively painlessly at the ass-crack-of-dawn on a Saturday morning, this area of downtown San Francisco predominately offices. Had the feds missed something or someone on their checks?

Typing fast and furious, Lauren tapped into a security feed on the opposite side of the apartment building. One of the wall monitors flickered, changing its vantage point. She glanced up from her laptop, relaying, "Two masked individuals carrying assault rifles."

The dryness crept down Nic's throat, memories of heat and sand and blood at the edge of his consciousness. Always associated with combat, always there when he was worried, and right now, with new armed players on the scene, his worry for Cam and the teams was magnified.

"Approaching south stairwell," Lauren said. "Ninety seconds until they reach your position, Alpha."

"Part of the crew?" Cam said.

Nic swallowed, forcing saliva into his mouth, uttering a single word. "No."

He'd investigated this crew for over a year. He knew every detail of every member—height, build, weapon of choice, how they moved—and these two were no one he'd studied. "Third-party rip-off," he surmised.

"Charlie team, move to intercept," Cam ordered. "Alpha team moving on primary. Priority one, victim rescue. Two, secure the target. Three, apprehend suspects."

The target was a portable voice-activated safe containing priceless Serbian artifacts for a museum exhibit next weekend: millions in jewels, historical texts and sheet music, and textiles that had been rescued from war-torn Kosovo two decades ago. The victims were a Serbian dignitary and his wife whose voices were required to open said safe. They'd only just arrived in town last night, the artifacts and their safe not yet moved to the museum's secure cage.

"Suspect Monroe is not to be harmed," Nic reminded him. Abigail Monroe was their confidential informant inside the crew.

"Roger that," Cam replied. "On my count…"

Cam got as far as "two" before a hail of gunfire erupted.

Everywhere.

Inside the target apartment, on the floor below, and outside the surveillance van. Shots pinged the metal grill and raced up the hood toward the windshield.

And inside Nic, fear and worry exploded—heat everywhere—before his military training kicked in and his emotions morphed into action. He was fine, he wasn't in the desert, he'd been trained in urban combat, and fuck it, he needed to protect his position. Once that was done, he'd help Cam whether the bullheaded ASAC wanted him to or not.

"Go, go, go!" Cam shouted, dispensing with quiet.

In Nic's ear, heavy boots pounded up metal stairs, doors slammed open, and gunfire continued to pop, shattering what sounded like wood and glass. Nic's balance wavered, whether from the strangled shouts in his ear, from a similar clenching of his chest, or from the sway of the van under assault, he couldn't say.

Lauren's shout of "Comm under fire!" snapped him out of it.

And back to the on-monitor view from Cam's helmet cam, which abruptly wobbled, the agent's step faltering.

"Boston, go!" Nic yelled. "I got this."

"Beta, secure Comm. Charlie, intercept third party, back up Alpha. Go!" Cam said, before charging out of the stairwell with his team.

Nic tore his gaze from Cam's screen and focused on the others, searching for the shooter who'd paused firing on the van. "Sweep the area," he told Lauren, as he mentally rewound and counted the previous shots. He needed to know how long the next barrage would go on before he could make a move.

Her glittery nails flew across the keyboard, new angles and views of the surrounding Financial District blocks appearing on the monitors.

A bright glare on one screen nearly blinded him.

"Stop, there!"

Early morning sunlight bounced off glass—a sniper's scope—on the second story of the under-construction building across the street.

Nic reached for his sidearm, then thinking better of it, grabbed a rifle and scope out of the van's cage. Darting to the front, he crouched between the seats, behind the dash, as bullets slammed again into the windshield. Cracks snaked across the outside but the reinforced glass continued to hold. Assured of its strength, Nic lifted his head and peered through the scope, spying the shooter's nest. "Lauren!" he shouted back into the van, as he attached the scope to the rifle. "Tell Beta team to lay down cover."

Lauren relayed the order, and suppressive fire sprayed from the roof of the apartment building. Nic shoved open the driver-side door and rolled out of the van, using the door as a shield. Shots pinged the outside while Beta team's answering fire whizzed overhead. He counted the sniper's shots as he lowered the window.

Reload in three, two, one… Another break in the fire.

Fist raised, he signaled Beta team to hold and rose, bracing his rifle on the window ledge and lining up his shot. At the first glimmer of sunlight on the shooter's scope, Nic fired, unleashing a full mag into the nest.

Weapon emptied, he crouched behind the door and waited. No return fire came.

"You're clear," Lauren confirmed after several seconds. "No sign of movement."

Standing, Nic tossed the rifle on the driver's seat and drew his pistol. "I'm going after the shooter."

He was halfway across the street when "Alpha team. Agent down! Civilian down!" echoed through the van's open window. "Radio for EMS!"

Cam.

Nic's already racing heart sped with another burst of fear-soaked adrenaline. He hung a U-turn and sprinted for the apartment building.

"Get someone in that other building," he shouted to Lauren, as he passed the van. Inside the building, he yanked open the stairwell door and took the steps three at a time, racing toward Cam and the scene. Weapon at the ready, he exited onto the penthouse hallway.

To eerie quiet. No gunfire. No shouts. Until an anguished cry broke the silence.

Nic ran the last few feet to the target apartment, heart in his bone-dry throat, and skidded inside across the slick marble foyer. The place looked like a disaster area. Sunlight reflected off broken glass, splintered furniture littered the space, and blood stained the walls and floor.

Nic half scrambled, half tip-toed around the cavernous apartment, seeking the source of the blood while trying not to destroy evidence, heart climbing his throat with each step. Past the foyer, he saw the crew's ringleader handcuffed to the dining bar's footrest, and next to him, similarly restrained, their breaking-and-entering special-ist. The former's right arm was covered in blood, but the graze on his outer shoulder didn't look life-threatening.

Groaning to Nic's right drew him into the living room. On the other side of the couch, an agent knelt over another, treating a leg wound. They hadn't removed their helmets, but Nic could tell neither was Cam. They were thin and lanky, not the broad build of the former baller.

Was this the agent down? Or was Cam down some-where too?

"Where's—"

"Here, Price."

Nic's eyes shot up, connecting with Cam's black ones across the room. Helmet off, dark hair ruffled, Cam looked fine, if tousled from a fight. A quick up and down of his person revealed no obvious injuries.

"Boston," Nic breathed on a grateful sigh. "You okay?"

Cam nodded and Nic wanted nothing more than to close the distance between them, to claim that second kiss, to wet his worry-parched mouth with Cam's lips and breath. The epitome of stupid and unprofessional. His haywire instincts were derailed by another agonized cry like the one he'd heard from the hallway. Grim, Cam tilted his head toward the room behind him. "You bet-ter come see this."

Civilian down, Nic recalled, dread racing up his spine. Was it Abby?

Following Cam into the room, Nic was relieved to see Abby kneeling on the bed, her springy dyed curls unmistakable, bouncing in the breeze from the open window. Relief, however, died a quick death as she shifted back onto her haunches.

Abby's hands were covered in blood, but they were nowhere near as coated as the Serbian dignitary's, pressed to his wife's chest, fighting a losing battle against the life draining out of her.

Hours later, Cam stood outside a sleeping Stefan Kristić's hospital room, watching through the door's narrow window as a nurse tended to his IVs. After they'd told him his wife had died, the inconsolable husband had had to be sedated and his ruptured stitches resewn. Kristić had been shot in the shoulder—a through-and-through, not a fatal chest wound like his wife's—but painful nonetheless.

"He sure did make a mess of things," the nurse muttered, as she stepped into the hallway, closing the door behind her.

"He'll be okay, though?" Cam asked.

"As well as can be expected," she said with grim sympathy for the man in the bed, and for a beleaguered Cam.

He tried to put on a smile, figuring she'd had enough bleakness for one day. "You got a soda machine around these parts?"

The smile, or his accent, must have been convincing enough, drawing a small grin from her. "Soda *and* snacks." She snaked an arm through his and tugged him down the hall. "Follow me, handsome."

His own gray mood unfortunately returned as he stared at the little red lights on the vending machine.

Thank God Nurse Adams, who'd slipped him her number, had been called away before his horror at the prices registered. After eight months in the Bay Area, he shouldn't be surprised—everything cost a fucking fortune here—but two-fifty for a can of soda? Resigned, and in desperate need of caffeine, he pulled his wallet out of his back pocket. A lonely dollar was all that greeted him. The horrors today just kept mounting.

Though Cam only had himself to blame for the earlier one.

What was supposed to have been a straightforward takedown had turned into a bloodbath. He'd had three teams in position, all his best agents, and the tip had been solid. Scott Chestnut's crew had moved on the artifacts. What Cam hadn't foreseen was one of Scott's crew turning on him, his second-in-command, Rebecca Wright, who it appeared was working with the third party who'd tried to rip off the heist. The artifacts hadn't been stolen, and all but one of their primary suspects were in custody, but things had gone sideways as fuck in the process.

Maybe he should have let Nic lead. The ex-SEAL was certainly capable, even if an Assistant US Attorney leading an FBI team into a raid wasn't exactly protocol. But if that had been Nic in the middle of the firefight…

Cam banished the thought, only to hear Lauren's voice in his head, shouting that Comm was under fire. At the pop of rifle fire hitting metal and glass, he'd faltered a split second, feeling disconnected, helpless and overcome with worry for Nic. Was that when Stefan or Anica Kristić had been shot? Or his agent? Had someone taken a bullet because he was distracted? He'd made that mistake before, getting distracted by what he wanted, and someone's life had been stolen in the process.

Someone dear to him.

Wallet still in hand, he withdrew the laminated library card he always carried, running a thumb over a name that wasn't his. The card had been faded and wrinkled decades ago—well-used—and if not for the effort to preserve it, he wouldn't have this reminder of what—*who*—had been lost, when he'd been young and distracted.

This was why he had rules.

This was also why you weren't supposed to get involved with colleagues. Granted, it had worked out for his best friend, but Jamie and Aidan were no longer colleagues.

Not that he and Nic technically were either—colleagues or involved. They worked for separate agencies and one kiss did not a relationship make, even if they had been dancing around an attraction to each other for months.

An attraction that had boiled over in that one kiss…

Slipping the card back in his wallet and pocketing the leather billfold, Cam slumped against the wall and closed his eyes, recalling the icy hot glare of Nic's blue ones from across a hotel elevator. Returning to their rooms after Jamie and Aidan's wedding, he and Nic had been arguing when Cam's beer-and-whiskey-addled brain decided the best way to win the argument and shut the other man up was to put his mouth to better use.

Two strides across the elevator cab and he'd shoved Nic against the mirrored wall, grabbing his sharp, angular jaw and slamming their mouths together. Never one to back down, the prosecutor had argued back, as was their way, but with his tongue instead of words. Forcing his way into Cam's mouth, he'd taken control of the kiss and owned it. Owned him. Seconds later, when Nic had pushed him out of the elevator onto his floor, Cam had been an aching, turned-on mess.

Neither had spoken of the kiss in the two weeks since. Nic probably thought he didn't remember it; there had been hours of beer and whiskey shots and dueling pianos preceding it. Nic sure as fuck remembered it, though. His pale blues strayed to Cam's mouth more often, he stood just that bit closer whenever they were in the same room, and he argued with him more hotly, like he wanted, consciously or not, to incite another explosive reaction.

Another kiss.

Cam never corrected Nic's assumption, nor did he rise to the bait again, intentionally laid or not. Between his new role as San Francisco ASAC, and his new two-fifty-a-soda life in the Bay Area, which his government salary did not cover, his plate was already full of complications. And there was also the matter of Nic having once dated Aidan Talley, who was both Cam's new partner and his best friend's new husband. All signs pointed to danger.

So of course his fucking dick wanted to run right to it. He'd had those impulses, that other side of himself, under control. Work hard, play hard, but not like the punk kid who'd sacrificed something precious for what he'd wanted, or the hotshot college athlete who'd fucked his way through every fraternity and sorority at Boston College, still wild and desperate to blot out the past. Before he'd found the FBI and atonement avenue. Now, he worked hard as a kidnap specialist, rescuing himself and others in trouble, and limited his play to the occasional man or woman in his bed. That was how he stayed focused at work, how he avoided distractions that ended in tragedy.

Then into his life walked Dominic Price, and Cam wanted to throw all his rules out the window.

And look what that distraction might have cost them today.

Groaning, Cam scrubbed his hands over his face, trying to block out the sight of Kristić in his hospital bed and the memory of his wife bleeding out, only to have the object of his distraction appear in the vending room doorway. Nic stood over the threshold, all six foot plus of him looking cool, calm, and perfectly suited, not a brown or gray hair on his head out of place, despite the rough-and-tumble morning.

No, no thinking of *rough*.

And definitely no thoughts of *tumbling*.

"Bowers is here," Nic said. "In the waiting area."

Cam's thoughts instantly righted. "Fuck. I thought he'd at least wait 'til we got back to the Federal Building."

Nic shook his head. "We interrupted his day on the greens. He came straight here from the club." Nic's asshole boss was going to be extra salty. "I can deal with him myself," Nic offered.

"No." Cam pushed off the wall. "This is a joint op."

"And your charm seems to have worn off, where my boss is concerned."

"He likes you any better?"

Cam wondered if San Francisco's US Attorney had always been chilly toward his best AUSA or if he'd only become frigid in recent months, as Nic's ties to the FBI grew stronger. Both agencies were under the Department of Justice, often working side by side, but Bowers liked to think he was top dog. Since taking the helm as Special Agent in Charge, Aidan had disabused Bowers of his top-dog notion, frequently. And Cam, who Bowers used to like, had taken his partner and friend's back. As had Nic. Their names had since skyrocketed up Bowers's shit list, which Cam didn't doubt was long.

"Conceded," Nic said, holding an arm out toward the hallway.

Cam strode past, ignoring the other man's tempting body heat. "Why is he all over our ass on this one?" Even given their shit-list perch, this was more oversight than usual.

"High-profile, Aidan's gone, hoping DOJ doesn't re-appoint him. Take your pick."

"Lot to pick from," he said, as they made their way down the hallway to the waiting area. "How do you want to play this?"

"Like any other debrief. We did nothing wrong."

"Tell that to Stefan Kristić."

Nic paused midstride and turned directly to him, blocking Cam's path. "You ran a clean op. We had no indication of other parties on the scene." His conviction was fierce, and Cam appreciated the support, especially as Nic had wanted to run the operation himself.

"We should have checked the surrounding areas more closely," Cam said. "Or dug deeper into Becca's background."

"One, the third parties came up through the BART tunnels after we'd cleared the area. Two, all we've done for months is dig into background. There was no indication Becca had turned against Scott. You know that as well as I do."

Cam cast his gaze aside, rubbing a hand over his rough jaw, long past shave time. "We must have missed something."

Nic's hand at his elbow, gently tugging it down, startled him out of his self-recrimination. "We didn't miss anything," he said, voice soft, comforting, like his thumb caressing the inside of Cam's elbow was probably supposed to be. And it was. But it was more too, and Cam's body reacted, rampaging pulse doing its best to pump all his blood south.

"Price! Byrne! In here now!"

Nic's eyes flashed—equal parts desire and fury—before he snatched his hand away and turned, putting himself between Cam and Bowers. "On our way," he returned. Cool, calm, all trace of fire gone, he'd tucked it away behind that smooth professional mask.

Cam marveled at the skill, so much more refined than his own, while also appreciating the extra time to compose himself. Rolling down his shirtsleeves, he buttoned the cuffs and caught up to Nic outside the waiting room. They entered together, a united front.

"Where's Talley?" Bowers barked, beady eyes staring them down.

"On his honeymoon," Cam said, telling Bowers what he already knew. Aidan's out-of-office days had been on all their calendars for months.

"He should have come back for this," Bowers said. "Or you should have waited."

"And how would that've worked?" Cam replied, irritation bleeding through his thinning patience. "Were we supposed to call up Scott and tell him it wasn't a good day for the feds to bust his crew? I guarantee the heist would have happened in that case."

Bowers's round face reddened. "Maybe no one would have died."

"On the contrary," Nic said, "more than one person

would have probably died if Cam's team hadn't intervened."

"Some consolation," Bowers huffed. "I've got a dead dignitary's wife on my hands and the Serbian consulate and DOJ breathing down my neck."

Cam's bravado waned, reminded of Anica Kristić bleeding out as her husband tried to stem the flow, and of Stefan Kristić, thrashing in his hospital bed when the doctors told him his efforts had been in vain.

"You can tell the Serbian consulate we have the parties responsible in custody."

"Not all of them," Bowers said. "Rebecca Wright's still out there."

"I'm on my way to question Abby next," Nic said. "We'll find Becca."

"*And* who she's working for. DOJ wants this operation, all the way up the ladder, shut down for good."

Cam bristled at being told again what he already knew, especially when he and Nic had put in far more hours than Bowers had on this case.

He held his tongue, though, until Bowers disappeared into the elevator at the end of the hall. "I hate that fucker."

"Not half as much as I do," Nic answered through gritted teeth.

Cam sensed there was more there, but now wasn't the time to press. "I need to get to the office. See what the team's got on the other shooters."

"And I need to talk to Abby."

"I want to be there for that." Cam wanted to know how their CI hadn't had a clue her girlfriend was about to turn on the crew.

Nic, however, shook his head. "She's better one-on-

one. Let me talk to her first, then you can question her tomorrow."

Cam didn't like it, but she was technically Nic's CI, his play. And the prosecutor did seem to trust her. "All right," Cam said. "Debrief first thing tomorrow?"

Nic nodded, turning toward the exit, already onto the next task, just as Cam had suggested, but Cam wasn't ready to let him go, yet. He shot out a hand, grabbing the other man's biceps. "I'll catch the rest of 'em," he said, finding the words he should have said to Bowers.

"And I'll prosecute them." Bitterness belied Nic's words.

Cam slid his hand down to Nic's elbow, mimicking the earlier touch through the superfine wool of the dapper prosecutor's suit coat. "I'm sorry about the way this turned out today, for Kristić, his wife, my agents, but I'm not sorry I took the lead. And I'm not sorry you were in the van."

"I still got shot at."

"By one shooter. You weren't in the middle of the firefight."

Nic pressed his lips together, like he was measuring his words, eventually settling on "I could have helped. Maybe saved—"

Cam tightened his hold, fingers digging into sinewy muscle through layers of fabric. "You could have maybe died. I'm not risking that, Price. I'm not risking you."

Chapter Two

Hands clasped behind his back, Nic stood in his war room, ignoring the long conference table littered with legal pads and file folders, and stared at their suspect board instead. His and Aidan's scribbled notes covered half the whiteboard—timelines, bank accounts, travel itineraries. On the other half, they'd hung suspect photos in pecking order.

Scott was at the top. Directly below him, Becca, his second-in-command, who'd turned on him and escaped with the rip-off crew. On the next line down, below Becca, was the crew's "talent." Mike, the B&E guy, who was also keeping mum in a cell, and Abby, Nic's confidential informant and now star witness.

As Becca's girlfriend, and the key to the operation, she'd had a front row seat to everything. And a little sister she was trying to protect. That had been what led Abby to the courthouse to find Nic, sent to him by another contact he'd worked a deal for. She'd been the break in the case they'd sorely needed.

Bowers apparently thought she was the key to today's mishap as well. "Why aren't you interrogating Monroe already?" he blustered from over the threshold.

Nic forced his lip not to curl. "Abby just got here from

holding an hour ago. It took some time for the legal paperwork to process on a Saturday. I checked on her. She's understandably upset, after this morning. I'll question her when she's calmed down and able to focus."

"She's not a witness, Price. She's a suspect. Take off the kid gloves."

Nic rubbed a hand over his mouth, trapping his retort.

"Maybe I should question her," Bowers said, misreading Nic's restraint as hesitation. "Maybe that scene today shook you up too."

It had, not that Nic would ever admit it to another soul, especially Bowers, and especially when Bowers was wrong about why the botched raid had thrown him for a loop. For fuck's sake, he was ex-Special Forces and a fifteen-year prosecutor, first with the JAG Corps and then the US Attorneys' Office. He'd unfortunately seen worse—more blood and guts and foul play in his lifetime than anyone should ever witness. Anica Kristić bleeding out, Becca turning on her crew, even the shots fired on the surveillance van, were not why his mouth had gone dry and his skin still felt like it'd baked in the desert sun. No, the source of Nic's earlier distress was now safe two floors above in the FBI's offices.

Thanks to that, the scene earlier today no longer affected him, and he'd have no trouble questioning Abby. His only trouble now was his goddamn boss. Bowers wanted him to go in there like a bulldog, which was Bowers's style, and it worked, most of the time. For Nic too, when he needed to go on the attack. But this wasn't that situation. Abby was his CI; he knew her and Bowers didn't. Bowers thought she was just another suspect, another lead to work, and that would be his primary focus with DOJ breathing down his neck. He didn't see Abby as a victim too. Blaming Abby and strong-arming her was not the best way to the answers Bowers wanted.

"We need this one, Price."

"Understand that, sir," Nic said. "Scott's in custody, as is their B&E guy. With Abby's testimony, Mike will flip and Scott will plead out too."

"And Rebecca Wright? The new crew she's working with?"

"No activity, according to the Bureau. We're aiming to extract possible locations, among other things, from Scott and Mike in exchange for pleas."

"We could use Kristić and those artifacts as bait. Or your CI."

Bulldog was one thing; bait another. No stopping Nic's lip curl this time. Do whatever and sacrifice whomever to make the case. There had to be a line, and he and Bowers disagreed frequently where that line was.

But at least he generally knew where it would land with Bowers. As ready as he was to be rid of Bowers, who would DOJ appoint next? It sure as fuck would never be him in the boss's chair, not that he wanted it. He had more flexibility and more court time as an AUSA, picking and trying cases, putting away criminals, versus admin bullshit and political ass-kissing. Besides, he'd ruffled too many feathers, had had too many lovers, and had too many skeletons in his and his family's closets to clear full-blown hearings. More than that, he was gay, very out about it, and that wouldn't fly with the current administration, even at a post in San Francisco. Maybe if he were bi, like Cam, he could pull it off, but he wasn't. He liked men, period. He'd never wavered, even when his sexual orientation had gotten him disowned.

"I don't think that's the right move, yet," Nic answered, a hedge without being in open rebellion. There'd been enough of that last year. He was lucky to still have his job, even if the chain of command had soured.

"Monroe thinks she's bait regardless," Bowers said. "Why not use her?"

"Doesn't mean she should be. Let's try the less dangerous route first. Avoid any more deaths, if we can help it. Abby will come around and give us what we need. She's just a little rattled still."

Bowers's glowering visage indicated he wanted to argue more, but he deferred, for now. "Fine. So long as you get her unrattled and ready for the arraignment."

"Working on it, sir."

Following his boss out, Nic closed the war room door behind them. At the elevator bank, Bowers boarded a cab down, probably back to finish his round of golf. Good, less chance of him interfering. Nic walked on across the main floor, empty on a Saturday afternoon, to the small conference rooms at the far end.

"How's she doing?" he asked Tony, the guard posted outside the room where Abby was waiting.

"Gave her the iPod with an audiobook on it, like you suggested." The big man smiled, shaking his head. "Peeked in a few times. Never seen anyone take notes like that except in class."

Nic opened the door and sure enough, Abby had both earbuds in, listening intently, while filling a yellow legal pad with barely legible script. Spotting him, she breathed out a relieved sigh, then held up a single finger, signaling him to wait.

He gestured for her to continue and slid into the chair across from her. With her free hand, she absently twirled a ringlet of hair around her finger, the purple streaks complementing her brown skin and olive eyes. A minute later, she paused the playback and popped out the earbuds, looking up at him.

"What'd you detect?" Nic asked.

"Narrator's from California. When she does the British accent, there's no underlying lilt or drawl, like the little extra twang when an American from Texas or the South tries to pull off the Queen's English."

"Can you mimic it?"

Tucking one earbud in her ear, she offered him the other and pressed Play. Nic only needed to listen for a second, a smile stretching across his face. "I know it well."

"Fantasy fan?"

"That, and I have a traffic-filled commute to work every day."

She grinned, tired but true, then started repeating the couple of sentences she'd played for him, the accent getting closer each try, until on the fourth, it was an exact replica of the narrator's put-on British.

And that was why Scott's crew needed her. A military brat who'd been dragged all over as a child, Abby had grown up to be a languages and accents savant who could speak and understand multiple languages and who could mimic nearly any accent, including Anica Kristić's unique Romani-Slavic dialect. He'd never heard anything like it, nor met anyone with Abby's skill.

"Nice work," he said with a smile.

She wrapped the cord for the earbuds around the device. "Thanks for this. It helped, a lot."

"Knew a guy in the Navy. He was younger so I wasn't in with him long, but he hummed aloud on flights and in his head when he lined up a shot. Centered him."

"That's exactly it." She relaxed back in the chair, iPod in her lap.

With Abby finally wound down, Nic approached the topic that had brought them here. "Tell me what happened today."

"There was so much blood." She wrung her hands, staring down at them as if they were still covered in blood. "That wasn't supposed to happen."

"Take it from the top. We'll get to where it went wrong."

She clasped her hands on the table, fingers laced to still their movement. "We were in the vacant condo across the hall. Where I'd called you from."

She'd called in the wee hours of the morning, once she'd had a second alone. They'd had less than an hour to clear the area and move into position. Cam's operation prep had been solid, ready to move at a second's notice.

"The portable safe was in the living room," Abby continued. "We were supposed to go in quiet and take the safe if we could. If we couldn't, Scott had been practicing the husband's part. I had the wife's down. They should have never heard us."

Cam's team had tried to warn the Kristićs, but there'd been no answer to their calls, texts, or emails, and they couldn't approach to warn in person without tipping off Scott's crew. It'd been a calculated risk—based on Abby's intel that the op would go down quiet, as she described. Cam's team would be waiting to pounce in the hallway, once they'd exited.

Except gunfire had erupted inside the apartment first. "Someone did hear?" Nic asked.

"The husband opened the bedroom door, and Becca..." Abby closed her eyes, face turned away. She started again after another hard swallow. "Becca shot him, Scott shouted, and the next thing I knew, they were shooting at each other."

"The gunfight that drew the tactical team?"

Abby nodded. "They stormed in, after Scott and Mike first, and Becca rushed us into the bedroom."

"That's when she shot Anica?"

"She was distraught, screaming after her husband. Becca shot her point blank." Abby's voice quieted to a whisper. "I couldn't believe what I was seeing. She's threatened before, but never…"

"How'd you get loose? How'd Becca get out?"

"She ran to the window. Said the cops were shooting at something across the street instead and that we could jump to the balcony below. Some guys would meet us there."

Nic hung his head. They'd been covering him and Lauren in the van. He'd drawn Beta team off the exterior, and Charlie team off the third floor and the rip-off crew. "She went out through the window?"

Abby nodded again. "I'm terrified of heights; she knows that. Cops were closing in, so she left me helping the wife. Made me promise not to cooperate, or she'd…" Abby lost her words again, and Nic understood why.

"She threatened to hurt your sister?"

"Yeah." Abby reached for the iPod again, unwinding the earbud cord and weaving it through her fingers, a nervous tic not limited to her hair. "She said she'd come for me. She's not gonna let me or the job go."

"She's down you, Mike, and her ringleader."

Abby laughed, short and harsh. "You thought Scott was the leader?"

"We traced the payoff funds to his accounts."

"Becca let him front as the lead, to protect her own ass, but she called the shots. As for Mike, B&E guys are a dime a dozen. She's probably already found a replacement and muscle to replace Scott."

Maybe the two rip-off guys who'd helped her escape.

"Why didn't you tell us Becca was the real lead?" Nic asked.

She shrugged, eyes downcast. "I hardly knew you. If *you* turned on me, all I had left was her. And she's the one holding a felony over my little sister's head."

Nic couldn't trust Abby completely, especially after she'd held back this crucial information, but he understood why she'd done it. Yes, Abby was a criminal—he had no delusions there—but from everything he'd seen and heard since Abby had sought him out, including today, she'd gotten into this for love, not for the money or to harm anyone, and now she was stuck, a victim of Becca's emotional manipulation. And actual blackmail.

"All that's left is for her to come for me," Abby said, fear making her voice tremble. "Then she'll make another run at the artifacts."

"Which are now locked up tight in the museum's vault."

Abby tapped the iPod on the table, the repetitive *knock-knock-knock* loud in the otherwise quiet room. "Nothing is as secure as you think."

Nic reached across table, stilling her hand. "We've got eyes on your sister, and we've got a safe house ready for you."

Sliding her hand out from under his, she patted the back of his as if he were an idiot. "Which I guarantee she'll case. The courthouse too."

"You think she'll make a move there?"

She gave him a "duh" face, and Nic conceded the point. Abby was invaluable, not just for this job but for others too, as voice recognition technology continued to grow in popularity for high-end safes.

He drummed his thumbs on the table, contemplating alternatives. "I can't move the arraignment from the courthouse, but I can talk to the clerk about keeping the exact time and courtroom under wraps. We'll change it at the last minute, where we're holding you too, if we need to. Throw her off a bit."

"And the safe house?"

"We'll move you each night. I'll also coordinate with the feds to add more guards to Tony's protection team."

Abby lifted the iPod. "Could use some more audiobooks too. Good distraction."

"I think we can arrange that."

Worries seemingly allayed, Abby braced her forearms on the table and tilted toward him, flashing her cleavage. "You single, Attorney Price?"

"Yes, but this—" he gestured between them "—would be a clear violation of attorney ethics rules."

She flapped a hand like she was swatting a fly. "Rules."

"You're also not my type."

She twirled an errant ringlet of her hair again. "Blondes instead?"

He leaned forward and lowered his voice, like he was about to tell her a secret. Building a sense of trust with his witness. "Men instead."

Her eyes rounded and her mouth dropped open in a silent *Oh*.

He laughed out loud as he pushed to his feet.

"That's cool," she said, recovering. "Good for you."

"Good for you too. I'm a terrible boyfriend."

She reclined back in her chair, tucking an earbud back in her ear. "I don't believe that for a second."

He didn't correct her, choosing instead to be amused at the end of this long, terrible day. He was still grinning when he walked back into his war room and found Lauren at the head of the table, face hidden behind her laptop screen, long brown hair escaping from the wobbly pencil bun atop her head. His smile grew wider, then died when she glanced up, blue eyes filled with worry.

His earlier distress came roaring back, mouth dry and skin on fire. He almost voiced it, almost asked *where's Cam*, then caught himself, correcting and asking more vaguely, "What's wrong?" and praying the answer didn't involve the ASAC.

"The shooter who targeted the van," Lauren said, "I don't think he was with either crew."

"What do you mean?"

"He left behind this phone." She disconnected the generic burner model from her laptop. "I cracked it."

Nic eyed the device like it was poisonous. Ridiculous— it was just a piece of handheld electronics—but judging by Lauren's wariness, his caution was warranted. "What's on it?"

She held the phone out to him. "It's wiped clean, except for these."

He slid it from her hand and stared at the picture on the screen.

Of him.

He swiped his thumb left, across the screen. Again and again.

More pictures, of him.

At the Federal Building. At the UN Plaza food trucks. At the gym where he worked out.

Lauren closed her laptop, the click loud like the gun-shots that had hit their van earlier today. That had been aimed at him. "You were the target."

Chapter Three

Nic swung his truck into a parking spot near the front entrance of Gravity Craft Brewery. Five years ago, when his friend and SEAL teammate Eddie Vasquez transferred out of the Navy to the local Coast Guard unit, they'd tapped their savings, bought a couple old warehouse buildings in Redwood City, and opened the microbrewery they'd dreamed about while stuck in the desert together. It wasn't easy, working the equivalent of two full-time jobs, but Nic wouldn't have his other job forever. The writing was on the wall at the US Attorneys' Office. He didn't want it forever either, or a similar job in private practice. As much as he loved the courtroom, he'd started to itch for a different challenge. In Gravity, he was building something with his teammate and friend, a future they could call their own. Every hour Nic spent at the brewery, even the hours doing paperwork as Gravity's business manager, were worth it. For perhaps the first time since he'd stepped into the Navy enlistment office the day after high school graduation, Nic felt like he was taking control of his destiny again.

On his way to the door, he peered between the brewery buildings to the back lot where tonight's band and food trucks were shutting down. The music and variety of food options, together with the hanging lights and electrical spools-turned-tables and barrels-turned-stools, created a festive atmosphere that drew a steady crowd on weekends when they were open to the public. One of Eddie's more brilliant ideas.

He keyed in his access code, the electronic lock switching from red to green, just as the hanging lights over the back lot darkened, leaving only the sodium lights glowing in the main lot behind him. Slipping inside, Nic waited for the lock to reengage, then followed the wail of nineties grunge toward the expansive tasting area.

"Yo!" Eddie called from behind the bar.

Par for the course, Eddie's black brewery tee was about to bust at the seams, the falling-apricot logo on the short sleeve peeling and cracking with each swipe he made over the bar top. Eddie's shirts had always been two sizes too small. Just like his gravity-defying pompadour of jet black hair had rarely deflated since he'd grown it back out.

Nic grabbed another bar towel and began wiping down the stools and pub tables around the tasting room. "Good crowd tonight?"

"Packed. Only a couple cases left of the Imperial Stout, and the public stock of IPA is selling fast too. Few more weeks, at most."

More than half their award-winning IPA had already been committed to restaurants. The fast-moving other half was a good sign. "You brew a mean beer," Nic said with a nod to his brewmaster.

"Damn right I do." Eddie grinned, fist out for a bump. Nic returned it—top, bottom, then knuckles. "Didn't think you'd make it in tonight."

"Work thing," Nic replied.

Eddie shot him a disapproving glare, and Nic shot him one back, plus the middle finger. Eddie was the last person to give him shit for working too much. Gravity aside, Eddie's Coast Guard hours, while more predictable than other service branches, were far from nine-to-five.

"Went tits-up?" Eddie asked.

"That's being generous."

Whistling low, Eddie drew a pint of pilsner off the tap and passed it across the bar. "Guessin' you need this, then."

"No question there."

As if the shoot-out, asshole boss, fretting CI, and apparent attempt on his life hadn't been enough, Nic had spent hours filling out paperwork for rotating safe houses and rousing court clerks about rotating courtrooms. By the time he'd left the office, once Tony radioed in that Abby was secure in tonight's location, he'd angered more than just Bowers.

Taking a long draw of his favorite brew, Nic forgot about all that shit for a few heavenly seconds. With a higher malt concentration than other pilsners, Gravity's Alto Pils was less sweet and more spicy, "a stand-out in its class" according to *Beer Advocate*. He took another swallow, savoring, before his happy sigh turned weary.

"And I've still got another call with the feds." He needed to touch base with Cam and see if he'd gotten anywhere with Scott or Mike. He also needed to find out if Lauren had said anything to Cam about the shooter. Nic had sworn her to secrecy, but technically her duty was to the FBI, not him. He should have called Cam on the drive down from the City but he'd taken the rare, traffic-free forty-five minutes for himself, enjoying the relative silence after an otherwise very loud day.

Eddie yanked Nic's bunched-up bar towel out from under his fisted hand. "I stand by my earlier glare. You work too much."

"Whatever you say, Pot."

Chuckling, Eddie ran the towels over the bar once more, then tossed them into the laundry basket beneath the back bar. "Speaking of, I'm due at Alameda at oh-five-hundred."

"Then what the fuck are you still doing here?"

He stretched out a hand to Nic, as if for a handshake. "Hi, Kettle, I'm Pot, nice to meet you," he said with a brown-eyed wink.

Nic swatted his meaty paw away, laughing. "You know how long?"

"Captain thinks a couple weeks."

Probably a drug interdiction matter then—chasing illegal drug vessels around the Pacific—which meant it'd land on Nic's desk eventually. "I'll check the schedules. Make sure we're covered here, since I won't be around much either. Trial."

"Already done. Ang and Steph will hold down the fort." They'd lucked out in the staff lottery, finding not one, but two, UC Davis grads who were talented apprentice brewers and competent assistant managers.

"Good deal." Nic finished off his beer and handed the pint glass to Eddie, who rinsed and put it in the dishwasher.

"Owe the team a couple of cases." Eddie stepped out from behind the bar. "Help me load 'em?"

"Sure thing." Nic shrugged out of his coat and tie, pushed up his shirtsleeves, and followed Eddie into the warehouse. They carried two cases of Belmont Red Ale out to Eddie's sand-crusted Wrangler, surfboards still stacked on top. Nic liked the coast all right—had spent plenty of time there as a kid—and Eddie's place in Half Moon Bay was great. As nice as it was though, Nic could never live there. Not in a place where sand in his shoes was a daily occurrence. Not again.

Eddie slammed the trunk door shut, snapping Nic out of his thoughts. "How much longer you gonna be?" he asked.

"Need to make that call, then I'll be on my way." Nic followed him to the driver side, waited for Eddie to climb in, then held out his fist. "Don't run to your death."

Eddie bumped back. "Hooyah."

Once Eddie's taillights cleared the lot, Nic started back to the main building, pausing halfway when his phone vibrated.

Unknown lit up the screen.

"Nic Price," he answered.

Silence greeted him.

"Hello, is anyone there?"

Still nothing.

"Who is this?"

A male voice answered, but not from the phone. "I'd be more worried about who's here than who's on the phone," he said from behind Nic.

One look over his shoulder and Nic spied a shiny-suited man rushing toward him. The big guy wrapped his arms around him from behind, and though he'd gotten the jump on him, Nic thought someone was a fool for not telling this idiot who he was up against. Even without the Ka-Bar and Beretta he'd left in his truck, Nic could take this guy.

Or maybe someone had warned the goon, because a second one came barreling out of the back lot, pistol aimed at Nic. "I'd stay still if I were you."

"Why don't you stay still for me?" Nic replied.

Using the big man behind him as a support post, Nic crossed his arms, grabbed the stranger's biceps, and curled up with his abs, lifting his legs off the ground. One swift scissor kick and Goon Two's weapon was gone. Another swift kick to Goon Two's blond head, and he hit the pavement. One threat neutralized, Nic swung his legs down with as much force as he could muster and used his momentum to flip Goon One over his back, laying him flat out next to his partner. Nic plucked his sidearm free in the process, so by the time the two idiots staggered up, Nic had a pistol leveled on each.

The Silicon Valley version of "muscle," their trainer-honed physiques were decked out in designer suits and Italian loafers, capped off with three-figure haircuts. They looked like TV G-Men, not real-life enforcers, but the weapons in Nic's hands were very real and very high-powered. Jacked as they were, the handguns were also highly illegal.

"Gentlemen." Nic widened his stance. "You want to tell me who sent you here?"

The dark-haired one tried to skirt around Nic to the door. "Your father give you the money for this place?"

Nic blocked him. "Not a single goddamn dime."

"If he did——" Goon One talked over him "——we'd have to take our cut. Your father's debts are growing by the day."

Nic schooled his features, more to hide his anger than any sort of surprise. He'd heard the rumors float-ing around. His father, Curtis Price, was selling off his real estate holdings. Most speculated he was cashing out, old age and a booming real estate market hastening the sell-off. Nic knew better. One, cashing out for what? Curtis sure as shit wasn't putting the money away for him. And two, his father never gave up control of anything, unless he was forced to. Now whatever upside-down deal he'd made was blowing back on Nic."

"Wonder what this property would sell for?" Goon Two said. "I suspect the value might decline, if something unfortunate were to happen. Alcohol burns fast, I hear."

"Bet the insurance proceeds would be significant," Goon One added.

Red-hot rage surged through Nic, but he kept a lid on it, barely, taking a measured breath and keeping his aim steady, an idle tune flitting through his head. "I asked who sent you here."

Goon One reached into his jacket pocket and withdrew a card. He held it out to Nic. "Our employer wants to be sure you're aware of the issue."

A mind-boggling dollar amount was scribbled on the back of the heavy ecru cardstock. Nic turned it over and bit back a curse as he read the printed block letters. VAUGHN INVESTMENTS.

He should have fucking known. Duncan Vaughn, the man Nic's father was apparently indebted millions to, was a prominent "real estate investor," among other things. *Crook* was more accurate. "That what those shots at me earlier today were about?" Nic asked.

Silence from the Goon Squad.

"I haven't spoken a word to my father in twenty-seven years," Nic carried on, "and I don't want a fucking cent of his money. Never did. He sells his properties,

Vaughn can take the money. Leave me and my brewery the fuck out of it."

"Your last name *Price*?" Goon One said.

Nic gritted his teeth.

"We're just here to remind you."

"Take your reminders and shove them up your ass."

Goon Two smirked. "I hear you're fond of shoving things in asses."

Nic snapped. He shot out a leg, sweeping the thug's out from under him, dropping him to the ground, and shoving the pistol in his face, all the while keeping the other weapon trained on Goon One. "I don't want to see either of you here again. If you set one foot on these premises or inside the brewery, or harass any of my staff, I've got weapons deadlier than these. And I know how to use them."

He stepped back, far enough for Goon Two to scramble to his feet. He could take these two into custody right now. Cuff them and call the cops or Cam to come get them. But in the past he'd seen Vaughn's goons get off with barely a slap on the wrist. Nic would get more out of this encounter by letting them go, tracing the weapons, and fishing for more information, without letting on that he was going to cause trouble.

"Give those back to us," Goon Two said, jutting his chin at the pistols.

"No way in hell." Nic's aim didn't waver. He'd held weapons aloft for much longer than this before. "Now get the fuck out of here."

The dark-haired one moved, preparing to attack, but blondie had had enough. He put a hand out, holding him back. "Another time, Mr. Price."

Nic sure as fuck hoped not.

They disappeared out the back lot, a car roaring to life and peeling away seconds later. Clicking on the pistols' safeties, Nic shoved them in his back waistband and picked up the phone he'd dropped in the scuffle.

The unknown caller had hung up. No way to call back either.

"Shit!"

Hurrying inside, he slammed the door closed behind him, the plate glass rattling, and forced his keyed-up self to wait for the lock to reengage. Once it glowed red, he headed for the tasting bar, laying the handguns and phone out on a bar towel, then poured himself another pint of Pils. He quenched his dry mouth and waited for his pulse to slow. For his mind to move past worry—for his brewery, his business, his future—and onto formulating a plan to save it.

He needed information. And backup.

The unofficial sort, if he wanted to keep whatever mess his father had gotten into from fucking up his own life. Or worse, threatening someone he cared about, the list of targets having grown alarmingly long over the past year. Before, it'd been a short list—his SEAL team, Eddie, Gravity, the handful of people who worked for them. He'd held everyone else back, had avoided relationships beyond the professional or very casual nonprofessional context. People got hurt in his orbit, even when he tried to do right, and after the pain he'd caused already, he didn't deserve more than what he allowed. He didn't want to cause anyone else that sort of pain again.

But then he'd gotten tangled up with Aidan's lot, including the ASAC Nic wanted, against his better judgment, to know in a decidedly more than professional or casual context, whether he deserved to or not.

Taking another long swallow of beer, Nic picked up his phone and activated the secure call app. He scrolled to the most resourceful person among the six contacts listed there.

"Price," Melissa Cruz answered, instantly alert. "Talk to me."

They'd worked together often when Mel was the FBI SAC before Aidan, and their working relationship had continued despite her retirement from the Bureau. Chief of Security for the Talley's shipping company by day, bounty-hunter—maybe also mercenary, Nic knew better than to ask—by night, she'd delivered more than one wanted criminal to him. Now he needed her assistance dealing with the criminal element threatening his own life.

"I need your help."

"With?"

"Couple things."

Headlamps blasted through the plate-glass windows, lighting up the interior entryway. Nic's pulse hammered, two beats of worry that the goons had returned—perhaps with reinforcements, or worse, with tanks of gasoline and a lighter—before the rattle of a blown-out muffler reached his ears. He released the breath he'd been holding, shaking his head, as he wondered how Cam had made it cross-country in that junker.

"I've got company," he said to Mel.

"Friendly or foe?" she asked, voice clipped.

"Friendly."

"What you need, can it wait until morning?"

A trace on the handguns and unknown call? He didn't see how eight hours was going to make much difference on either. And he could do some searching of his own during that time. "It'll hold."

"I'll text you a time and place." She clicked off, just as the noise outside died.

Nic wrapped the pistols in the bar towel and hightailed it to his office. He swung aside the framed map of the world's beer regions and opened the safe behind it, shoving the weapons inside.

He was readjusting the picture when Cam banged on the main door.

"Let yourself in," Nic hollered. This time of night, Cam should be able hear him. And hopefully he remembered the key code Nic had given him a couple months back. Sure enough, by the time Nic reentered the tasting room, Cam was behind the bar, helping himself to a pint of the Imperial Stout.

"Make yourself at home," Nic greeted.

"Don't mind if I do." Cam set a full pint of stout on the bar top, then tipped another glass toward him. Nic nodded, and Cam filled the second glass with pilsner.

"I was about to call you," Nic said.

"I'd rather debrief over a beer, if it's all the same to you?"

"No complaints here."

Approaching, Nic let his eyes rove over the agent, checking for any cuts or bruises he hadn't noticed earlier. Cam's dark hair was mussed and exhaustion weighed down his broad shoulders, but otherwise he looked as he had when they'd parted ways in the Federal Building elevator that afternoon. More important, nothing in Cam's demeanor indicated Lauren had told him about this morning's shooter. If she had, Cam would have stormed in here in high-gear-agent mode, demanding protection for Nic.

"How'd you know I was here?" Nic asked, climbing onto a barstool.

Cam set the pint of pilsner in front of Nic, next to the phone. "You weren't in your office when I left." Rounding the bar, he claimed the stool beside Nic. "Thought I'd swing by on my way home."

"You could have called."

"One, you're on the way."

True. Cam's house, which he rented from Aidan, was a ten-minute drive, at most, from the brewery, right off the highway exit Cam would take to get home.

"And two, beer," Cam added, before taking a long swallow of the stout, cheek dimpling on a satisfied smile. Lowering the glass, he licked the foamy head from his full upper lip, and Nic had to look away, remembering the heady taste of his beer on Cam's lips the night they'd kissed. He silently cursed the charmer for not leaving a stool between them.

"How long you been here?" Cam asked after another sip.

"Fifteen minutes." If he didn't count the Goon Squad's attack.

"Went that well with Abby?"

"Needed to give her time to calm down, then we talked, and then I had to fill out a reams-worth of paperwork to get her into rotating safe houses. I think she's settled, for now."

Cam gave him a sideways glance, then a once-over he didn't bother to hide. Nic turned the curses on himself, realizing he hadn't bothered to straighten his hair or shirt since the altercation in the parking lot. But by the dark look spreading over Cam's face, the other man's brain had gone an entirely different direction. "What'd it take to get her settled?" he asked.

"I don't swing that way," Nic replied, staring into his beer. "Also helped Eddie load some cases when I got here."

"You're lying. Your tight-ass shoulders are up to your ears, you're avoiding my eyes, and you're drumming your fingers on your glass."

Fucking well-trained FBI agents. Nic stilled, forced his shoulders down, and tore his gaze from his phone where they'd drifted. "Don't FBI me."

"Don't attorney me." Cam nodded at the phone. "What's going on?"

He could give him part of the truth; maybe it'd satisfy the hound. "Odd hang-up, right after I got here."

"Connected to the case?"

"Don't know." It was possible, though Nic suspected it was more likely a diversion by the goons so they could sneak up on him. He needed Mel to run an off-book trace to confirm it.

"Get Jamie to hack it." The former Cyber agent, who now coached college basketball, still "consulted" on the side, for the FBI and Talley Enterprises.

"Think he's probably pretty busy at the moment."

The last thing Nic wanted to do was draw them near his father's shit. Let them believe the sanitized version in the media, that his father was a Bay Area real estate tycoon who was winding down his business. Certainly safer than the unsanitized version Nic suspected and had further proof of tonight, that Curtis Price was a real estate failure up to his eyeballs in debt. Nic would get to the bottom of that mess with Mel, without putting the rest of them in the crosshairs.

"What'd you get out of Scott and Mike?" Nic asked, diverting Cam to the promised debrief.

"Not a damn thing. Flipping them is going to hinge on Abby."

"She's convinced Becca will make another run at her, and at the artifacts."

Cam raised a brow. "At the museum?"

Nic nodded.

"They're in a voice-activated vault there too, right? The prototype of the one in the Kristićs' apartment?"

Nic nodded again.

"Then Abby's right. Becca will need her." Cam drained the rest of his beer. "She'll have to make her move soon. The show opens next weekend, assuming Kristić doesn't take the artifacts back home with his wife's..." Cam's words drifted off, as did his gaze. Twisting on the stool, back to Nic, he slid off and cleared his throat. "You in tomorrow?"

"After I get some paperwork done here."

Or rather, after he met Mel.

"We'll go over security plans for the arraignment then. I want everyone safe." Cam slapped the bar with the flat of his hand, a parting gesture.

Wanting to offer some comfort, Nic shot out a hand, covering Cam's on the bar. "Kristić's lucky to be alive. He has you to thank for that."

"They both should be alive." Cam brushed his thumb along the side of Nic's, and Nic barely hid his shiver.

Barely stopped himself from closing the distance between them.

But he had to get his father's shit sorted before he

started anything with Cam. Probably not a smart play either, definitely more than he deserved, but he wanted that second kiss, badly.

After he cleared the other hazards from the road.

He withdrew his hand, wrapping his fingers around his glass and hiding his words behind the rim. "See you tomorrow, Boston."

Chapter Four

Cam paused the playback of yesterday's operation footage. On the monitor, Nic froze midstride, halfway between the surveillance van and buildings, standing in the middle of the street. Exposed, in the line of fire, with only Beta team overhead for cover. The image had plagued Cam all of yesterday, only waning in Nic's presence at the brewery last night. It'd come creeping back in his dreams, haunting him straight through to morning. It should have been the memory of Anica Kristić, pale and bleeding out on the bed, that tormented him, but every time he'd closed his eyes, he imagined Nic bleeding out in the street instead.

"Byrne!"

Aidan's sharp bark from the speakerphone snapped Cam out of his waking nightmare. He was so used to Aidan calling him by his first name now that the last name address was jarring. Rankled more than a bit too.

Taking a measured breath, Cam leaned forward and braced his elbows on his desk. "This isn't my first rodeo, Talley."

Aidan sighed heavily on the other end of the line, and Cam pictured him raking a hand through his red hair. "I know that, and I didn't mean to imply it was, or that you couldn't handle this. Just please tell me you're not blowing smoke up my ass."

"I blow smoke up Bowers's ass, not yours. Everything's under control, partner."

There was a sharp knock on his door, and before he could answer, Lauren stuck her head inside. He flagged her in and gestured at the visitor chairs.

"I want status updates every four hours," Aidan said.

Lauren dramatically rolled her eyes and Cam bit back a grin. "Roger that," he managed. "Now get back to enjoying the whiskey. Both kinds."

Irish expat Aidan had taken his new husband, nicknamed "Whiskey," to the motherland for their honeymoon. The jokes were too easy.

Lauren's hands flew to her mouth, trying and failing to stifle her laughter, as Cam hung up on Aidan's Gaelic curses. She spoke behind her fingers, nails a shiny shade of purple this morning. "Sorry, I couldn't help it."

"At least someone found it funny."

"Aidan would too, if he weren't a control freak not in control right now."

"No shit." Cam wasn't one of the FBI's best K&R agents for nothing, but he could also understand that this was Aidan's first big case as SAC and it'd gone sideways without him, not that any of them could have predicted Becca's betrayal.

"So's that one," Lauren said, pointing at the freeze-frame of Nic. "Do you think he wears a suit on his days off too?"

Not always. Cam remembered that tasting at the brewery a few months back. Remembered Nic dressed down in beat-up jeans and a snug Gravity tee, his muscles outlined in black cotton, and dark ends of a tattoo peeking out from beneath his short sleeves and crew neck. Lord only knew what was hiding beneath his daily suits and business wear.

"For what it's worth," Lauren said, "I'm a fan of the weekend dressed-down policy you've got going while the boss is gone."

Cam tried not to wince. It was a professional rule he hated breaking and would have never considered it in Boston. But dry cleaning here cost twice what it had back home, and he'd frankly run out of clean dress clothes. Seeing as designer jeans and a vanity tee counted as business casual in San Francisco, his washable Dockers and knitted polo certainly fit the bill, and lowered his dry cleaning costs.

"Enjoy it while it lasts." Cam snapped closed his laptop and gave Lauren his full attention. "What'd you find on Becca?"

She ran a hand across the computer in her lap. Not standard issue, given its alien-head logo and plethora of stickers. "Don't ask how," she said.

Cam held up his hands. "Not asking." With a hacker for a best friend, he'd learned that lesson years ago.

Opening the laptop, Lauren spoke as her fingers flew across the keyboard. "Before, we were focused on Scott's accounts."

He peered at the account numbers on the case board in the conference room between his and Aidan's offices. Nic had a bigger war room two floors down, but they had a robust setup here too. Including teetering stacks of financial records. "We checked each crew member."

"We did, but once we identified the job down payment in Scott's, we paused our deep dive into wonky finances of the other crew members."

"Wonky?"

She glared up at him, kohl-rimmed eyes narrowed. "Yes, *wonky.*" If Cam didn't know better, he'd take her for a smart-mouthed teen. But the thirty-year-old analyst-turned-agent was wicked smart, too observant for her own good, and a frighteningly good marksman with a Colt 1911 in her tiny hands.

Almost as good as she was with a computer, which was truly frightening.

Chuckling, he relaxed back in his chair. "So there's wonky stuff with Becca's financials?"

"Not exactly." She slid her laptop onto his desk, turning it to face him. "This is an account statement for Rebecca Monroe."

It took less than a second for it to click. "Rebecca Wright and Abigail Monroe. A joint account?"

"Yes and no." Lauren rotated the laptop half around so he could see while she clicked through windows, reaching one with an Account Holder Agreement opened. "Becca's listed as the account holder and signatory. Becca and Abby are both listed as beneficiaries."

"Did Abby know about this? Did she access it?"

Lauren shook her head, long strands of brown hair escaping from her pencil bun. "Only one user has ever logged in, from a single mobile device we don't have on record. I'd bet that's Becca."

"On a burner." He ran a hand over his jaw, prickly since he'd skipped his morning shave two days in a row. "They could have shared the log-in." While Nic seemed convinced of Abby's cooperation, Cam wasn't sold. Even less so now that they'd found a bank account with her name on it.

One with multiple *sizable* deposits. "Are those—"

"The third-party payoffs," Lauren said with a nod. "We were only looking at Scott's account for the bank-roll."

Cam glanced back at the board and the list of deposits. "He had them."

"The payouts to his crew too, but these—" she pointed at her screen "—don't match up. They're bigger than Scott's fee."

"By a lot," Cam said. "Have you traced the origin yet?"

"Hitting private bank walls. I've got calls with Switzerland and the Caymans on my agenda tomorrow when they reopen."

"We need to update Nic."

"Already texted him that we had a development." She closed her laptop, slid it off the desk, and stood. "He said he had a meeting this morning and would be in around noon."

As keen as she was at reading people, Cam hoped Lauren's own movements had distracted her from noticing his. Nic had told him he was doing paperwork at the brewery this morning. Maybe he was meeting someone there. Or maybe the prosecutor was lying about something. The same something that had ruffled Nic last night, even if he hadn't wanted Cam to see him off his cool, collected game. How was Cam supposed to help the man who'd grown to mean more to him than he should if Cam didn't know what the fuck was going on?

He shook his head. Beside the point right now. He needed to focus on the case, not distractions.

"All right," he said. "I want all our bases covered. Keep running down that account and dig for others with wonky aliases or activity." Lauren smiled at his use of her word, the deflection working. "Dig deeper into Abby too. I'm going to bring her in for questioning. Would be great to have more to go on."

"You got it." She breezed out the door, and Cam waited for her to turn the corner before drawing his own laptop back in front of him. He logged back in and the screen came to life.

To the picture of Nic.

The man who was hiding something from him.

Nic clutched his steering wheel, debating whether this was the right call. Last night, in the heat of the moment after Vaughn's thugs had tried to jump him, consulting Mel had seemed like the best plan. He trusted Mel more than most, professionally and personally, and she had the connections, and discretion, to get him what he needed. Answers. But would her other connections— to the Talleys—require disclosure when Nic required secrecy? She wouldn't put her family in danger, which was exactly what Nic was also trying to avoid, but would she see it that way?

That said, he didn't really see any other option. He couldn't trace the handguns and call himself without triggering flags, and there'd be a dozen more of those if he took this to the feds. He'd be walled off, ethically, and Aidan and Cam would be so far up his ass that he wouldn't get another moment's peace, much less what he really wanted from the latter. Or worse, they wouldn't want anything to do with him at all. He didn't want to admit he'd become attached, but yeah, that list was fucking growing all right.

He pulled Vaughn's business card out of his pocket, turning it over in his hand. He'd have to play this care-

ful. Try to feel Mel out with the handguns and call trace
before he showed all his cards, this one in particular. He
resigned himself to losing—up against someone so well-
trained in interrogation and torture—but with his SEAL
training, he could hold out longer than most.

Maybe.

Pocketing the card, he grabbed the briefcase off
the passenger seat and climbed out of his truck. He
approached the private marina's guardhouse, badge
in hand, ready to prove his identity to the rent-a-cop
on duty, but the uniformed guard greeted him with a
smile and waved him on through. He didn't need to ask
which of the dozen or so docked yachts was the one he
wanted. The American and Irish flags flying from its
stern were a dead giveaway. As was the striking and im-
posing woman waiting for him on deck, her brown skin
glowing under the morning sun.

"I'd heard you and Danny moved." He tucked his
briefcase under his arm and climbed aboard.

"We did," Mel replied, brushing back her windswept
curls. "But *ay dios*, living and working with him, I
needed a space of my own."

Nic laughed. "So you turned the floating bachelor
pad into your office?"

"Let me show you the improvements," she said with
a smirk.

He followed her below deck, through the showcase-
worthy living room, past the kitchen that looked rarely
used, and into the main cabin area. Where the bedroom
should have been was instead one of the most advanced
private command centers—there really was no other
word for it—Nic had ever seen.

He turned a full three-sixty in the middle of the room, trying and failing not to gape. "Should I be seeing this?"

"Probably not." She claimed one of the ergonomic desk chairs and used her high heel to toe over a second. "Now, what did you need help with?"

Right to the chase. He took the offered seat and lifted his briefcase onto the long metal table that ran the length of one wall. Mel rolled beside him, as he snapped open the locks, lifted the lid, and removed the false bottom, revealing the two handguns from last night, snug in foam.

She pulled one free. "Not your weapon of choice."

"Not my weapons."

She flipped it over, running a French-tipped nail over the scratched-out serial number. "Other one like this too?"

"The same."

"I might be able to salvage something, but no promises." She laid the pistol on the table and sat back in her chair, nail tapping the armrest. "This for a case or personal?"

"Personal." He mirrored her faux-relaxed posture, the both of them taking the measure of each other. Friends, yes, but how much to say? Or better question, judging by her dark assessing eyes, how much did she know already? "You don't seem surprised."

"The FBI has a very thick file on Mr. Vaughn."

Nic forced himself not to gape again. "I didn't—"

She nodded at the handguns. "His weapon of choice. Right down to the make and model and the half-assed scratched-off serial numbers. They came after you?"

He could play dumb, but she was already halfway down the trail. And she gave no indication of stopping. "Last night. And possibly yesterday morning too."

"At the Kristić raid?"

Apparently that police ban radio in the corner wasn't just for nostalgia.

Nodding, he lifted the other handgun out of the case, set it next to the first, and removed the foam. He withdrew the evidence bag containing the phone Lauren had hacked. "We took fire in the surveillance van. Thought it was connected to a third-party rip-off, but then this was found in a sniper's nest." He took it out of the bag, powered it on, and handed it over, photos open. "Only thing on it are pictures of me."

She swiped her thumb over the screen, a crease forming between her dark brows. "And you said they came at you again last night?"

"At the brewery. Distracted me with a call from an unknown number, then tried to jump me."

"Idiots," she muttered, handing the phone back. "Do you want me to trace the call?"

"Please." He sealed the phone back in the evidence bag and dropped it in his briefcase. "Came into my cell number, around ten thirty."

"Easy enough." She spun to one of the keyboards, typing in commands that lit up the closest monitor, a call search running on-screen. "Does Byrne know about any of this?"

He clicked shut the briefcase. "No."

She turned from the wall of computers, angling toward him. "Because you think this has to do with your father's debts. To Vaughn."

He startled this time, no hiding it, at just how far down the trail she'd already sprinted. Mel, it seemed, knew just as much, if not more, about his father's financial situation than he did.

"Your father was also being monitored by the Bureau," she added, shocking him further. "No surprise the sharks are circling. Those are some dangerous fish, Price."

Nic was still hung up on his father being under FBI investigation. He was surrounded by FBI agents these days, and not just in a professional context. None of them had said a thing. "Does Aidan know? About my father? About Vaughn?"

Mel shook her head. "Walled off. Conflict of interest."

That statement was too absurd, too accurate, for comment. He did anyway. "Because *that's* stopped Talley before."

"Different department, low level, relatively. Which was why the matter never got to him. Before I left, I turned everything over to Assistant Director Moore, with the recommendation to keep Aidan, and Cam, for that matter, walled off."

"Is the case still active?" he asked.

"As part of a bigger one to nail Vaughn, yes," she said with a tilt of her head toward the pistols. "But if Curtis's situation gets worse, if he gets desperate, he might get back on the radar in his own right."

Nic debated whether to ask for something he had no right to. The FBI and the US Attorneys' Office were both DOJ, and while they often worked together, they were separate agencies. Sometimes, logistical and ethical walls between them were necessary. This had been one of those times. But if the FBI knew the full scope of his father's financial dealings, and failings, he needed to get his hands on that information. To assess how it might blow back on him.

Before he could ask, Mel carried the pistols across the

room to a corner wall safe and tucked them inside. Nic prayed her lock-pick husband couldn't crack that one or his secrets wouldn't stay secret for long.

"I'll see what I can find out," she said, turning back to him. "About the call and guns. Usual searches?"

He nodded. "Acquisition, ownership, used in other crimes, etcetera." The other ask still hovered on the tip of his tongue.

She beat him to it, making the offer. "I'll make some additional inquiries too. Discreetly, of course. See where the agencies are on Curtis."

"I have no right to ask."

"But you were going to. Friends and family benefit." She folded her arms. "And I don't want Bowers to get his hands on it and blindside you."

He pushed to his feet, hand extended. "Thank you."

She pulled him into a hug instead. "What's your plan, once I get you this information? Believe it or not, certain people do care about you. No one wants to see you step into the line of fire."

The sentiment both warmed and chilled his heart. The last time someone had cared for him, had stepped into the line of fire, or rather fists, for him… He banished the memory and answered her question instead. "My father and Vaughn aren't giving me much choice. So I'm trying to build a shield, for myself and for those who care for me." He swallowed hard, forcing the truth out of his arid mouth. "Who I care for too."

"You're building a case," she correctly surmised.

"I don't want to have to bring it. I don't want to air my family's dirty laundry for everyone to see."

"For Cam to see."

He turned away, grabbing his briefcase and hiding

the truth she was perilously close to. He headed out of the command center and across the living area, toward the stairs that'd take him above deck.

"How much do you know about the ancient Spartans?" Mel asked behind him.

The *non sequitur* halted him midstep. "Not much," he said, turning back to face her. "Beyond what I've seen in movies."

She leaned a hip against the end of the nearest leather couch. "The Spartans were famous for their shield walls."

"Shield walls?"

"When under attack, a Spartan phalanx would lock shields and advance together. As one. They were nearly impenetrable. Saved countless lives."

Not so *non sequitur* after all.

"Before you dig into this further, Price, think long and hard whether your shield of one is enough. For both—*for all*—our sakes."

Chapter Five

Nic didn't wear suits on his day off, but it was a near thing.

The prosecutor barreled out of the elevator bank in charcoal dress slacks and a navy V-neck sweater, the latter making his ice-blue eyes glow.

Or maybe that was just the cold, hard anger burning there.

Cam pushed back from the conference room table. "Control freak incoming," he mumbled to Lauren on his way to the door.

Nic ate up the bullpen floor with his long-legged stride, meeting Cam a mere two steps past the threshold. "Why the hell was Abby brought in here? I didn't spend hours doing rotation paperwork last night, trying to keep her safe, for you to fuck it up. Are you trying to get her kidnapped?"

The jab at his professional competency hurt, poking Cam's sorest spot, especially after yesterday. But it angered him even more. Nic fucking knew him better than that, professionally and otherwise. And even if he didn't, it was a fucking low blow. He didn't go around accusing Nic of cratering his own cases. Seeing red, he stepped nose to nose with the attorney. "Don't you ever say that to me again," he gritted out through clenched teeth.

"We need to question her," Lauren added at their sides, having followed him out.

Nic's steely-eyed gaze stayed trained on Cam. "She's my fucking witness."

"Okay, Bowers," Lauren retorted, voice mocking.

Fury flashed in Nic's eyes, Lauren's insubordination testing his clearly strained patience, ratcheting up his anger. It was enough to turn down the heat on Cam's own boiling rage, for the moment.

He shifted his gaze from Nic to Lauren. "A minute, please."

"I don't get to watch the pissing contest?"

"Agent Hall," Cam said in his command voice, brooking no argument. "Don't you have bank accounts to trace?"

Her blue eyes bounced between them, seeing too much. "You'll regret it if you hurt each other," she said, before spinning away on her booted heel.

Cam returned his attention to Nic, reining in his boss voice and speaking to the other man as an equal, even though the earlier dig still burned. "We're on the same team here. Abby's the Bureau's witness too."

"You should have cleared it with me first," Nic said, shoulders dipping slightly. "Before bringing her in."

"Maybe so, but you weren't here this morning."

"I was at the brewery."

"You told Lauren you had a meeting."

"At the brewery."

Lie.

Nic's shoulders had ticked back up the tiny measure they'd relaxed, giving him away. Right now, though, they had bigger issues. "I didn't want to disturb you, either way." He raised his hands, palms out. "Look, every precaution was taken, and I'll do the reset paperwork for the safe houses."

The way Nic held his stare, Cam wondered for a second if they would come to blows, but then Nic stepped back, sucking in a deep breath. When next he spoke, it was level and calm, the mask slipping back into place. "Why *did* you bring her here?"

Cam held out an arm toward the conference room, and Nic entered ahead of him. "Give him the rundown," Cam said to Lauren.

"Glad you didn't kill each other," she mumbled, before launching into her recap of the latest developments.

By the time she was done, Nic's thumbs were drumming a steady rhythm against the table. "You're right," he said. "We need to question her again. Make sure she's not planning an escape *with* Becca."

"Or another heist, from the inside," Cam added.

"Fucking hell," Nic cursed again as he stood. "Where is she?"

"Holding Room Two," Lauren answered.

That was the other reason Cam wanted to question Abby in the FBI's offices. Holding Room Two was equipped with specialty audio and video instruments designed to read a suspect's or witness's biometrics during questioning. "Analytics running?" he asked Lauren as they rose.

She nodded.

"Double-check 'em," he said. "We're right behind you."

"You know, you could've just said you wanted another moment alone." She swung the door closed before either of them could call her out on the repeated insubordination. Not that either of them would. She was too valuable to the team, and usually the lighter mood was appreciated.

Turning to Nic, Cam opened his mouth to make sure they were okay, here in the office at least, but Nic spoke first. "I'm sorry I came in here…" he waved a hand between them, then let it drop to his side "…like that. And I'm sorry for what I said. I was way out of line."

"You were," Cam acknowledged, but didn't dwell, at least not on the words, digging for the reason instead. "Meeting this morning went south?"

Nic wiped a hand down the length of his face, thumb snagging on his rough, angular jaw. The brownish-red scruff, flecked with gray, was already well past five o'clock. Cam wanted to run his fingers over it, desperately.

He shoved his hands in his pockets instead. "That bad?"

"Productive, but everything I didn't want to hear."

Concern blotted out the flare of lust. "Is it something I can help with?"

"It's personal."

"And?" Cam stepped closer. "We're friends, aren't we?"

Nic's eyes darted to his, darkening, and Cam's lust crept back in, but then Nic cast his gaze aside and opened the door. "It's fine."

Cam paused over the threshold, right in front of Nic, the tight squeeze forcing his gaze again and drawing out a sharp inhale. "If you change your mind, you know where to find me."

A door clicked open across the bullpen. "We're ready," Lauren called from the observation room.

"Coming," Cam replied, only to have his step falter when a light hand brushed over his lower back, Nic's soft "Thank you" floating past his ear.

He was thrown further off-kilter in the interrogation room by Lauren's voice in his ear, and by Nic's one-eighty in demeanor. He'd turned off the tired, worried man, leashed the legal bulldog, and was all charm and patience, greeting Abby warmly.

"I'm sorry for having to bring you back in here."

She wound her earphone cord around her thumb. Nervous, put on alert by the change in schedule. "What's happened?"

"Something we hope you can help us understand," Nic said.

Was this how he manipulated suspects and witnesses on the stand? How he got them to do his bidding for him? How he got a jury to eat out of the palm of his hand and give him the conviction he wanted?

Presently, though, his palm was literally held out to Cam, eyes on the folder of redacted bank account ledgers Lauren had passed him on the way in. Cam handed it over, and Nic opened it on the table, pushing the top sheet toward Abby. "This is from a bank account ledger we discovered this morning."

She pulled the paper closer. "For Rebecca... Oh." Her eyes widened, locked on the top right-hand corner where the account holder's name was printed.

Beside him, Nic slid back in his chair and gave him a small nod. Time for him to play bad cop. Normally, Cam was the charm to Aidan's Irish fury, but in this case, Nic needed to maintain the rapport with his potential witness, leaving Cam to press to determine if she was also a potential suspect.

"When did you and Becca set this account up?" Cam asked.

Her head whipped up, dyed curls bouncing. "Me and Becca?"

"Are you playing us, Abby?"

"What's that supposed to mean?"

"I'm starting to wonder if Becca is still your number-one priority."

Her fiery gaze darted to Nic. "He does know I'm the CI, right?"

Cam propped his elbows on the table, leaning forward. "Because Becca sent you in here. She set up that third-party rip-off during *our* raid. Perfect chaos for her cover. And you were in a position to know all about it."

Abby angrily jabbed a finger at her chest. "*I* could have been killed in that chaos. Becca may still kill me for turning on her. I *did not* set it up."

"Then why is this account in both your names? You're both listed as beneficiaries."

"I don't know."

Cam reached out, in front of Nic, and pushed the second page from the folder over to Abby. "And why are there deposits from Friday for twice as much money as Scott received?"

Her eyes grew impossibly wider, taking in the amounts. "I had no idea about this." She looked back up, first at Cam, then to Nic. "I had no idea she was going to turn on us."

"Biometrics say she's telling the truth," Lauren reported in his ear.

Cam's gut reported the same, at least about the account.

So where had that money come from? And when was Becca coming for Abby? Because that account, and the money in it, meant Becca still had a job to do. And she needed Abby to do it.

Legs crossed, Nic sat waiting in one of the leather chairs in the lobby of his father's building. Or was it? Price Holdings was still listed on the lobby directory as occupying Suite 200, and PH still technically owned the building. Nic had checked the assessor's records first thing this morning. But now there were a dozen other companies listed on the building directory with PH too. While the first floor had always been rented out—the downtown Burlingame location drew premium rents—the second story used to be solely occupied by the family office. No longer, according to the directory, and evidenced by the stream of twentysomethings in branded polos bouncing down the stairs and out the doors.

Nic squinted against the flare of bright light, the sun reflecting off metal, marble and glass. His father's first major real estate purchase, the building had been significantly renovated since Nic had last visited. More than once, according to the assessor's records. In its present incarnation, it bore every appearance of wealth, but if one looked closely, the carpet was worn thin on the side stairs tucked out of sight, the grout between marble slabs needed repair, and the tech at the reception desk was at least five generations out of date. The building receptionist manning the desk probably had better tech on the phone she'd hardly glanced up from.

When Nic's sight returned, it was to a smartly dressed

young man—smug business school attitude written all over him—striding across the lobby toward him, ignoring the other two gentlemen in the next set of chairs over. "Mr. Price," he said, hand outstretched. "Harris Kincaid. I work for your father. He's not in at the moment."

Nic knew that. He'd waited in the coffee shop across the street until he'd seen his old man leave, then waited another thirty to make sure he hadn't come back before entering. "I actually came here to speak to you," he told Harris.

The kid, who couldn't be more than twenty-five, fresh out of business school if Nic had to guess, buttoned his jacket and stood taller, which still left him a half-foot shorter than Nic. Looking up, he jutted out his chin, defiant. "About?"

"Let's go up to the office," Nic said, arm out toward the stairs. The cocky little shit looked like he was going to argue, until Nic reminded him who his boss was. "I don't think my father would appreciate his business discussed in public, do you?"

Harris paled, confirming to Nic that his father remained an uneasy man to work for. And he wasn't Harris's only boss.

"Of course," Harris conceded.

Upstairs, it was as Nic suspected. Only one corner of the second floor remained occupied by PH—two offices, a conference room, and a reception area, the desk unstaffed. By the layer of dust gathering there, it hadn't been staffed in a while. Harris led him through the small lobby, past his father's office—the solid wood door with the brass nameplate closed—and into the other smaller office, which was meticulously neat.

Nic claimed a visitor chair as Harris circled to the

other side, unbuttoning his coat as he sat. "What can I do for you, Mr. Price?"

"You knew who I was, in the lobby." Unless Harris hung out at the courthouse, there was no reason he should. They'd never met, and Nic hadn't set foot in this building since he was eighteen.

"The guard called up."

"You ignored the other two men in the lobby and headed straight for me."

Harris lowered his chin, hiding a small smile. "He talks about how smart you are." Before Nic could get over that shock, Harris delivered another. "And I knew it was you from the picture in your dad's office." Which must have been recent for Harris to recognize him, because other than his blue eyes, Nic did not take after his blond-headed father at all. And certainly no longer looked like the gangly eighteen-year-old in his graduation photo. Harris righted his face, some of the earlier smugness gone, asking again, "What can I do for you, Mr. Price?"

"I'd like an update on PH. You signed the last corporate filing as the asset manager."

"I'm sorry, but I'm not authorized to provide you that information."

Nic relaxed back in his chair, resting an ankle on his opposite knee. He was going to enjoy this, especially after a day spent preparing court documents for tomorrow's arraignment. This would be a good warm-up, not that he expected to question witnesses tomorrow, but never walk into a courtroom unprepared.

"The company is still a limited liability company, is it not?" Nic asked.

"As are many real estate holding companies."

"And the sole member of the holding company is the family trust, correct?"

Harris inclined his head. "You've done your research."

"I am an attorney, who checks corporate filings on the Secretary of State's site regularly." Nic dropped his leg over his other knee. "And last I'd heard, I'm also the secondary beneficiary of the family trust, after my father. So you see, I have a vested interest in this company, and I want to know its status."

"I thought you weren't interested in your father's money."

"Your boss tell you that?"

Harris rested his forearms on his too clean desk. "Your father hasn't—"

"Your other boss, Mr. Kincaid."

The kid's gulp was audible in the otherwise silent office. He laced his fingers together, which only made his whole fist shake.

"You're married to Duncan Vaughn's niece, aren't you?" Nic didn't give him a chance to answer, going right for the hammer instead. "While I was checking the property records on this building, I also checked the records on your million and a half dollar Silicon Valley hovel. Not one but two loans from an entity that traces back to Vaughn Investments." He hadn't actually had time to dig back through the corporate filings and peel back the layers of ownership. He was hoping Harris would confirm his suspicions for him.

Which he did. Giving up the ghost, Harris curled in his shoulders and slumped forward, deflating. "I don't know anything, okay? The day Duncan forced me on your father, Curtis boxed up all the financial documents, took them home, and put a lock on his office door."

"So what are you still doing here?"

He waved a hand at his inbox on the corner of the desk. "Answering calls, going through the mail, signing whatever corporate documents Curtis's attorney puts in front of me. Collecting a paycheck on the off chance your father decides to pay me, and when he does it just goes to pay Duncan." Harris ran a shaky hand through his dark hair. "I did not kill myself in business school to be an executive assistant for a shell of a company."

"Duncan's forcing you to stay here?"

"I know what he is." Harris dropped his arm, the thump of it on the desk a resigned exclamation mark. "You saw the deeds of trust. We got upside down on that house, and Duncan had to bail us out, just like your father. Now we can't get out from under him."

Excitement trilled up Nic's spine. Finally, a break. He leaned forward, offering the life preserver Harris so obviously needed. "What if I could help you?"

Chapter Six

Scott and Mike's arraignment was scheduled to start in ten minutes, and Cam had no idea where it was actually going down. Ear pressed to the stairwell door on the sixteenth floor, Cam could hear the muffled chaos on the other side, a crowd of people as equally confused as him. He checked his phone again—still no reply from Nic. The court calendar listed the arraignment on the seventeenth floor, but that federal courtroom was empty. Probably why all the squawking press had trampled down to the clerk's office on sixteen. Cam had known this was the plan, for Abby's safety, but this morning's radio silence from Nic was complicating matters, for him at least.

Taking a fortifying breath, he swiped his all-access card over the security lock and pushed out of the stairwell. He flashed his FBI badge at the guard posted on the door, nodded at the cute law clerk he passed in the melee, then smiled and cajoled his way through the crowd of reporters to the court clerk's front desk.

"Agent Byrne," the desk attendant greeted him. "Please tell me you're here to rescue me." Mandi usually delivered that line with a wink and toss of her long blond hair, but today she looked like she actually meant it. Expression pinched, hair yanked back in a severe bun, she'd put the kitten away and unleashed the tiger. And it was a very tired and grumpy cat. Not that the press weren't still trying to shove proverbial chairs at her.

Cam had come prepared with a different, hopefully more effective, strategy. He reached into his inner coat pocket and withdrew a bar of dark chocolate from one of those ridiculously overpriced San Francisco factories. Aidan would probably never notice it'd disappeared from his desk drawer. Flirt turned up, Cam held out the bar to Mandi, tempting. "How about I rescue you, and you return the favor?"

She snatched the chocolate out of his hand and sniffed it, eyelashes fluttering in ecstasy. "Well, it's not an air-lift, but it'll work." She unlocked the service counter swing door and held it open for him to pass through. "Karen, cover me for a minute," she said to one of the other attendants before leading Cam around the corner, out of earshot.

Out of view and out of earshot, Mandi ditched her heels with a relieved sigh and propped a bare foot against the cinder block wall, giving Cam a view of her toned thigh under a hitched-up pencil skirt. Not the only show she was putting on either. Pretty brown eyes with lips that were just this side of decent, she slowly peeled back the foil candy wrapper, eyeing him through long lashes. "You looking for Attorney Price?" she said. He'd un-wrapped the bombshell a time or two, back when he'd only just swing through town for a case or to visit Jamie. Before he'd moved here, before... Mandi spoke again, saving him from jumping through avoidance hoops. "He's down on fifteen, Courtroom C."

"Magistrate's chambers?"

"You saw that out there." She waved the chocolate bar toward the lobby. "It's worse on seventeen." Where the main federal district courtrooms were. "Vultures won't look for them on fifteen."

Grinning, he leaned in close, a forearm against the wall by her head. "I always did say you were the smartest person here."

"Don't you forget it." Her cherry-red lips closed around the chocolate bar, over the line of decent, but his mind was already a floor away.

She read him like a book, dropping the seduction and chuckling. "Use the internal staircase," she said, tilting her head back and right. "Thanks for the chocolate."

"Thank you for the assist," he said with a wink, before he took off for the stairs.

He exited onto the fifteenth floor, in the staff hallway behind the courtrooms. Halfway down the corridor, Tony stood outside one of the holding rooms. "Agent Byrne," the guard said.

He blew out a dramatic huff. "Had to run the gauntlet to get here."

The door opened, and Nic stood there, in all his fullsuited glory. Light gray three-piece, crisp white dress shirt, and monochrome blue tie that matched his eyes. Sharp. Add to that the barely contained excitement vibrating through him, the hype of the coming courtroom, even for a perfunctory arraignment, and Cam forgot how to make words.

Nic filled the silence, albeit with a knowing smirk. "Sorry, the gauntlet was my fault." He opened the door wider for Cam to step through. "Just give us a minute."

Closing the door behind them, Nic turned back to Abby, who sat at a small table reading through a stack of documents. She wound an iPod cord through her fingers, the motion gaining speed when she looked up and caught sight of Cam. He'd backed off the bad cop routine but she was still skittish toward him. He leaned back against the wall, as nonthreatening as possible, while Nic claimed the chair across from her. "Do you have any questions on the affidavit? On your testimony?"

Cam had thought that was what the papers might be. Nic had spent the rest of Sunday in Holding Room Two with Abby, taking her official statement and preparing her for questioning. Yesterday, he'd been a ghost, locked in his own war room preparing court documents, save for a brief meeting with Scott's and Mike's attorneys, then an early departure to take care of something at the brewery, he'd said.

"I didn't misrepresent anything you said, did I?" Nic asked gently.

She abandoned the iPod and cord for the pen next to the papers, mashing the clicker-end against the table. "No, everything's right."

"Clearly something isn't. What's got you nervous?"

"Besides the obvious," Cam added, gesturing at their surroundings, then at Nic. "He lives for this shit. Fucking junkie. The rest of us…" He wrinkled his nose in exaggerated disgust. "Not so much."

"Hey!" Nic twisted in his seat, looking over his shoulder. "You give your fair bit of testimony."

"Because your ass drags me in here." He pushed off the wall and slid into the chair next to Nic. "It's not just you, sweetheart." People tended to overlook his suit and badge when he lengthened his vowels, letting himself sound like a blue-collar garage rat from South Boston.

Which he was. Before he'd become an Assistant Special Agent in Charge at the FBI.

Worked on Abby too, finally chipping through her nerves, and also it seemed, her reluctance toward him. Good; if she betrayed them again, he'd use that. She chuckled, relaxing in her chair and laying the pen down. "Do I have to go in there, with Scott and Mike?"

"I'm going to try to avoid that." Nic nudged the stack of documents with his index finger. "This is your statement about Saturday's events, plus my and Agent Byrne's recommendations to waive any charges against you, as a cooperating informant and witness. You sign the affidavit and the recommendation, which Agent Byrne and I already signed, then I'll hand the papers, together with Stefan Kristić's statement—" he pulled a trifold sheet of paper from his inner coat pocket "—over to the judge."

"Then why did I have to come here?" Abby asked.

"In case the judge has questions about your statement or our recommendations. Same reason I asked Agent Byrne to join us. Mr. Kristić, unfortunately, hasn't been released from the hospital yet."

"Isn't this just an arraignment?" Cam asked, mentally scratching his own head, not that he minded seeing a pre-court-jazzed Nic. "Scott and Mike walk in, plead not guilty, and you move for prelim or trial." He'd seen more than a few of these too.

"It's felony murder," Nic explained. "Someone was killed in the act of committing a felony, the attempted robbery. Neither Scott nor Mike pulled the trigger, but they're on trial for murder." Abby shivered, no doubt realizing that could be her on trial for murder too. "I'm covering all my bases," Nic said.

"Where do I sign?" Abby said, almost a squeak.

Nic walked her through where she needed to exe-
cute each document, finishing just as two swift knocks
sounded against the door. Tony opened the door to the
court bailiff. "Attorney Price," the bailiff said. "Judge
O'Donnell is ready to start. Courtroom C."

"We'll be right there," Nic replied.

Seeing Abby jolt, Cam reached across the table, covering her trembling hands. "Hang tight. Shouldn't be
more than fifteen minutes, twenty at most."

"Can Tony wait inside?" she asked.

"Don't see why not," Cam said as he stood. The big
man could do his job on either side of the door.

Nic followed Cam to his feet. "How far are you into
the book?"

"Chapter eleven, I think."

"That's a good one." He collected the legal documents, putting them all in a bucket folder, and left behind the pen and a legal pad. "Big conclave between the
warring factions. Lots of interesting voices."

Abby had the earbuds back in before Tony even closed
the door.

As they walked down the hallway toward the courtroom, an air of confidence came over Nic that made Cam
doubly wish the damn bailiff wasn't waiting for them by
the courtroom doors. Nic's firm, round ass in perfectly
fitted suit pants didn't help either.

"This is the part you like best, isn't it?" Cam said.

"It's the one thing I've always been good at."

"Arguing?"

Nic smirked. "Exactly."

Outside the courtroom door, the bailiff turned to head
in, and Cam gave in to the urge, as much as he could

under the circumstances. He darted out a hand, copping a feel of Nic's ass in the guise of a "Go lock 'em up" tap.

"You'll pay for that," Nic murmured, smirk tipping up into a smile.

Biting back his own, Cam slipped into the courtroom behind Nic, impressed to find the room all but deserted. Just him and Nic, the judge, clerk and bailiff, and Scott and Mike, and their attorneys. Nic's ploy had worked, and the clerk's office had definitely done them a favor, more than a few.

The pounding of the gavel called the court to order, and true to Cam's word, it was eighteen minutes, start to finish. Not guilty pleas. A short argument over whether Scott and Mike would be released on bail, which Nic obviously won. The criminals were too much of a flight risk, and with Becca still at large, too much of a risk for another attempted felony gone wrong. Then some back and forth over calendaring to set the preliminary hearing for next Monday.

"I'm surprised opposing counsel didn't want to push the prelim out," Cam said, as they walked back to the holding room.

"Part of that gauntlet you ran earlier was the press on sixteen, yes?"

"Yeah, it was a fucking nightmare up there."

"That will only get worse the longer this drags on," Nic replied. "Scott's and Mike's attorneys aren't stupid. This is a relatively open and shut case, especially if we capture Becca in the meantime. Now, I spend the next week negotiating plea agreements. That should be enough time. And if it isn't…"

The gleam in those blue eyes was telling. Maybe the prosecutor didn't want to agree on the pleas. "If it isn't,"

Cam said, "you get to trial faster." Nic's smile could have lit the hallway. As it were, it lit Cam's blood to boiling. "You are good at this."

"I know."

That confidence, that smile, and that fucking suit and tie finally got the better of Cam. Fuck but this man made him want to break all his rules. And truth be told, he'd never been that good with them when it came to sex, the wild side he'd buried long ago needing some outlet. And right now, Nic was the matador in an irresistible cape of gray and blue.

He intercepted Nic's arm midreach for the holding room door, using it to swing him around, back against the wall. Cam closed the distance between them, pressing Nic against the wall. "You're good at other things too. The way you handle case assets. Legal strategy. Making beer." Cam's gaze roved over Nic's face. Blue eyes wide and darkening. A blush staining his high cheekbones. Parted lips that Cam couldn't shake the taste of.

Wanted to taste again.

"Kissing," Cam whispered.

"Boston, there are cameras in this hallway." It wasn't so much a warning as barely restrained desire, Nic's voice low and gravelly.

"How much do you really care right now?"

Nic's gaze strayed to his mouth, and Cam had all the answer he needed. He clasped one side of Nic's freshly shaven jaw and angled the other man's face so he could devour him. The muted whimper from the back of Nic's throat made Cam even hungrier.

He moved to rid the inches between them, to slake his hunger with Nic's mouth, only to have the distance spring back into reality, the holding room door banging open.

At first, instinct startled them apart.

Then shock kept them that way, attention suddenly focused elsewhere.

Tony fell through the open doorway, hand slipping off the inside doorknob, as he collapsed onto the floor.

They both kicked into emergency mode.

"Tony!" Nic slid onto his knees next to the unconscious guard, ripping through layers of clothes, searching for a wound, while Cam leaped over them.

Into the empty room.

No sign of Abby anywhere.

Just the legal pad and iPod left behind.

Chapter Seven

"Are all lawyers screamers?" Cringing, Lauren shrank in her seat across the conference table from Cam. "I can't believe I used to think Aidan was bad. He's a fucking Chihuahua compared to…" She waved a hand the direction of Bowers's office, and Cam couldn't agree with her more.

Nic and his boss had been going at it—Cam checked his watch—a solid hour, their voices escalating, louder by the minute. Two offices lay between them, yet Cam could still make out every few words between the two bulldogs.

"Fucked up…more resources…irresponsible… what you wanted…turned on you…forced us… We're screwed… Fix this…" The tirade went on.

Cam and Lauren weren't the only ones privy to the shouting match. In the war room with them were another attorney and paralegal working on a continuance, neither of whom seemed all that fazed by their bosses' argument, and a team of agents Cam had brought down to brief on kidnap and extraction scenarios. He should have sent them back up to thirteen when he'd finished the debrief, but he wasn't sure what Nic might want to run through once he escaped Bowers.

The answer to that question was an emphatic "Clear the room."

Everyone scurried at Nic's bark, and Cam could tell it was a struggle for the other man not to slam the door behind them. As it were, once he'd forced himself to close it gently, Nic stood with his rigid back to the room, arms spread, hands clutching the doorframe.

"Breathe, Price."

It took a good thirty seconds of measured breaths, Nic's long torso heaving up and down, before he dropped his arms and turned. He rounded the table and collapsed into the chair next to Cam. "We're fucked," he said.

Acting on impulse, more and more of those sneaking through in Nic's presence, Cam rolled his chair closer, their knees brushing under the table. Nic's hand came down on his leg, and Cam was certain he was going to shove him away, the impropriety here in the office a step too far, but Nic's fingers dug into his thigh instead. All of that frustration needed an outlet; Cam was happy to provide it. "I got that much."

"Did you figure out how this happened?"

Ignoring the warm, tempting weight of Nic's unmoving hand, Cam drew the laptop over and opened the playback of the courthouse security footage. The time stamp was three minutes after the judge had called them to order. Cam pressed Play and the stairwell door he'd earlier entered, the one from the clerk's office, opened. A young suited woman appeared first.

"That's Judge Booth's law clerk," Nic said. "Lily Kramer."

Cam nodded. "Passed her up on sixteen when I first came in. Looked like she was waiting for someone outside the clerk's office."

"Him," Nic said, eyes glued to the young man who'd appeared on-screen, following Lily through the door.

With his shaggy black hair and too-huge suit, the man didn't look like another lawyer or anyone Cam recognized from the Federal Building elevators. Steno pad in hand, glasses perched on the end of his pointed nose, most people would mistake him for a reporter, or given how young he looked, maybe an interested law student. Interested in more than just the law, judging by the way he'd brazenly flirted with Lily. And she'd bought it, letting an unauthorized person onto the chambers hallway.

"I don't recognize him," Nic said.

"I didn't either," Cam replied. "The hair and glasses may be a disguise. The suit certainly doesn't fit." In any event, he was attractive enough to catch Lily's attention. On-screen, he moved in for a kiss, much the same way Cam had on Nic in the same hallway, only when the stranger got close to his target, he slipped something out of his coat pocket. A second later, Lily's weight collapsed against him and he lowered her to the floor.

"She okay?" Nic asked.

"Probably out of a job, but otherwise, yes, she's fine. He drugged her with something and stashed her in Judge Booth's chambers."

When the stranger emerged into the hallway, he headed straight for Abby's holding room, pretended to be the bailiff in the accompanying audio, and Tony opened the door for him. The guard's gut met the business end of another syringe. Not long after, the man dragged Abby out by the arm, disappearing with her into the stairwell.

"Where'd they go from there?" Nic asked.

Cam flipped to another security footage view. "Down

to the parking garage and out. He swiped the clerk's access card and keys."

"Fucking hell we're fucked." Nic fell back in the chair, withdrawing his hand and scrubbing both over his face. "Who even was that? Is he working for Becca or someone else?"

"Facial recognition didn't register, but we found the syringes in a parking garage trash can. Partial print. Lauren's running it now."

Nic dropped his hands into his lap. "Let's just hope it pings."

"How's Tony?" Cam asked. A sad reprieve from the immediate issue but one nonetheless. Cam was genuinely concerned about the guard, whose status was being reported to Bowers.

"Triple dose. Doctors were amazed he managed to fight through it and open the door. They're monitoring him overnight for complications. Barring any, he should be released tomorrow."

"Good, good."

Nic hung his head, stretching out his neck, then rolled his head and shoulders, face angled toward Cam. "Prelim is in a week. We'll move for a continuance, but we need to get Abby back." The concerned weariness in his eyes said he was worried about more than just his case. Abby had not looked like a willing participant on that tape; she'd looked like a hostage. But still, Cam had to ask... "Are we sure that wasn't an act, on Abby's part?"

His eyes narrowed. "Did that look voluntary to you?"

"That's why I asked if it was *an act*. Why do you trust her?"

"Because Becca's got leverage on her sister. You know that. Cooperating with us is in her best interest."

"And allying with Becca's not?"

"All the biometrics on Sunday reported she was telling the truth. She's a victim too, of God only knows what emotional blackmail, or worse, that Becca's put her through."

The prosecutor's voice and shoulders had risen as he'd gone on. And it wasn't the first time Cam had seen Nic go to bat for a victim witness. There was more there, more Cam wanted to dig for, but now wasn't the time, not when their witness was missing and Nic had already gone twelve rounds with Bowers. "Look, I agree, all signs point to Abby telling the truth, and I do not want to blame the victim either. I hear and respect you there. All I'm saying is, Abby's number one priority is her sister, and we can't completely dismiss the possibility that Becca is still her best bet. Abby may not trust us either."

Blue eyes stared back at him, icy and hard, until Nic blinked and the calm mask fell back into place. "Okay, so how do we get Abby to trust us? Get her out of the current jam, right?" Cam nodded, and Nic went on. "Perfect. This is your specialty. You're one of the Bureau's best kidnap and rescue agents. So, how do we get Abby back and get ourselves unfucked?"

Crisis averted, Cam relaxed back in his chair, crossing a leg and angling toward Nic. "The context of each kidnapping is different but they generally fall into one of a few categories. Assuming Becca arranged Abby's, or that this person who took her is after the same thing— a way at the artifacts—relatively this is one of the better sort."

"Yeah, Boston? How's that?"

"Kidnappings for ransom or kidnappings where the

victim is needed for something depend on the victim remaining alive. At least for a time."

"And the other kind don't," Nic said quietly.

No, they didn't, and Cam wouldn't wish that sort of pain on anyone. A search and rescue that turned up a dead body, or worse, no body at all. A family left to always wonder what had happened to their missing partner, friend, son, or daughter. That kind of loss tore families apart, was enough to send parents and siblings spiraling, especially when *someone* had broken the rules, had failed to be where *he* was supposed to be and lost someone dear to all of them as a result. Those cases, Cam knew, personally and professionally, were the worst, and not something you ever got over. Distractions cost lives.

Ignoring the sick bubbling in his gut, Cam closed his laptop and laid a forearm on the table. "Unfortunately, this isn't a ransom situation, so I don't know what we can offer to persuade the kidnapper—short of the actual artifacts, assuming that's what they're after—to trade for Abby or to set a trap."

Nic shook his head. "Neither Kristić, the museum, nor the Serbian embassy are going to let us risk the artifacts, so where does that leave us?"

"We have to find out where they are and go in after them."

"A raid?"

Cam nodded. "Never my ideal rescue scenario—the chance of collateral damage is high, as we saw with the last one—but that's all we've got here, unless we find another in. The perps in custody still aren't talking, and even if they were, they're clearly not privy to Becca's plans."

"And probably not to her current location either."

"I'm guessing not. I've got agents out checking their previous hideouts but ten to one she's someplace new."

"So, we've got nothing," Nic said over the door opening and Lauren flying in.

"Maybe you've got nothing, but not me," she said. "Wait, is that right, or did I fuck up the double negative thing?"

"Lauren," Cam snapped, probably sounding as irritated as Nic looked. It was only noon, and it already felt like one of the longest days of Cam's career. "What've you got?"

She set her laptop on the table and turned it around to them. On the screen was a young man with overly styled blond hair, dressed in khakis, flip-flops, and a polo bearing a tech company logo. The picture looked like it'd been snapped at airport security. "Percy Hunter," she said. "Print matches the one on the syringe. He's a breaking and entering specialist we have under surveillance."

Cam squinted, looking for the same guy underneath the ridiculous frat-boy-slash-tech-boy outfit. "That's him? And he's a B&E guy? You sure?"

"Number one rule of Silicon Valley," Nic said, "never judge a person based on their attire and appearance. That guy you think looks like a stoner-fuck is probably an iPO millionaire. Or a criminal mastermind. Or both."

Cam shook off the cognitive dissonance, asking Lauren, "Is he connected to Becca?"

"His accounts are flagged too." She had that hacker gleam in her eyes; she'd caught the trail they needed. "Rebecca Monroe made a deposit, this morning."

Cam shot to his feet, as did Nic beside him. "Do we have a location on him?"

"Noodle Stop. Right around the corner."

Dining at the pho place where half the Federal Building employees ate lunch was a colossally stupid crook move. Then again, according to Lauren, Percy Hunter had no idea he was under investigation.

That was about to change.

Hoofing it up the street, Nic could already see the long line outside the tiny noodle shop.

"We can't go in there hot," Cam said from beside him. "Not with that many people. He'll either hear us coming or someone will get hurt. Or both." He glanced over his shoulder at the two agents behind them. "Go around back. We'll go in the front, flush him to you. Weapons holstered." The agents broke left, down a side street, while Nic followed Cam up the hill. "No badges either," Cam said to him, and to the agents through the comms in their ears. "I don't want to start a panic."

They didn't need to worry about a panic so much as a riot. As soon as they hit the line, and ignored it, heading straight for the door, the angry "you can't jump" shouts started, in more languages than Nic could decipher. But they needed to get in there. Percy had paid ten minutes ago, which was the exact amount of time it usually took to fill an order here. And today was no exception. From his vantage point above most heads, Nic saw sandy-haired Percy up front, still in that poorly fitted suit, grabbing his order.

"He's at the counter," Nic said to Cam.

The crowd complaints grew louder as Cam used his bruiser-build to cut a path forward. Enough that Percy twisted to check out the commotion. When his gaze fell on Nic, his eyes widened and all the color drained from his face. Becca must have shown him a picture.

"He's running," Nic said, anticipating Percy's next move.

Sure enough, noodles hit the floor with a *splat*, followed by the metal *clang* of upended tables and chairs on linoleum, as Percy darted for the back, creating a trail of hazards in his wake.

Need for discretion gone, Cam shouted, "FBI! Out of the way," and charged one direction around the small interior, leaping over the flipped table and noodles. "Move, move, move!"

Nic cut the other direction, upending a table and chair himself, in case Percy tried to run toward them, instead of away, though the rest of the patrons bolting toward the door would make a front exit difficult.

Percy, however, did exactly what they wanted. Ran straight for the back door. "He's headed out back," Nic shouted across the room at Cam.

"Intercept," Cam called, as Percy slammed through the exit door.

Right into the waiting arms of the other agents.

By the time Nic and Cam reached the alley, the other agents had cuffed Percy and shoved him, face-first, against the cement wall.

"Hey, you can't do this!" Percy struggled against the agent's hold. "What about my rights?"

Cam took the other agent's place, wrapping a hand over Percy's cuffed wrists and pressing him harder against the wall. "He's not going to object," Cam said with a nod at Nic.

"You're an attorney," Percy spat his direction. "Do something."

"Sure," Nic said, then proceeded to read him his Miranda rights.

Cam smiled wider with each word. "Nice not to have to do that for a change." He flipped Percy around and pushed him back against the wall. "Becca told you who we are?"

Percy tried to play dumb. "Becca who?"

Failed.

"He recognized me, back in the restaurant," Nic said. "Maybe not you."

Cam had been masked at Stefan and Anica Kristić's condo, and this was technically Nic and Aidan's case, even though Cam had been regularly briefed. Becca wouldn't know Cam was the one chasing her now. Unless Abby… He banished the thought, wisely put there by Cam, but not wanting to think about Abby turning on them, or cracking under pressure. Or worse, torture.

"I got no idea who you are," Percy tried again.

Failed again.

"You know," Nic said, "you're also in the running for stupidest crook of the year. Eating a block away from the scene of the crime, and you didn't even change out of the fucking suit that's too big for you. Just ditched the wig."

"I have no idea what you're talking about."

"Then how'd you know I was an attorney? How'd you recognize me?"

"I work around here. I've seen you before."

"Give it up, Percy," Cam said. "We've got your prints at the scene, and Becca's deposit in your account."

"So let's see, then," Nic said, holding up a hand and ticking off charges on his fingers. "Evading arrest, breaking and entering, assault and battery, kidnapping, attempted murder."

Percy changed his tune real fast, going on the defensive. "I didn't break and enter. The big dude let me in. And I wasn't trying to murder him."

"Near thing that," Cam said. "Giving him a triple dose."

"He was a big motherfucker," Percy argued. He probably thought he was helping his case, not digging his own grave. Confessing.

"Add accessory after the fact," Nic said. "To attempted robbery and felony murder."

Percy went white as a ghost. "What murder?" The kid's voice shook, finally properly scared. Properly informed of the pile of shit he'd stepped into. "I ain't trying to kill no one."

"Then you better help us, Percy," Cam said.

Percy's eyes slid from Cam back to him. "Help you with what?"

Now that they had a pawn, they could set a trap for the queen.

"Stop the next robbery."

"Thank you for delivering my package." Becca's satisfied smile was evident in her voice, filling the war room from where it echoed out of the speakerphone. "I've just sent the second wire."

"And the third?" Percy replied.

"The third?"

"You want me on your next job."

"I like the confidence, Mr. Hunter."

From where Nic sat, Percy looked anything but confident. Blond hair matted with sweat stuck to his pale forehead. Cuffed hands clasped in his lap, shaking. Eyes full of fear, locked on the script in front of him.

But the kid could front like a pro. "Getting Abby out was a test, wasn't it?" he read off the cheat sheet. Nic and Cam had drawn up the list of assembled prompts and questions, designed to draw out a confession. Something Nic could use against Becca in court, once Cam captured her.

"You passed." Not exactly a confession, and Bowers knew it too. From across the table, Nic's boss mouthed, *Ask again.*

Percy ran his wide eyes down the page once more. "I broke your girl out of the courthouse, just like you wanted," he said. "Proved myself. I want in on the next job."

Becca dodged again but opened another door. One infinitely more useful. "We should meet. Make sure our interests align."

"And the third deposit?"

"You seem awfully focused on the money, Mr. Hunter."

"It's Percy," he said. "And do you know what the average monthly rent is in San Francisco these days?" He didn't read that off the sheet.

Beside Nic, Cam nodded. Nic didn't think the sympathy a show.

For her part, Becca chuckled, seemingly convinced and amused. "After we meet, Percy."

Cam shifted forward, reaching over his laptop and pointing at the first potential meet location he'd scribbled on the script. All the places he'd listed had limited ingress and egress points, giving them the best chance for rescuing Abby and taking Becca into custody.

For springing their trap.

Percy proposed the first location. Becca shot him down, offering someplace else. Not unexpected—she held all the cards—and by the way Cam's brows raced north, she'd played a surprising one. Good or bad, Nic couldn't tell, and Bowers didn't give them time to assess or counter, giving Percy a thumbs-up and gesturing for him to continue.

"I know where that is," Percy said. "When do you want to meet?"

"You be there at midnight."

"Does that mean you'll—"

Becca hung up, cutting off the rest of Percy's question. Nic reached out and slapped off the speakerphone, cutting the call on their end as well.

Hunched forward, Percy was still waiting for an answer. "What the fuck did that mean?"

"It means she'll show up when she's ready," Cam answered. "Sometime before sunrise." He shifted in his chair toward Lauren. "Take him upstairs to Comm and get him fitted for eyes and ears. Then call in the tactical teams. Debrief in an hour."

"On it." She snapped shut her laptop and stood. "Let's go, blondie."

Percy looked her up and down, and not in the appreciative sort of way. Not that that would have been any more acceptable. Either way would get him neutered, by the lady herself.

"Don't even think it," Cam said, reading his thoughts. "Her favorite weapon is a Colt 1911 and she's trained in hand-to-hand combat."

"She'll drop you faster than either of us could," Nic added.

Cam jutted a thumb at him. "And he's a former Navy SEAL."

"Don't make me ask a second time," Lauren threatened, indulging in the talking up. Nic didn't begrudge her the attitude.

Percy snapped to it, following like a well-trained puppy.

Cam tossed her the keys to the cuffs. "I'll be up shortly."

The door closed behind them, and when Bowers didn't speak, Nic turned the floor over to Cam. "All right, Boston, lay the tactical out."

"We proposed Transamerica Park," Cam started as he opened his laptop. "Exits with gates on three sides, only three buildings hemming it in, and lots of vantage points, especially from the lower scaffolding of the Pyramid."

"Becca shot it down," Nic said.

"As we expected she would."

"But you were surprised by her alternative."

"At first." He turned the computer around, a layout of the South Park neighborhood on-screen. "You wouldn't think South Park much better, for her. An oval green, buildings on all sides, two exits at either end."

"You know the area?" Bowers asked.

Fair question. Cam hadn't been in San Francisco long and he lived down on the Peninsula, not in the City.

"Chased a suspect through there this past winter," Cam answered. "It's a real bitch to cover."

"Why's that?" Bowers asked.

"Because there're more than just two exits," Nic said, his military training kicking in, the urban landscape coming to life in front of him.

Cam nodded. "There are narrow alleyways between,

his usual calm and collected self, a tall dark-suited form by the window, speaking quietly with Mel. But Cam recognized the tension in his frame. The rigid, slightly lifted set of his shoulders, his hands clasped behind his back, his moonlit eyes glowing eerily as they tracked Bowers around the room.

Mel was even unhappier about their uninvited guest. Bowers had shown up an hour ago, silently looming over the op as if he were waiting for them to screw up again. Danny, for his part, was making conversation with Percy, one lock-pick to another. Cam appreciated the younger Talley's attempts to ease the jittery kid's nerves. But as the midnight hour approached, not even ringmaster Danny could hold Percy's attention, his gaze jumping everywhere, always landing back on the clock by the door.

Keeping an eye on all the moving pieces, Cam shuffled into the kitchen Lauren had claimed as Comm. She moved back and forth between the long granite countertops, assembling Percy's accessories in the dim glow cast by the under-cabinet lights. Standing behind her row of open laptops, Cam zeroed in on the screen with the interactive satellite map. He touched his ear, activating his comm. "Teams, report."

Alpha team, in the cars closest to the center of the park, radioed in first, their position lighting up on the map. The rest of the teams—around the oval, on the roof, outside the perimeter—cycled through their checks, ending with Cam in Command. "Snipers in place. Next report before go in fifteen." Cam toggled the comm off, staring at the screen as boots shuffled overhead, their lookouts shifting as the snipers moved into position.

"Everyone's set, boss." Lauren stood beside him, tightening a screw on a pair of glasses exactly like the

in front of and behind buildings, and it's a straight shot through on the ground floor of most. That's what the perp did in January. Smashed through a plate glass window, ran the length of the place, and out the back door. This time, we'll put teams on the rooftops with wider vantage points to cover."

"And teams on the surrounding intersections." Nic pointed at the corners where Second and Third met either end of Bryant and Brannan. "Catch her there, if we can't capture her inside the target area."

"That's how we captured the last perp," Cam said. "The street parking will also help." He hovered his cursor over the cars bordering the center green. "At rush hour, most of these cars clear out, and the residents flood in. My agents will flood in with them, go undetected during the switch."

Not a foolproof plan—urban combat never was—but Cam had covered as many bases as he could. It would give them a better than decent shot at capturing Becca and rescuing Abby. They devolved into tactical planning, pointing out the best rooftops for optimal vantage points, until Bowers shifted in his squeaky chair, reminding them of his presence.

Would be pretty damn hard to ignore him after his next words. "That's not how it's going to go down. I want the person Becca's working for."

"*If* she's working for someone," Nic said. "Maybe she's the one calling the shots."

Bowers gestured at the whiteboard. "Your case board says otherwise."

Nic cursed himself for the fucking question mark he'd scribbled above Becca's picture. It was a fifty-fifty shot Bowers was right.

"What about Abby?" Cam said. "Percy? They third on your list now?"

"Both criminals," Bowers replied, and Nic bristled. "You two keep forgetting that." His black eyes bounced from Cam to Nic, then back to Cam. "Why not let Becca take them, and see where they lead us?"

"No way," Cam said. "This is my op. And it's a trap, not an insertion."

"This is *our* operation," Bowers said. "And with Aidan gone, I outrank you, *Assistant* Special Agent in Charge Byrne."

"Abby's *our* informant," Nic argued, interrupting the pissing match. "Percy is *our* bait." He hated the word, but he'd use it, if it brought Bowers around to his and Cam's plan. "They could both end up dead, if Becca figures us out. We can't lose any more lives to this; that would get us more of the wrong kind of attention from DOJ. Once we capture Becca, we'll question her about her boss."

"If there is one," Cam clipped, voice harsh, his patience with Bowers wearing thin.

As was Bowers's with them. "You're confident you can flip her? You haven't flipped Scott or Mike yet."

"Because they don't know jack shit," Cam replied. "Becca's had her own plans for a while now."

"We can flip her," Nic said. "Without risking anymore lives."

Bowers stared them down several long seconds before pushing to his feet. Nic was sure he was going to overrule them. What he gave them might be worse.

"Fine, I'll give you this one shot." He stopped over the threshold, his dark eyes cold and hard. "It's a short rope, gentlemen."

Yet just long enough to hang themselves.

Chapter Eight

When Cam helped move Mel and Danny into their South Park condo, he never imagined using his friends' loft as a command center, but it was perfect for this op. Situated on the two floors above a street-level design firm, the condo with its floor-to-ceiling windows and private rooftop provided clean sightlines of the lamp-lit green. Good thing too, as their surveillance van would have stuck out on the single-lane loop around the park.

Granted, Cam would have rather been on the ground himself, directly able to counteract any variables that arose, but from this vantage point, he could view the entire field of play. He'd be better able to direct the agents hiding in cars along the loop and those in the cruisers covering each outside corner of the block. Short of stationing an agent in front of every building, which would be too obvious, he had his bases covered.

Mel and Danny's place was also big enough, with its open floor plan and giant windows, shades pulled back to let in the moonlight, to accommodate their command team traipsing around in the shadows, Lauren's wide array of surveillance equipment, and one very agitated Assistant US Attorney.

A casual observer wouldn't know it. Nic appeared

ones Percy was wearing. "Being real, I'm more worried about a fight breaking out in here."

He ignored her very real, very accurate assessment of the tension in the condo. "This needs to go off without a hitch."

"Couple of hours, we'll have Becca in custody, Abby safe, and you and Nic can ride off into the sunrise together."

"I hope to God we're not here until sunrise."

"True dat."

Cam was still chuckling as a narrow-eyed Nic rounded the dining bar into the kitchen. "Finish wiring Percy," he said to Lauren. "It's almost time."

She grabbed her gadgets and ducked out of the kitchen.

"I don't like him here," Nic said.

Cam didn't have to ask who *him* was. Nic's gaze drilling holes into Bowers's back was indication aplenty. "I don't trust him either." Cam clicked through surveillance feeds on the computer, checking positions again.

"Why aren't you more worried?" Nic asked.

He was worried, but one of them had to keep their shit together. And this was far from the most high-risk op he'd coordinated. "You're worried enough for the both of us."

Letting out a low huff, Nic turned and rested his ass against the counter. "Didn't think I was showing it."

Cam glanced up. "Most people don't see through the mask." Their gazes locked, held, tension of a different sort filtering in, only broken when a chair scraped back across the floor.

Nic twisted, looking over his shoulder at Bowers, who stalked toward the windows. Nic righted himself on a curse. "There's no reason for him to be here. We can run this operation. He's gonna fuck it up."

"So we run it." Cam paired one of the spare comms by the computers and handed it to Nic. More information, more control over the situation, might help him settle. "And we roll with whatever curveball Bowers throws at us. Better to anticipate it and plan for the worst."

Nic tucked the device in his ear, one corner of his mouth hitching up. "You're good at this."

Cam met the half smirk with a grin of his own. "This is my domain."

"Well, technically," Mel interrupted, her high heels clicking on the hardwood as she approached, "it's mine."

Danny twisted in his chair, playfully glaring at his wife. "Hey now!"

Their banter acted like a valve, releasing some of the pressure in the room, but not for long. Charlie team radioed in from the roof. "We've got movement at the west end of the park."

It ran against Cam's every instinct not to rush to the window, not to look out and assess the situation with his own eyes, but the shadows could only conceal so much. A herd of people standing next to the condo's glass would stand out, even in the moonlight.

Cam activated his comm again. "Local?" He wouldn't put it past one of the neighborhood millionaires to take a late-night stroll with their pocket-sized pooch. No doubt why Becca picked this location. The cover of normalcy, together with plenty of exits, witnesses, and objects she could use as roadblocks if a chase ensued.

"Negative," Charlie replied. "Muscle, two of 'em. Bulges under both arms."

"She's early," Nic said. "I thought she'd make us wait."

Mel shook her head, short curls bouncing. "She's scoping out the area. Putting her people in first."

"Or so she thinks," Cam said, then to Lauren, "Go time."

"All right, Weasley." Lauren hauled Percy up and held out the enhanced glasses to him. "Swap your current ones for these."

Percy pocketed his old glasses and adjusted the new ones on his nose. "They're heavier, but I'm not seeing the bells and whistles."

"Because they're on our end." She pointed at the computer on the left. "Hit F3 on that one."

Cam bumped Nic's hip, shifting him out from in front of the computer. He tapped the key as directed and the front window retracted, displaying a zoomed-out version of the desktop. In one of the other open windows, Lauren's pixie features filled the picture. Cam brought that window forward, the view changing as Percy rotated his head. "We're good on visual," he said.

"Now cough," Lauren said to Percy.

He cleared his throat and a sound bar on-screen registered the noise.

"Sound's good too," Cam confirmed.

Bowers ambled over beside Lauren. "You're sure the tech can't be detected?" he asked.

"It's all in the glasses," she answered. "Unless Becca takes the glasses off him and feels their weight, we should be in the clear."

"Has it been tested in the field?" Bowers followed up, narrowed eyes not on the tech but on Lauren, doubt coloring his voice and every feature.

Beside Cam, Nic tensed, his hands curling around the lip of the granite counter. Cam shifted closer, brushing his arm against the other man's, containing him as much as he could under watchful eyes. The last thing Percy needed was to doubt the competency of the people who were supposed to keep him alive.

But before Cam could step in, Lauren shut the matter down. "Multiple times," she said, standing tall, not giving an inch, despite being a good foot shorter than Bowers. "It'll work."

"Let's hope so, Ms. Hall." Nose in the air, Bowers headed up the stairs.

Once he was out of earshot, Lauren muttered, "That's Agent Hall, asshole," and Cam was pleased to see the answering smile on Percy's face. Whether she'd meant to or not, she'd eased their bait's jangled nerves.

Hoping to do the same for Nic, Cam crossed behind him, trailing a hand gently over his lower back. At first, Nic's hands tightened around the counter lip, knuckles going white, but then they relaxed, along with his shoulders, and he leaned back into the touch. Mission accomplished, Cam stepped on past him, meeting Lauren and Percy at the end of the bar.

With a piece of Jamie's tech.

He pulled the two-ply card out of his pocket and held it out to Percy. "Find a way to give this to Becca or Abby."

Percy flipped over the simple black card, running his thumb over the white embossed number on one side. A number that would ring to any of the team's encrypted phones. "What if she won't take it?"

Mel slunk past them, whispering "Try harder" in Percy's ear.

Eyes wide, Percy's Adam's apple bobbed, struggling to swallow his nerves as he pocketed the card. He lifted his other hand to adjust the glasses. Lauren slapped it away. "Don't do that. Draws attention."

Static crackled over the comm, and those with a device in ear snapped to attention. "Two women approaching from the west," Charlie radioed.

"That's your cue," Cam said to Percy. The kid started to tremble, and Cam began to seriously question whether he could pull this off.

Sensing the same, Nic stepped closer, hunching slightly to bring him eye level with Percy. "You're the key to this, Mr. Hunter." Calm and soothing, the same way he'd handled Abby the other day. Getting his witness, his CI, what-have-you, to do what he needed. "All of us—" Nic gestured around the room "—are here to back you up."

Head down, Percy stared past his wobbling knees to his shoes. "I don't even want to be in this."

A partial lie. He'd accepted the first job, had wanted it and the sizable payoff. He was a B&E guy with a record. Only this time, he'd accepted the wrong job. "After tonight, you won't have to be."

Percy's head snapped up. "What about that guard, the one from the courthouse? What about what I've done already?"

"You're not our target, Mr. Hunter." A partial lie on Nic's part. Percy had been under FBI surveillance. He was a target, they'd caught him, but in this case, he wasn't *the* target. "Your cooperation will be noted."

"There a problem, gentlemen?" Bowers called down the stairs. "We need to get moving."

Nic straightened, eyes locked on Percy, who gave a slight nod. "Not at all, sir," he called back to his boss.

After a last round of checks, Percy was ushered out the condo door. An agent would take him down the stairs, to the back exit of the building, and from there, Percy would pretend to break into the ground-level commercial unit on his way to the park. In reality, Mel and Danny owned the entire building and had given the other agent a key to the downstairs unit.

Once there, however, Percy ignored the agent's offer of the key and picked the lock. "Calms him, probably," Danny said, as they watched Percy's progress on-screen. "Kid's good. Knew a few tricks even I didn't."

"Daniel," Mel called from the couch. "Let the professionals work." Far enough back from the window, she wouldn't be spotted, but she likely saw everything through her night-vision goggles.

Danny rolled his eyes, but left them to it, loping over and plopping down on the couch next to her.

Eyes back on the screen, Cam watched as Percy made his way through the design firm's premises and out the front door, approaching the park.

"Comms hot," Cam ordered. "Percy, cough for us."

Percy did as instructed, and each of the teams confirmed the audio. Cam had proven Nic's point, that Percy had backup, and the younger man's spine got a little straighter, his step a little surer, with each report.

He was near the jungle gym, Becca in sight on the other side, sitting on a stone bench, when her two bruisers converged.

"Arms out, Mr. Hunter," one said.

Cam waited as the guard patted Percy down. But only

up to his neck. Cam breathed easier. Their surveillance was clear. And so was Percy.

"Nice little demo you put on there," Becca said, as he rounded the jungle gym.

"You didn't seem to think the courthouse was enough. You got a safe? I can crack that too." The kid had memorized the new script well. Another opportunity to get a confession out of Becca, otherwise they would have cornered her the minute she walked into the zone.

"That's what I have her for." Becca scooted to the side, and the new view through Percy's glasses caused Nic to inhale sharply. Cam too. In the lamplight, Abby looked like she'd been put through the wringer. Bruise on one cheek, hair straggly, eyes red-rimmed and bloodshot.

Nic clenched his jaw so hard that Cam heard the grinding of teeth. Saw it too in the sharp relief of Nic's sunken cheeks and in the way his eyes were locked on the screen, on his witness who, by her haggard appearance and her jerky motions each time Becca moved, was definitely *not* a willing participant. She wasn't acting now; she was afraid. Nic's gaze didn't stray, even as he toggled off his comm and said to Cam, "Move the teams in now."

Cam inched his hand over, brushing the back of Nic's where it'd curled around the counter's edge again. "Teams, we have eyes on the target. Treat Monroe as a hostage, nonhostile. Approach quiet."

Those long fingers relaxed, twining with his, until Bowers's voice came over the comm. "Hold."

"What the fuck?" Nic said, at the same time Cam demanded, "Bowers, stand down."

"We need someone on the inside," Bowers replied.

His argument from earlier today rearing its head. So much for that rope he'd given them. He wouldn't let them hang themselves. He'd hang them himself.

And Nic was having none of it. "I promised Percy this was over for him tonight. Once he put himself on the line for us."

"Change of plans. DOJ wants the person at the top. Percy will have to roll with it."

"Wait, what?" Percy said, and Cam's eyes whipped back to the screen.

Becca had heard it too, her eyes narrowing with suspicion. "Who are you talking to?"

The view on-screen tilted, and Lauren cursed. "Percy! Stop touching your glasses."

Whatever Percy's reaction, probably a swift jerk of his hand down, gave him—*gave them*—away. Becca bolted to her feet, dragging Abby with her.

Bowers's plan was shot. And his last-minute change had possibly also shot the entire plan if Cam didn't act fast.

"Teams converge!" he ordered. "Go, go, go!"

But they weren't close enough yet. Becca twisted, yanking Abby in front of her and pressing a knife to her throat. Their CI used as a shield.

Nic was out the door before Cam could get out a "Wait!" He cursed, then ordered his teams to hold.

"Who sent you?" Becca demanded of Percy.

"You did," Percy improvised. "Gave me this location."

Becca hustled backward, hauling Abby with her. "I think I'll be demanding a refund."

"Who's got a clean shot?" Cam asked.

"Command, Beta, clean shot from the west side."

"Take it," Cam said. "Disarm only," he added, in deference to Bowers. They needed to question Becca, not kill her.

"Hold!" he shouted a half second later, before his sniper got off a shot. At the corner of his screen, Nic barreled out from behind a building, gun drawn. He was headed straight for Becca and Abby, whose attention was drawn the other direction by Percy. Nic had a better angle on the situation, and Cam didn't want him caught in the crossfire.

No one, however, counted on the car that suddenly revved. That flashed on its high beams, blinding Nic in the middle of the street, and pedal to the metal, aimed right for him.

"Dominic, watch out!" Cam hollered.

But it was too late.

The car caught him midstride, tossing him over the hood like a rag doll.

Cam couldn't tell if it was his scream or the screech of Nic's comm that rattled his ears more.

He ripped the device from his ear and hauled ass for the door. Mel stepped in front of him, blocking his path. "Run the op, Agent Byrne."

Every one of his cells screamed a different objective. "I need to get to Nic."

"You need to tell your agents which way is up."

"What the hell is going on?" Bowers hollered behind them, steps thundering down the stairs.

Mel snatched the comm from his hand, tucking it in her ear. "I'm headed down."

A sheathed knife hurtling through the air, tossed by Danny perfectly into Mel's outstretched hand, snapped

Cam out of his panic-induced haze. "We're on it," he answered Bowers, then to Mel, "Go to him."

She nodded, and disappeared out the door, while Cam ignored a glowering Bowers and hustled back into the kitchen. Lauren tossed him another comm, and he shoved it in his ear, fighting to get his focus back, to look at all the screens, when all he wanted to do was watch the screen that showed Nic lying motionless in the street. "Teams report."

Grinding metal was his answer. Lauren's fingers flew across the keyboard of the far right computer, and a second later, a street level view appeared on-screen. A second crash of metal and the car that had hit Nic rammed through two police cruisers on its way out of the oval.

Orders were called down the line to pursue, but the two most able to give chase were out of commission.

Cam whipped his gaze to the center computer, to a sideways view of the park, Percy's glasses on the ground. Percy was in the frame, writhing on the ground with his hands over a bloody nose. Nowhere in the limited view did Cam see any sign of Becca or Abby.

"Where are our suspects?"

"They disappeared into one of the south side buildings," an agent on the ground reported.

"Fan out," Cam ordered. "Search them all."

"Lost your suspects again, did you?" Bowers said from the other side of the kitchen bar.

Cam bit back the *No thanks to you* on the tip of his tongue. There'd be a time for arguing later, and he'd prefer to do so with Nic—

"Agent down!" Mel's voice came over the line. "We need medical, STAT."

Cam finally let himself look at the third screen. Then immediately wished he hadn't.

He'd needed eyes on the scene, and now he needed some way to erase what he'd seen.

Because the sight of Mel crouched next to Nic's unconscious body, lying crumpled in the middle of the street, was going to haunt him forever.

Chapter Nine

Nic woke to Cam's Boston brogue, harsh and drawn out with unleashed fury. "What the hell was that?"

From Nic's other side, Bowers spoke, his words clipped and strident. "I'm trying to find the person calling the shots."

Eyelids heavy, Nic listened to their voices echo around him in stereo, the beeping of a heart monitor like a metronome keeping the cadence of their argument. "You lost us Becca and Abby," Cam said. "And you got Percy and your best AUSA injured in the process."

"My best." Bowers scoffed. "*You* were the one running the op. *Your* agents should have adapted to the change in course."

"Percy is not a fucking agent. We didn't prep him for an insertion."

"Whose fault was that?" Bowers retorted.

"We had a game plan, and *you* called an audible without warning."

"I warned you yesterday."

"Then you said we could run the op our way."

A third voice entered the fray, Irish lilt pronounced. "We cannot change an op in progress if we don't have the right personnel in place," Aidan said. His thicker-than-usual accent, startling but not surprising after ten days in his mother country, had finally unstuck Nic's eyelids so that he witnessed the direction of the SAC's chiding.

"You're back," Nic croaked, and three faces swung to him.

"We're back," came a fourth voice.

Nic lolled his head on the pillow, following the direction of the Southern drawl. In the back corner of the hospital room, Jamie and Lauren huddled behind two laptops open on the tray table. Nic gave a nod, then movement at his side drew his attention forward again.

"Hey," Cam said, stepping closer, all trace of harshness in his voice gone. "How do you feel?"

"Like I was hit by a fucking car." He braced a hand in the mattress, wincing, and assessed the physical damage. Sore, but no sharp pains and no casts on his limbs. Some bruised ribs, judging by the wrap around his torso, and scrapes and bruises under more bandages elsewhere. But nothing broken, on him.

"Easy there," Cam said, lifting a hand toward his shoulder.

Nic batted it away, pushed through the ache and levered himself up to seated. He leaned back against the mound of scratchy pillows.

"Percy's injured?" he asked, recalling Cam's earlier words.

"One of Becca's guards knocked him out as they made their escape. Broken nose and a concussion. He's shaken up more than anything."

"Escaped? Into the car that hit me?"

Cam shook his head. "Oddly, no. They used the confusion to take cover in a shop, then gave us the slip."

"And the car?"

"Rammed two cruisers as it sped out of the west end of the park."

"I did get a partial on the plate," Lauren said. "Running it now."

"A distraction," Bowers said. "So Becca could make a break for it."

Which meant the car would have had to have been there already, the driver lying in wait. Just like their people had been. Did that make any sense? Wouldn't the driver have noticed them and warned Becca away?

Wasn't it more likely the car was unconnected, like Saturday's shooter? Another attempt to threaten him, personally. Maybe an attempt to eliminate him altogether. But how'd they know where he'd be? About the bust? And for that matter, how had they known about the last raid?

"You're lucky you survived," Aidan said from where he stood at the end of the bed.

"No, I'm lucky the Navy taught me how to roll." Yanking the IV out of his arm, he tossed it aside and moved to swing his feet off the bed. Cool air hit his back, and he belatedly realized he was wearing a hospital gown. He'd have to wait for some privacy unless he wanted to show his ass, and his ink, to everyone. Which he did not. He straightened against the pillows instead.

"Do we have a location on Becca and Abby?" he asked.

"Yes," Cam said, finally delivering some good news. "A condo in SoMa. Percy planted the card on the guard just before he took Percy out." Not perfect, but as long as the guard stayed with Becca, and didn't find or otherwise toss the card, they could track them.

But Nic guessed everyone's presence here meant they

weren't going directly after Becca again. "What's our next move?"

"We are going to change the game plan, but we're going to do it right," Cam said, eyes cutting to Bowers and back. "Becca's going to lead us to the person in charge."

"How do you know she's not?"

"We cracked the money trail," Jamie answered behind him.

Nic rotated, wincing. "To?"

"Not a person, yet," Lauren replied. "But a place. Serbia. And it's the same place the deposits to Scott originated from."

Nic's mind whirred, fighting through the painkillers to make the pieces of his case fit. "So, one, someone didn't trust Scott to get the job done."

"Or hired Becca to eliminate him," Aidan speculated. "Once the job was done."

"Has to be considered," Nic said with a nod. "And, two, someone in Serbia is trying to steal the Serbian artifacts."

"My guess," Cam said, "before the exhibit opens."

"Close the exhibit," Nic replied.

"Tried that," Aidan said, then proceeded to lawyer back at him, counting off the issues. "One, it's a fundraiser. Two, Kristić still wants to do it, as a tribute to his late wife."

"We need someone inside," Cam said. "And if we're gonna do an insertion, we have to do it right this time, like you said. One of ours, not another Percy."

Nic agreed. "I'd go—"

Two sharp *Nos*, a strange Boston-Irish mix in one stern word.

"—but they know me," Nic finished his sentence.

Aidan raised a hand in apology. "And there's no way Becca will believe you've flipped."

"We need a B&E guy who is already ours, who we trust. One of your agents? Or assets?"

"Danny's had enough excitement for one year," Jamie chimed in.

"Mel will have my ass if I risk his on this," Aidan agreed.

Cam's suggestion was the last thing Nic expected. "I'll go."

Nic's first instinct was to argue but he bit back his *no* at the last second, not wanting to second-guess him in front of Aidan or Bowers. And besides, Jamie, blasting out from behind the tray table, was objecting loudly enough for the both of them. "No way, Cameron."

"It's fine, Whiskey," Cam tried to soothe Jamie.

"Talents I don't know about, Boston?" Nic asked.

Dark eyes shot to his. "There's a lot you don't know about."

If Cam had the skills, he was certainly qualified, and there was no one Nic would trust more as their inside man. No one he'd trust more to rescue Abby, capture Becca, and help close this case.

Before Nic could say so, Jamie grabbed Cam by the arm and tugged him out of the room. Aidan broke the astonished silence that had settled in their wake. "Has Becca or any of her new crew seen him?"

Nic shook his head. "I don't think so. He was kitted out in a mask and helmet at the condo raid. I don't think he took them off until after Becca fled." He craned his neck to glance at Lauren again. "Anywhere else I'm forgetting?"

"The arraignment, maybe?" she said.

"Negative." He turned back to Aidan. "Becca wasn't in the courtroom, and I don't remember seeing her anywhere around the courthouse yesterday. We can check security footage to confirm, but I'd be willing to bet Percy was the only one there. And when we cornered him, he recognized me but he had no idea who Cam was."

"She still could have had eyes on him," Bowers said, as the door swung open.

"I won't look the same to those eyes," Cam countered, stopping at the foot of the bed next to Aidan.

Fuming, Jamie stalked back to his spot beside Lauren, and Nic could tell it was all the former agent could do not to make a remark.

Nic wanted—needed—to know what was up, for the sake of the mission, if not his sanity. But he wouldn't ask Cam in front of Bowers. "Are you sure about this?" Nic said instead. "Your call, Boston."

"It's the quickest, surest way to infiltrate, to find out who Becca is working for, and to rescue Abby. This is my job. This is what I'm good at."

Nic sank back into the pillows. No use arguing. Cam's mind was set, and if his best friend couldn't change it, Nic wouldn't be able to either.

"All right, Boston, it's your rescue."

Cam kicked down the volume on his headset before the screeches of "Uncle Cam!" blew out his eardrums. "Bobby," he tried again, hoping his older brother could hear him over the kids. "I just need five fucking minutes of your attention."

"You try sparing five minutes with three kids always

hanging off you," Bobby replied, weary but laughing. "They miss their favorite uncle."

Truth be told, Cam missed them too, more than a little. He slumped on the end of his bed, next to his go-bag stuffed with the rattiest clothes he still owned. Torn jeans, threadbare T-shirts, ribbed tank tops, an old BC hoodie, and his ancient army surplus camo jacket. He held the coat to his nose, inhaling the lingering scents of shop grease and pot smoke. Two decades later, any smells should have been long gone—maybe they were and it was all in his head—but this jacket would always smell that way to him. Remind him of that part of his life—a mix of bitter and sweet. Vestiges of a life left behind, even before he'd moved here.

He was lucky he'd kept this stuff. Luckier still that he'd brought it out with him to California. Then again, he'd had to make the U-Haul worth it. A bed frame and mattress, treadmill and weight bench, and a couple suitcases of clothes barely filled half the trailer. So the shit in the back of his old closet had moved cross-country to the back of his new closet. Would unearthing it all now unearth his old life too? A life he and his brother had vowed never to revisit.

"Say a few words to them?" Bobby said, snapping Cam back to the present. "Ma's on her way over to babysit while Josie and I go out."

Cam set the coat aside. "Yeah, I'd like that."

A little comfort from home was due, especially after the past few days. A raid gone wrong. A kidnapping on his watch. Seeing Nic's body tossed across the hood of a car. He'd thought his imagination was bad before, when it kept showing him Nic bleeding out in the street. Now he didn't need his imagination; he had the real thing to go on, sans the blood. Nic's unconscious form, lying motionless in the middle of the road, was there every time he closed his eyes. That sight was a big part of the reason he'd volunteered to take point infiltrating Becca's crew. He'd be damned if Nic walked into the line of fire again on this case.

Going undercover would also require him to play his full accent. Nothing like the unchecked Southie drawls of his nieces and nephews to help bring back his own. Full-strength, not the watered-down version his friends here thought was thick but sounded pitifully thin to his ears. A call wouldn't be as good as being back there, but every minute on the phone helped.

He asked each of them how they were doing in school. How his nephew was doing on the Pop Warner football team. How far his niece could kick the same football, determined to play with her twin brother. Cam held out hope the youngest of Bobby's kids would follow his uncle's footsteps onto the court—Cam had even put a tiny basketball in little Jack's hands at Christmas—but with the way he worshipped his older siblings, Jack would probably go the way of the pigskin too.

He'd have to hold out hope for his own someday.

Just as Bella finished telling him about their field trip to Salem, a door slammed and Cam's mother called out, "I'm here, with cannoli!"

Shouts of "Nana" and "I get first pick" rang out as they all abandoned him for his mother and pastries.

Laughing, Bobby came back on the line. "Now you know where you rank."

Cam couldn't blame them, his own mouth watering. "Everything ranks below cannoli."

"We are the worst Irish family ever."

"Yeah, us and half the Irish families in Boston."

Bobby laughed out loud. "Only half?"

"Truth, brother, truth."

Standing, Cam grabbed the straps of his bag and started to lift, only to be swatted by a clawed paw. Green eyes in a white-and-orange tabby face glared at him from inside his open bag. "Shoo, fur ball," he said, patting the cat's rump until it vacated his bag and room with an angry *meow*.

Slinging the bag over his shoulder, Cam carried it down the short hallway to the front bedroom he'd set up as a home office and gym. No way he could afford the gym memberships here. Not that it ever got cold enough he couldn't run outside. No snow and relatively little rain to contend with either. He should ditch the equipment and rent the room out. Bring in some spare cash. Buy an extra suit or two with it.

"Hey, brother," Bobby called. "Where'd *your* attention go?"

"Sorry, sorry." He dropped the bag in his desk chair. "Getting ready to go on assignment. Let me switch you to FaceTime." He swapped the audio call for visual and propped the device against the stack of unopened mail on his desk. "Just got a lot going on here."

"You got a woman you're not telling us about?"

A man, *maybe*, but until that maybe became a firmer *yes*, he wasn't going to spring his bisexuality on his family. He'd never been serious enough, with anyone to bring them home, and he'd kept his college partying to campus. So, he'd chickened out and never corrected his family's assumption. He felt like a coward every day for it, especially after Jamie had been brave enough to come out last year, and with the rest of his friends here who were out and proud. Another way he didn't measure up. Granted his family had taken Jamie's coming out in stride, sending wedding gifts and well wishes, but Cam didn't know how they would take his. Having caused his family more than enough strife already, he didn't want to create more unless and until he had someone special in his life. And it was too soon to tell with Nic.

"Work thing," he answered Bobby. "New assignment tomorrow."

"Where's this one?"

"Local." He bent at the waist, opening the lower desk drawer and unlocking his safe there.

"That why you called?"

Maybe he shouldn't have. He'd just worry Bobby, who, if he told anyone else in the family, would worry too. But Bobby knew better than anyone the Cam he was about to become again. He was the only one Cam could talk to about how much that fucking scared him.

From inside the safe, Cam withdrew the bag of tools long since retired. "Remind me, best way to jack an AmSec 8000 series vault door?"

Bobby's blue eyes widened, then the dark brow above them furrowed, a deep crease forming between them. "Why do you need to know that?"

"The assignment I mentioned…undercover gig."

"Not someone else who can do that?"

"'Fraid not." He had the skills, and there were people he had to rescue. Others he needed to protect. This *was* his job.

"You really need me to remind you?" Bobby said.

Of course he didn't. Despite the intervening years, Cam had done it so many times it'd be like riding a bike. If he'd really needed pointers, he would have asked Danny instead of worrying his brother.

He tossed the tools into his bag, tossed the bag onto the treadmill, then sank into the desk chair. "Called for another reminder." He pulled out his wallet and the library card again, smoothing a thumb over the name preserved in laminate. More than could be said for the owner's body, which two decades later was still missing. When he glanced back up, Bobby's eyes were likewise on the card, as sad and heavy as Cam's chest felt. "We made a deal," Cam said.

Bobby blinked, casting aside the same memories likely plaguing Cam. "This is for work."

"Still, we said never—"

"You got backup?"

"Yeah, my partner." The memory of Nic rolling over the car hood streaked behind his eyes again. If he'd go to those lengths for their CIs… "And the prosecutor on the case. He's ex-Special Forces."

"Tell them about our deal," Bobby said.

Cam hung his head as his heart raced, turning the card over in his hands. Aidan had to know; it would have been in his file, in his psych evals. He hadn't hidden the truth of why he'd joined the Bureau. No, that wasn't the reason why his pulse sped. It hammered at the prospect of exposing his grimy past to the man who always had his shit together.

"Tell them where your line in the sand is," Bobby continued. "Make sure they hold you to it."

But could they, if he was on his own—embedded, undercover and cut off? He righted his head, meeting his brother's concerned gaze. "If anything should happen—"

"Don't talk like that."

"You still ignoring what I do?"

"I know it's what you needed, for your sanity, but for the sake of mine, yes, I'm ignoring it."

They both chuckled, the tense mood lightening a bit, then more so when background calls of "Daddy" grew in volume.

"Duty calls," Bobby said. "You want to talk to Josie or Ma?"

"Nah, I'll just make them worry. Don't say anything about this, okay?"

His brother nodded his head of dark hair, going gray at the temples. "Call me when you get back. Or during, if you need me. I'm always here."

That devotion had saved both their lives, right when they'd been on the edge of throwing their futures away for good. "Love you, brother."

"Love you too."

Bobby clicked off and Cam reclined in his chair, closing his eyes and tipping his face to the ceiling, card held to his chest. What would Nic think when he learned that by-the-rules Agent Byrne was a figment of Cam's imagination? Created out of necessity, but a persona nonetheless.

Sighing, he pushed to his feet, pocketed the card and wallet, and checked his bag over once more. He zipped it up just as a knock sounded at the front door. He glanced at his watch. His appointment was early.

Flicking off the lights, he pulled the hallway pocket door partway closed and crossed the living area to the front door, opening it to…not the visitor he expected.

Not that this unexpected one was unwelcome.

Nic stood on his doorstep, dressed down in slacks

and rolled-up shirtsleeves, holding up a six pack of his favorite Imperial Stout. "Not much of this left," he said. "Thought you might like to share some with me."

Cam held the door open wider. "Won't say no to that."

Chapter Ten

Nic strolled into the familiar house, his gait a little slower than normal. His body was confused, sore like it would be after an intense workout, stiff as if he'd sat at his desk all day, and if he turned the wrong way too fast, sore and aching would give way to a sharp stab of pain. All in all, not too bad for having been hit by a car eighteen hours ago.

Cam shut the door behind him. "They give you some good drugs?"

They'd tried; he'd refused. He'd also tried to refuse the X-rays and head CT the doctors had recommended, wanting to leave with the rest of the team once they'd finished the debrief in his hospital room. Bowers had ordered otherwise, and for once Aidan had agreed with him. Bastard.

Hours later, he'd finally been released, but by the time he'd returned to the Federal Building, Cam had already left. After checking on Tony, calling Scott's and Mike's attorneys for perfunctory plea negotiations, and replenishing the caffeine and sugar stash for Lauren and Jamie, who was consulting on Cam's cover build, Nic had left the City too, detouring by the brewery to check in with his assistant managers. He should have gone home from there, to his duplex a few blocks away, but he'd driven to Cam's place instead.

Not the smartest idea—he was putting Cam in more jeopardy than he already was—but after being flung over a car, after the way Cam had looked at him in the hospital with those swirling black eyes, after Cam had volunteered to take point on a case that had already gone from bad to worse, Nic was getting that second kiss before it was too late. He was also getting an explanation for why Jamie didn't want Cam on this assignment.

"Wouldn't be here with these—" he lifted the beer bottles in their cardboard carrier "—if they had. I took worse hits in BUDs training." Worse falls too, including the one that'd ended his SEAL career. He stood in the middle of the living area, glancing around. "Didn't change much."

"Aidan left most of the furniture, which was good, since I didn't want to haul mine cross-country."

Cam shuffled past him, slipping the carrier from his hand. Nic stifled his gasp at the sizzle of heat running up his arm. If his hospital room hadn't been packed when he'd woken this morning, would he have gotten that second kiss, then? The way Cam had looked down at him, had spoken so softly, would have tempted Nic into pulling him down by the tie and forcing his tongue between his lips, if they hadn't had an audience. Cam's tie was gone now, as was the rest of his suit, replaced with a gray FBI T-shirt and worn jeans, the view of Cam's ass in the latter a sight Nic enjoyed immensely as he followed him into the kitchen.

Pulling free two bottles, Cam set them on the bar separating the kitchen from the dining area and shoved the rest in the fridge. Nic rooted around in the drawers for the bottle opener, and the mood was comfortable, until it was shattered by a furry beast jumping onto the bar. Nic fumbled the bottle opener, the metal clanking against granite. "Jesus, fuck, it's huge."

Cam stepped to his side, laughing. "I wanted a dog, but with the job, a cat made more sense."

"This is not a cat, Boston." Nic reached out a cautious hand. The animal ducked its head, then butted his curved fingers, nuzzling for a pet. Amused by the affectionate beast, Nic smiled as he scratched behind its ears. "This is a mini-mountain lion."

"Maine Coon, actually. He acts like a dog. As close as I could manage."

"What's his name?"

Cam grinned. "Bird."

Nic shot him a baleful side-eye. "You named a cat Bird?"

"I know you got hit by a car today, Price, but come on, put it together."

Nic glanced back at the cat. White and orange tabby, green eyes, thin green Boston Celtics branded collar around his neck.

Oh, in surprise, then *oh*, in disgust. Nic couldn't have stopped his eyes from rolling if his life depended on it. "Should have fucking known. Better than Larry, I guess. Or worse, Brady."

Cam hid a wider smile around the mouth of his beer bottle, and Nic couldn't stop himself from staring either. Or from the heat that warmed his cheeks when Cam made a satisfied hum in the back of his throat.

Tearing his gaze away, he forced himself to pause his desire's objective and address the other objective first. "You ready for this tomorrow?" he asked.

Cam looked like he wanted to swallow a whole bunch of conflicting emotions with his next gulp of beer. "Best way to rescue Abby."

"Thank you," Nic said, infusing his voice with all the gratitude he felt, "for keeping that as your priority, even if you still don't trust her completely." If not for Cam, he'd feel like he was shouting at the wind.

"Bowers isn't my boss."

"Lucky you." He took a long swallow from his own bottle and unfastened another button at the collar of his dress shirt. He should have snagged a T-shirt at Gravity, but his mind had been elsewhere. Here already, questions swirling, and Cam, whose eyes had drifted to the hollow of his throat, wasn't giving him what he wanted, at least in the answers department. "Also, you dodged my question," he said, calling the other man's bluff. "Tell me why Jamie doesn't want you going under on this one."

Cam's eyes shot up. "Boy, you don't beat around the bush, do you?"

"Not with most things." He held Cam's gaze, double meaning clear. They'd been beating around the bush of whatever this was between them for months. Nic intended to directly address that too, *after* he got any more case surprises out of the way. There'd been enough of those already; he wanted everything out in the open before Cam put his life in danger.

"I wasn't always Special Agent Cameron Byrne."

"I didn't expect you launched from your mother's womb as such."

Cam almost spit out his beer on a startled laugh. Nice to catch him off guard, and to break the tension that'd crept in.

Smiling, Nic climbed onto one of the padded barstools. "Tell me why you can fake it as a B&E guy."

"Caught that, did you?"

"I should hope so, as the success of this sting depends on it."

Cam took another long swallow of beer, then set the bottle down. "My older brother Bobby worked at a garage."

He'd put the last word in air quotes, and Nic caught on to his meaning. "So, a chop shop, then?"

Arms braced behind him on the end of the bar, Cam leaned back and stared into space, his reflection in the shiny double oven doors vacant, his mind far away from the here and now. "I worshipped him."

"You followed him to the garage?"

"Into it all. I could boost a car by the time I was thirteen. From there, it was a short jump to breaking into and boosting other things."

"What changed?"

Vacant expression vanished, Cam's face twisted into grief and regret. He shook it off a second later, but Nic had seen it. Felt a familiar stab of pain in his chest. "Some family shit went down, the same night Bobby and I were out on a job. If we'd been where we were supposed to be instead…" His words drifted off, struggling, as the emotion returned. "I might not be a practicing Catholic, but I'm Catholic enough to have a mountain's worth of guilt stored up. Bobby too."

Reaching out, Nic slid a hand over his. "You got out?" he asked softly.

Cam tangled their fingers, like he'd done in the condo last night. "Bobby and I made a deal. Never again."

"And you became an agent, because of what happened?"

"After a failed dream of playing basketball, no thanks to Whiskey Walker."

Nic let him have that dodge; he'd rather see a smile on Cam's face than that ravaged look from a moment ago. "What's Bobby do now?"

Cam rotated on his hip, facing Nic. "Installs security systems."

"I bet he's good at that."

"One of the best. It'll be useful for when his three kids become unruly teenagers like we were."

"He'll LoJack them, won't he?"

"You bet." Cam polished off the last of his beer and waited for Nic to finish his, hand out for the empty. "Another?"

Nic nodded.

Cam strolled to the far end of the kitchen, tossed the empties, then opened the fridge door. "We both swung the opposite direction. Playing by the rules. Bobby installing security, me as an FBI agent."

While his head was in the fridge, Nic slid off his stool and crossed the kitchen so he was right there when Cam closed the door. No more dodging; he'd seen the problem with Cam's story. Had suddenly grasped Jamie's well-placed concern.

"You're going back on your deal," he said. "With Bobby."

Twisting, avoiding his gaze, Cam grabbed the bottle opener. "He said I'm not. It's for work."

Nic stepped closer. "How's your head doing with that?"

"Still processing."

"That's why Jamie was worried. He knows about this."

"Some of it." Cam held an open bottle out to Nic. "I'm worried," he admitted. "I buried that part of myself, deep, and now I'm digging it all back up."

Nic knew a thing or two about that. He'd spent most of his life hiding one secret or another. Maybe if he shared some of those, the things that made him the man he was, Cam would feel more comfortable using his own past on this assignment without fear of losing the present. Because after hearing what he had, Nic was more convinced than ever that Cam was exactly the *right* person for this assignment.

He reached past Cam to place his bottle on the cabinet behind him, and with his trailing hand, lifted Cam's face, catching his dark, swirling gaze.

Considering.

Plenty of other men had seen what Nic was about to show Cam. He'd intended for Cam to see it tonight as it were, and had taken all the wraps and bandages from the hospital off at the brewery. But while other men had seen, Nic still hid their meaning from most, explained to only a few, and never the full truth to anyone. Cam, though, needed it. Or as much as Nic could give.

Decision made, he removed his hand from under Cam's chin, stepped back, and began to work free the buttons of his dress shirt. Cam inhaled sharply, bobbled his bottle, and Nic chuckled. The blush across Cam's cheeks was so beautiful Nic almost reached for him, to claim that second kiss, but that wasn't what Cam needed. Yet.

In the end, Cam made the decision for him, rotating to set his bottle aside. When he turned back around, he

full on gasped as his wide eyes roved over Nic's tattooed skin, leaving a path of fire in their wake.

Nic unhooked the last button, letting his hands fall to the side, shirt hanging open. "We've all got a past, Boston."

Cam's darkening gaze flickered up, seeking permission, and Nic granted it with a nod. Cam didn't think to warm his hands, cold from the beer bottle, and Nic hissed at the first touch. His fingertips warmed in seconds, though, as they trailed across a torso lightly sprinkled with brown and gray hair and painted in memories.

The eagle, flintlock, anchor, and trident insignia over his left pec, aka "The Budweiser," inked after he finished BUDs training, once he was officially made a Navy SEAL.

"You got a JAG one too?" Cam asked.

"Hip," Nic replied, voice full of gravel. He planned on showing Cam the oak leaves and mill rinde later tonight, Cam's hands on his body making that all the more inevitable. Now, though, Cam was tracing the list of names beneath his SEAL tat. His team members, including Eddie.

Cam glanced up again, eyes asking a question to which there was a good answer for a change, not a heart-breaking one. "All still here," Nic said. "I wanted to honor them. They saved me, when I was injured in the field. Didn't leave me behind, so I keep them with me too."

Cam flattened his palm over the names, a benediction that had Nic closing his eyes and sucking in his own breath, then exhaling again as Cam slid his hand to the other side of his torso, over the quote halfway up his ribs. *The Only Easy Day Was Yesterday.* A SEAL

favorite. And below it, the skeletal frog and trident also
favored by frogs like him, though he'd never seen another SEAL's inked in rainbow colors.

"Got it when Don't Ask, Don't Tell was repealed,"
he said with a smile. It died though, as Cam coasted his
hand the rest of the way up his torso, first over the bruise
where he'd collided with the car, then over the simple,
unadorned number on his right pectoral.

Nic shivered, and Cam placed his other hand on his
hip, grounding him. "What's this one?" he asked.

Nic turned his face away, hiding a face much like
the one Cam had made earlier. Full of pain and regret.
"The number of people I killed." It wasn't a small number. He'd been one of the Navy's best snipers during
those seven years before the injury had forced his move
to JAG.

Cam's hold on his side tightened. "Where's the other
one?"

Nic righted his gaze, swallowing hard to force
moisture into his mouth. "What other one?" he asked,
hoarsely.

"The number of people you saved." Cam flattened his
palm again, over the number. "Or the number of murderers you put away?"

Nic gave a small, sad smile. "We don't celebrate the
victories enough, do we?"

Cam ran his hand down, over the rainbow frog again.
"You did here." Nic's obliques quivered under his touch;
so did other parts south. "Christ, all this is under that
suit, every fucking day?"

And Cam hadn't even seen the half of it, but the story
etched on his back was for another time, if ever. Some
truths were better left in the past where they belonged,

though the situation with his father brought it closer to the surface every day.

Releasing his hip, Cam's hands met over his abs and coasted up. Nic inhaled sharply again, blood roaring under his skin and through his veins. He paused Cam's exploration over his sternum, hands around his wrists. "I—" he started, then cleared his throat and tried again. "I go out there, into the courtroom every day, and I use all this to atone, to try and be a better attorney and man." He moved one of Cam's hands over the kill count again. "I put murderers away, for those I…"

Black eyes shot to his, blazing with fury and indignation on his behalf. "You're not—"

"Use what you learned." He wove their fingers together over his skin. "Take the guilt and regret and the pain and let it help you be a better agent. Take who you used to be and let it help you do your job and rescue Abby."

Eyes downcast, Cam seemed to deliberate some decision of his own. "What if I can't come back?" he whispered, barely loud enough for Nic to hear. "Old me, he was distracted. I lost…" His face pinched in remembered pain, and when he started again, his voice was thin and ragged. "How do I not step over the line?"

Letting go of a wrist, Nic cupped the side of his neck, forcing his gaze. "I will pull you back."

"How?" Cam breathed, black eyes boring into his. "When you're the one who makes me want to break all the rules?"

Nic stepped closer, crowding him back against the counter. "We're not breaking any rules." Maybe they were breaking the laws of common sense, but Nic had thrown that out the window after their first kiss. They needed each other more.

Cam laid his rough, tempting cheek against Nic's. "I really want to kiss you again."

Nic smirked. "Why do you think I brought the stout?"

"'Cause it's my favorite."

Using his hand around Cam's neck, Nic angled the other man's face in and licked his lips. Tasting, teasing. "No, Boston. 'Cause I like the taste of my beer on you."

"Fuck," Cam groaned, then lunged, chasing after Nic's tongue.

Their mouths slammed together, lips and teeth clashing, weeks of pent-up desire rushing out. Their second kiss was as wild and desperate, as scorching, as the first, and Nic already wanted a third. Wanted them all.

Shifting, Cam slipped his thigh between Nic's legs, and Nic ground against it with a moan. Cam encouraged the motion, hand racing down his back to clutch his ass, yanking him up and closer, all but riding his leg.

"Fuck, Boston." Hand snaking into Cam's hair, fingers knotting in the dark locks, Nic held Cam's hot mouth to his, tasting every corner as their hips rocked impatiently together, demanding attention. Cam gave it to him, pushing off the counter and spinning them. Pressing Nic's back against the fridge, he rutted his dick along Nic's, driving Nic wild despite the twinge of soreness and the damnable wool and denim between their bodies.

"Is this what you want, Dominic?" Hard length against hard length, the teasing wonderful and horrible. The torture continued as Cam slipped a hand inside Nic's waistband, clawing at his ass, then diving into the cleft between his cheeks. "Or maybe you want this?" His finger circled Nic's rim.

Nic's head fell back, banging against the steel fridge door. Fuck yeah that's what he wanted, but good luck finding words right now. Groans would have to suffice.

Understanding well enough, Cam bit and laved the exposed tendon of his neck. "I didn't think it was possible to want you more than I already did, but all this…" The hand not teasing his asshole burned a path down Nic's torso again, around the edge of his belly button, just like how he was torturing his other rim, then farther down, palming his cock. "And this…" he said, stroking up and down through his pants. "My dick's about to explode."

Nic righted his head, catching Cam's lips. "Mine too." Fuck, he didn't know whether to go back or forward. Thrust into Cam's palm around his cock or ride the finger breaching his hole. "Do something about it."

"How is it possible my dick's getting harder?"

"Only one cure for that," Nic replied.

And it wasn't the ringing doorbell.

Nic ripped his mouth away. "Who the fuck is that?"

Cam's lips slid over his collarbone. "Aidan's stylist," he murmured against the sensitive skin at the crook of Nic's neck. "Here for some disguise work."

Sighing, Cam stepped back, a bit wobbly on his feet, but so was Nic, clutching the fridge door handle to stay upright.

Cam eyed his crotch. "You're gonna have to hide that."

Nic's eyes flickered down to Cam's own problem, then back up, right before he shoved off the fridge door, bearing down on the tease. Cheek to cheek, he cupped

Cam through the denim, returning the stroking torture. "Don't show up with red hair tomorrow," he whispered hotly into the agent's ear. "Not sure I can pull you back from that."

Chapter Eleven

Single coffee cup in one hand, tray of four in the other, Nic nudged the FBI conference room door open with his hip, biting back a wince.

He hadn't lied yesterday—he'd taken harder tumbles—but no matter the severity, a little spill or a big one, the next day always hurt worse. Not even the long shower he'd taken after getting home last night had helped. Probably because he'd spent most of it contorting himself, one soapy hand pumping his dick, the other fingering his ass, desperate for relief.

While he'd left Cam's place unsatisfied in that regard, he'd at least satisfied his primary objective. Learning what concerned Jamie and Cam about this assignment, and hopefully instilling in Cam confidence that he could use his past for good. Nic had to believe that for his own day-to-day existence, otherwise getting out of bed and putting one foot in front of the other would be awfully damn difficult. He might not believe he was the better man Cam thought he was, but he had to believe in atonement, if nothing else.

Right now, though, Nic couldn't be his own or anyone's focus. All their efforts needed to be focused on supporting Cam, on keeping their inside man grounded.

Judging by Lauren's and Jamie's rumpled clothes, and the plethora of soda cans and Kit Kat wrappers littering the table, that's exactly what they'd been doing all night.

"Have you two slept at all?"

The remnants of Lauren's makeshift bun joined the rest of her hair that had already fallen around her face. "That'd be a negative." She shoved the strands out of her face and held out a hand, not bothering to look up. He slipped a coffee cup into it, then pulled out the next, intending to hand it to Jamie, but was caught off guard midreach.

"They're almost done with my cover."

Nic whipped around, wincing again at the sudden movement. Good thing he'd inhaled on the turn because air was suddenly in short supply.

Cameron Byrne, minus the Agent part, had sucked all of it out of the room. Very minus the Agent part. He stood in the corner behind the door, a motorcycle-booted foot braced on the wall. His propped knee stuck out of worn, ripped denim, and the skintight tee he had on under a ragged Boston College hoodie might as well have been painted on his solid chest. And was that a Maori tattoo creeping out from under his collar and up his neck, bordering on more dark scruff that had grown in overnight?

Nic idly imagined how the thicker beard would tickle his palms, his lips, and other parts, his idle imagination stoked as Cam, following his line of sight, rubbed a hand over his jaw. Nic got distracted again, by the wide black buckle cuff on his wrist and the gel-spiked tips of his hair, highlighted blue. The look was topped off with just enough eyeliner to make Cam's dark eyes seem like limitless black holes he could fall into.

Nic was on his way to doing just that when Aidan brushed past him into the room, swiping the coffee cup from his hand. "Meet Brady Campbell."

That brought Nic back to his right mind.

He scoffed, remembering their first kiss that had been prompted by a time-honored East Coast versus West Coast debate—Brady versus Montana. "You just had to go there," he bemoaned.

The next coffee cup in his hand disappeared as fast as the first two, swiped by Danny, who'd followed his brother into the conference room. "Seemed appropriate," the younger Talley said. He held up a leather pouch in his other hand. "We're set in Aidan's office," he said to Cam.

"Set for what?" Nic asked.

Cam pushed off the wall. "Replica of the museum vault where the artifacts are being held." He pulled a small sack from the chair at the head of the table.

On his other side, Danny waved around what Nic now recognized as a lock-pick set. "Practice."

Cam approached, wiggling a coffee cup free from the tray.

"Thought you knew how to do that already?" Nic said.

"Taking the bike out, just to be sure I can still ride it."

The more he talked, the more Nic noticed his thicker accent. The vowels longer, the Rs dropped. Pure Southie.

Jamie rose from his chair and circled the table, tablet in hand. "Electronic locks."

"You have to hack it too?" Nic asked, gaze bouncing between the two.

"Some component of the museum security system, yes."

Thank God Cam had the best tutor. Nic wouldn't even

begrudge Jamie the last coffee. He tossed the empty cardboard tray on the table, as his gaze followed the three men out of the room, eyes straying to Cam's ass in those worn jeans. This Cam was dangerous, in more ways than one.

Aidan cleared his throat, and Nic righted himself on a curse, from the ache and from the fact he didn't have a coffee cup to hide behind. Words would have to do. "A replica or Danny bought a vault?" he asked.

"To-may-to, to-mah-to," Aidan answered.

Nic hoped Mel could put it to good use after. He rounded the table to the conference room coffee machine and started a cup brewing. Not great, but better than nothing. "Tell me about Brady Campbell," he said, leaning back against the built-in credenza.

"High school dropout from South Boston," Aidan began. "Started working in his brother's chop shop as a teen. Boosting cars led to boosting more valuable items." As Aidan rattled off the details, Nic recognized the pattern, the familiarity. Easier for Cam to keep his cover story straight the closer it stayed to the truth.

"I know where this is going," he interrupted. "How are we getting him in?"

"Whiskey found a connection." Aidan nodded toward the laptops, meaning Gray Hat Jamie had taken a walk on the Black Hat side. "Someone that can make an introduction."

The coffeemaker beeped and Nic slid his cup out. Taking a sip, he grimaced at the bitter taste. "Will he be wired?" There were more advanced devices—ones Mel, if not the FBI, could get their hands on—that were almost undetectable.

Aidan shook his head. "Too risky."

More bitterness. "Sending him in completely cut-off isn't?"

"What's this really about?" Aidan asked, brown eyes narrowed.

Head down, Lauren struck her computer keys harder and faster, counting off the seconds of their stare-down. No way was he getting into this with Aidan, because no way would it not get back to Jamie, and that was Cam's call to make, his friendship on the line.

For only two kisses. So far.

Lauren's click-clacking reminded him of something else he needed to know, not that he really wanted to get into that matter either. "What'd your trace on the car plates turn up?"

Her chipped nails halted their assault on the keys. "Nada. Stolen. Not a match to the car."

"What do you think they'll show?" Aidan asked, far too perceptive.

Nic's phone, for once, rang at just the right time. He drew it out of his pocket, checking the screen. Another *Unknown* caller.

"Excuse me." He tossed his cup of piss poor coffee into the trash and ducked out of the room. "Hello, this is Nic Price."

Dead air, same as last time. Though standing in the FBI's offices, he doubted any of Vaughn's goons were around to rush him. But was there someone else here on Vaughn's payroll? Or in his office downstairs? Someone who'd known where he was during both the prior ops? What other explanation could there be?

His eyes roamed the bullpen desks, looking for who might be on the phone, on the other end of the line. "Who is this?"

More nothing.

"You gonna keep calling and not talking?" he growled low. "Who do you work for? My father? Vaughn?"

Still nothing.

"You won't be able to hide for long," he bit out, before his thumb jabbed at the screen, ending the call.

As soon as the screen went blank, he cursed. Not long enough for a trace, he didn't think. But couldn't hurt to ask. He opened the secure call app and scrolled to Mel's number. Before he dialed, though, Aidan's office door swung open and Danny, Jamie, and Cam filed out.

His frustration at the call must have shown. Cam trailed behind the others, pausing at his side. "Another hang up?" He was a damn good agent, didn't miss a thing. "Talk to Jamie," he said.

Nic dropped the phone back in his pocket, then looked up, first over Cam's shoulder, at the open safe in the office behind them, then, when Cam cleared his throat, into those deep, dark eyes. Cam was who they should be concerned about right now, he reminded himself. The investigation into the shooter, the driver, and whoever was calling him could wait.

"Jamie's got more important things to worry about."

"I'll be fine," Cam said. "I'll keep an eye on Abby and find out who's pulling the strings. Make Bowers happy." He brushed his hand against the back of Nic's. "I'll catch them."

Nic smiled weakly. "And I'll prosecute them."

Cam gave his hand a firmer knock, then started toward the conference room. Before Nic could second-guess himself, he grabbed Cam by the arm, turning him back around. "Hold just a second." He fished his keyring out of his pocket and flipped through the various pieces of metal until he got to the one with the red bumper. Using a nail, he forced the ring apart and began sliding the key off.

Cam's choked "Dominic" made him look up, and his nail slipped, the key snapping back into place on the ring. Cursing, and ignoring the question in Cam's one word, Nic tried again and wiggled the key all the way off this time. Grabbing Cam's wrist, Nic lifted his hand and pressed the key into his palm. "Eddie's place," he said.

Cam blinked, once, twice, then the confusion seemed to clear, his eyes sharpening. "The beach house in Half Moon Bay? He's not home?"

Nic shook his head. "Out with his Guard team, at least another week. Use it as a safe house, if you need to." It wasn't on either of their offices' records as an official safe house. It wouldn't be compromised. "Or..." he started again, then paused, contemplating how to say this without second-guessing Cam or doubting his abilities. "Or if you just need a place to pull back."

Cam curled his fingers around the key. "Thank you."

"And I'll catch you, if you need me to."

"I'm counting on it." Those dark eyes lit, swirling with emotion and with the confidence Nic needed to see to let him walk out the door.

Cam was back in SoMa, at a night club in the formerly industrial, recently revitalized tech-arts area. Streets of warehouses had been converted to start-up incubators and art studios, and mixed in with them, plenty of restaurants, bars, and clubs to entertain the future billionaires. Cam had never felt more out of place, and it had nothing to do with his rag-tag disguise. There were people around him dressed in suits, people dressed like

he was, people barely dressed at all—a head-spinning mash-up. Like Nic said, you could never tell here, and for once, maybe that worked in his favor.

He snagged a stool at the bar, thankful it was as far away from the onstage DJ as possible. Back to the bar, he scanned the cavernous space, locating each of the exits and stairs, including to the mezzanine level. Layout committed to memory, he spun and flagged down the bartender.

"Stout," he ordered, only to be disappointed when he took his first swallow. The dark beer hit his tongue without the blast of bubbles and flavor he'd come to expect. Nowhere near as good as Gravity's, but to say he was biased was an understatement. That taste, especially when mixed with Nic's, would forever be burned on Cam's tongue.

Like the feeling of the unfamiliar key pressed into his palm earlier today. For a second he'd thought it was to Nic's place, or maybe to the brewery, and the prospect of either had stolen his words. As shocking and momentous as those prospects would have been, the key was something even more important. A safe haven. From their enemies, and from Cam's own cover, if things got too intense. A place where he could be and find himself again, if he got too close to stepping over his line. That escape valve, that tie to the Cameron Byrne of the here and now, would be critical, especially with how closely Brady Campbell mirrored the Cameron Byrne of old. At the end of this assignment, he wanted to climb out of the past and back into the present, where he'd advanced to FBI ASAC and kissed the smoking hot AUSA. He didn't want to lose that. Like the old Cameron Byrne had lost—

"You Brady?" a familiar voice asked behind him.

A slender arm snaked over the low back of his bar-stool, heat burning through the thin T-shirt, his coat and hoodie checked at the door. The better to know exactly where Abby stood. Cam hitched an arm back first, sliding a hand over her forearm, preparing to hold her in place, before he twisted his torso to face her.

"That's me, sweetheart." He shifted them so Abby's back was to the club and he was between her and the bartender, cutting off all lines of sight to her shocked expression. Holding her gaze, Cam gave a slight shake of his head, and Abby, catching on, reined in her reaction.

She listening? Cam mouthed.

Abby returned the slight head shake.

"She watching?" he asked low.

"VIP section, mezzanine."

"Then make like you're still getting cozy." He coasted his hand up her forearm, over her elbow, and around to her back, bringing them side by side. "What'll it be?" he asked, as he flagged down the bartender.

"Jameson, on the rocks."

"Woman after my own heart." Smiling, he pulled her closer, selling the show to a watchful Becca on the second level.

He thanked the bartender, who came right back with Abby's drink, then watched in admitted admiration as Abby downed half of it in one swallow. Unfortunately, the whiskey did little to relax her. "What the hell are you doing here?" she asked, incredulous. "You're a fucking fed."

Cam swiped her drink, draining the rest of it. "Do I look like a fed to you?"

She gave him a slow once-over, from boots to blue tips. "Not in the slightest."

He wasn't quite sure he liked the interested gleam in her eye. "Becca's never seen me, so I'm the best shot you got at getting out of this mess. Unless you're with her now?" The question had to be asked, given the way she'd greeted him. Looking for Brady, *for* Becca.

Abby looked away, toward the other end of the bar, and swallowed hard. "I'm with my baby sister," she said, voice rough.

Not a straight answer, but one Cam could understand. Abby, he hoped to God, was trying to make the right decision, the one that he and Bobby hadn't made. Cam just needed to convince her she could trust him and Nic; they were a better option than Becca. "I'll do what I can to get you both clear," he said. "But to make that happen, we have to find out who Becca's working for."

Incredulous returned with a vengeance. "She's the boss."

"Our evidence indicates otherwise."

"What evidence?"

He grinned—better than a grimace—for any prying eyes. "I can't tell you."

Stymied, Abby moved to yank free her hand and Cam gave it a squeeze, hoping to calm her. Hoping all this looked like a negotiation to Becca. "How do we play this?" he asked. He needed Abby on his side, and giving her some control over the situation would go a long way.

"I'm supposed to take you up to her, if you check out."

He lifted her hand, kissing the back of it. "Think she's buying this?"

Finally, one corner of Abby's mouth twitched, fighting a smile. "You're smooth, I'll give you that."

"Let's go then." He lifted his hip, drew out his wallet, and tossed a twenty on the bar. Sliding off the stool, he tugged Abby closer, whispering in her ear, "I won't let anything happen to you." Because that's what Nic would want, and because Cam didn't like the bruises on her face one bit either. "Or your sister." Because that's what the old Cam had failed to do, the reminder burning a hole in his wallet. He knew he shouldn't have brought the library card with him, the only truly identifying piece of information on him, but he hadn't been without it in twenty years. He wouldn't start now, when he needed it most.

She nodded, then stepped out from between the stools, hand in his, leading him across the floor and up the stairs to the mezzanine level.

In the VIP section, Becca sat in the middle of a long couch, her position providing a prime view of the bar where he and Abby had been. Cam hoped like hell they'd been convincing. Legs crossed, Becca bounced her knee-high leather boot their direction as they approached. Two bruisers closed in, separating Cam from Abby. Becca lifted her chin, ordering her girlfriend over, while her muscle searched him, including with a handheld transmission scanner. Aidan had been right not to send him in wired.

Once clear, he crossed to the couch and Becca gave him a blatantly hungry once-over, a Cheshire cat grin stretching across her face. "When Ax told me he'd found a new B&E guy for me, he didn't mention you were fucking stunning."

Ah, well, he hadn't factored this in, but he could make it work to his advantage. Use it to get closer to Becca. Smiling, Cam took a step forward, and Becca waved off her guards. "Let Hot Stuff through."

She stretched the arm not around Abby across the

top of the couch, and Cam slid into the spot next to her, letting his own eyes linger on the cleavage her bustier accentuated. She'd appreciate the appreciation.

"I'm fucking stunning all around, boss lady. And so are you." He held out a hand, together with his best grin, the one that had once been spread wide until he'd begun reserving it for a certain prosecutor. "Brady Campbell, at your service."

"Someone's a charmer." She placed her hand in his and laughed as he lifted her knuckles to his lips, same as he'd done Abby's at the bar.

"Irish," he said with a wink. "I come by it honest."

"And from Boston, judging by that accent."

"You got a problem with some Southie blue collar on your crew?"

"None at all." She crooked a finger into the cuff around his wrist and dragged his hand to her leather-clad thigh. "You come highly recommended."

He ran his hand a little higher, eliciting a rumbling purr. "Like you said, stunning."

"Good." Nail beneath his chin, she drew him closer. "I'm gonna need you to prove it. Tonight."

Chapter Twelve

It was early morning when Nic pulled his truck into the parking garage, the shift in light from outside to underground negligible, the heavy spring fog blanketing everything in soupy gray. Between the cement pillars and slanted ramps, the mist that rolled down the ramp played in the nooks and crannies, making the shadows come to life. Born and raised in the Bay Area, Nic was old friends with the fog, had greatly missed it during his tours in the dessert, but it had its creeptastic moments.

Palming his phone, he stared at the dark screen. Other than work emails, it'd been silent since last night. No more *unknown* calls, and no word from Cam either. Nic didn't expect it. Cam was deep undercover. They had to assume all communication would be monitored. His phone, a burner, had likely been taken and bugged. But not even knowing if the meet had happened, much less whether Becca had accepted Cam into the crew—or God forbid, taken him hostage—had kept Nic up until the wee hours. Sleep eluding him, he'd eventually dragged his ass into the brewery to do paperwork, which finally knocked him out.

A couple hours' shut-eye and more pain in his sore body to show for it. If he was going to be halfway functional in court later this morning, he needed coffee, STAT, but even those shops weren't open for another half hour. And he'd be damned if he'd get stuck with office sludge again today.

He climbed out of his truck, dug his briefcase from behind his seat and slammed the door shut. He'd taken two steps toward the elevator when something pinged his periphery.

Motion, in a dark corner, the other direction, diagonally behind him.

Were Vaughn's men stupid enough to follow him here? In a garage with a police car pool monitored by security cameras? Or maybe it was Vaughn's inside guy? Because the more Nic thought about that last night in his wide-awake hours, he was sure of it. Someone, in either his or Aidan's office, had to be tipping Vaughn off as to when and where they might be able to disguise an attempt or threat on his life. To pressure a father who couldn't give two shits about him. Someone's intel was wrong; he was not the leverage they needed. And if they did know that, then they were trying to pressure him, directly, to pay for his old man's debts.

Nic didn't turn toward where he'd detected the motion. Using his side-view mirror instead, he kept an eye on the area behind him while lowering his briefcase and reaching for his sidearm. As fog curled out of the suspect corner, Nic cursed himself for falling prey to the mist's tricks. Until he felt another pair of eyes on him, up the ramp to the next level. He nudged the side-view mirror, angling it for a better look. Was that someone skirting back from the ramp's edge?

He flipped the strap on his holster, fingers curling around the butt of his pistol. "Who's there?" he called out, voice echoing around the cement pillars and empty spaces. There were so few cars on this level at this hour, only a handful left from overnight. Hearing no response, only the whistle of the wind down the ramp, Nic crept cautiously toward the back of the truck. From the tailgate, he could dodge either direction for cover, if needed. "Hello! Who's there?" he called again.

Nothing, at first, then feet shuffling over concrete. In a hurry. A clank, metal on metal, like something falling. A second later, a pipe came rolling over the edge of the ramp, and in its wake, a loud click.

Like a pistol loading.

Nic yanked out his own, loaded it, and darted behind the nearest pillar.

In his mirror, he watched a shadow move down the ramp.

Crouching, Nic skirted from one pillar to the next, closing in.

Only to have his quiet approach shattered by squealing tires and shining LED headlamps. Nic thought for sure he was headed for a repeat of Tuesday night. But then the lights swung and a car pulled into a spot on the other side of the pillar. Black, sleek, with Irish punk rock bleeding out of the windows, louder even than the car's roaring engine.

Aidan.

Secure on that side, Nic whipped back to the other, only to see another car rolling down the ramp. A police cruiser from the pool parked a floor above. The officer drank from a travel mug as he drove past, like it was any other absurdly early morning. Was that all he'd heard before? An officer getting into his car, maybe knocking away a stray piece of metal pipe? But what about the click? Locks on the car, maybe? He made a mental note of the cruiser's license plate tag. He'd have Lauren run it, find out which officer had checked it out, and whether his accounts had any errant deposits. If it hadn't been the officer, whomever it was had surely dropped back by now, as the garage came to life.

"Dominic," Aidan called behind him. "Why's your gun out?"

He holstered his weapon and turned around with a tired half smile. "Not enough sleep, too many shadows."

Good enough, it seemed, because Aidan had bigger issues, judging by his thunderous expression. "Let's go."

Nic grabbed his briefcase and rushed to catch up, Aidan halfway to the elevator already. "What's happened?"

"Got a call about a robbery last night. Car dealership two blocks over from the club where the meet was supposed to be held."

No coincidence there. "Cam?"

Aidan nodded as they stepped into the elevator. "Left us a fingerprint."

Nic didn't bother punching the button for his own floor. "She had him boost a car?"

"Same security system as the museum. You wanna guess the model of vault door they lock the money, papers, and keys behind each night?"

He didn't need to guess. "AmSec 8000 series."

"Case closed, Attorney Price," Aidan replied, missing his usual flair of excitement at those words. They were both attorneys by training, Aidan getting more out of the trial part of a case than most agents.

"It was a test run," Nic surmised.

"A try-out." Aidan led them off the elevator onto the

thirteenth floor. "Though now I have to explain to the very angry car dealer and SFPD why a federal agent broke into a car showroom and vault last night."

Both their phones dinged at once. Nic scrambled for his, disappointed it was a message from Lauren, even if it was a valuable one.

"I'd say he passed." Ten thousand had just hit Brady Campbell's bank account. "When do you think they'll move on the artifacts?"

"Fund-raiser soft open is Saturday night. Opens wide Sunday." Aidan tossed various bits of pocket detritus on his desk—phone, keys, badge. "I'd say tonight or after the soft open Saturday. The latter would give them more time to plan and integrate Brady."

"Not much time for Cam to find out who Becca is working for."

"Byrne's good. Don't lose faith yet." Aidan shucked off his jacket, hanging it on the back of his door. "When's your motion for continuance?"

"Ten o'clock with Judge O'Donnell." The preliminary hearing for Scott and Mike was scheduled for Monday. Nic would prefer to try all the defendants at once instead of piecemeal, but that assumed he had all his defendants in custody. If they couldn't make that happen by the end of the weekend, a continuance would give Aidan and Cam more time to work. "Hopefully we won't need the delay."

"Better safe than sorry." Aidan gestured at the visitor chair as he circled behind his desk. "Have a seat."

"I thought you had cops and car dealers to appease."

"I do." Aidan pulled out his laptop and opened it on his desk. "But there's something else we need to discuss first."

Wary at Aidan's sudden shift in tone, his frustration seemingly redirected at him, Nic debated whether to take the offered seat. Had Aidan realized Nic and Cam were flirting with being more-than-friends? Hell, more than just flirting with the notion. Any judge would laugh him out of the courtroom if he tried to argue otherwise. Did Aidan have a problem with it? Was he going to shut Nic out of this case because of it? Determined to make sure that didn't happen, because no way would he go blind with Cam out there, Nic sat, unbuttoning his coat.

Aidan grabbed a file folder from his briefcase and tossed it on the desk in front of Nic, some of its contents spilling out. On top, a black-and-white crime scene photo showed the sniper's nest from the raid a week ago. "You didn't tell me he was shooting at you."

Nic schooled his features, staying silent.

Aidan pushed the file forward, the rest of the way off the desk and into his lap. "What's going on, Price?"

"Not your problem, Talley."

"Beg to differ, when my agents are caught in the crossfire."

Nic started to argue—the shooter was only aiming at him, the car only struck him—but then he recalled Lauren in the van that day, recalled the other agents on the scene at South Park, and bit back his retort.

"And I beg to differ," Aidan said, tone softening, "when my friend is being shot at." Nic glanced up, meeting Aidan's sincere, concerned gaze. Aidan wouldn't let this go, if Nic didn't give him something. And Nic needed him to let it go, before it got back to Cam.

"My father made some poor business decisions," Nic hedged, maintaining walls, professional and otherwise.

"His lenders want to be sure they recoup their investment."

"That's lawyer-speak for he's in hock up to his eyeballs." Standing, Aidan walked around the desk and dropped into the chair next to Nic. "Are you tangled up in any of it?"

"No," Nic answered. "I've been estranged from Curtis twenty-seven years. I haven't taken a cent of his money, and they can have it all, for all I care."

"Look, you never mentioned your father, so none of us said anything, and you probably don't need or want this, but I'm sorry." He reached out a hand, laying it on Nic's forearm. "And I don't mean that you're estranged. If you made that decision, I trust that it was for a good reason. I'm sorry he made you feel alone then and is doing so again now. And that whatever this is, is blowing back on you. That's not fair."

Aidan was right; Nic didn't want sympathy for having cut ties with his father. There'd been no other choice, if he wanted to be who he was and make a stand for everything his father wasn't. Sympathy, or regret for that matter, were wasted emotions. But what Aidan was offering was more than he ever thought he deserved. He swallowed, hard, forcing out a "Thank you."

Aidan withdrew his hand and slid back in his chair, one leg crossed over the other. "Do you need protection?"

Nic snorted, and Aidan raised his hands, a smirk turning up one corner of his mouth. "They're just threats," Nic said, and ignored Aidan's eyebrow racing north. "No one's actually trying to kill me. I don't think. That wouldn't serve their purpose. And I've got help handling it, in addition to Lauren."

"Cam?"

"No," he snapped too quickly. "I don't want him involved in this."

Aidan's other brow raced after its companion.

"He's got enough on his plate," Nic said. "So do you. I've got this."

"Tell me who's helping you, and I'll be the judge of that."

"Cruz."

That seemed to appease him. "Fine, but if it gets out of hand, you tell me."

"Thank you," Nic said, as he pushed to his feet. "Now, don't you have calls to make?"

Aidan rose as well, raking a hand through his auburn hair. "Yes, God forbid San Franciscans be deprived of their luxury cars for a day."

"Says the man who drives an Aston Martin." Chuckling, Nic headed for the door, only to be stopped by Aidan's hand around his biceps.

"I've said it before, and I'll say it again. You're family. Dominic. And we take care of family."

All the moisture in his mouth evaporated, worried he'd never be able to live up to that gift. "One day, maybe, I'll tell you all just how much that means to me, but right now, Cam's the family member in danger. He needs to be our primary concern."

"Agreed." Aidan released his arm. "So go to court and do your thing. Buy him and us some time."

That he could do, for his family.

Face buried in the crook of Nic's neck, Cam lapped up the salt and sweat, the hint of beer, and inhaled musk,

hops and man, the heady mixture making him groan
with need.

Everything he wanted was beneath him, around him.
All of it hot. Under his hands, on his tongue, around
his cock. Cam roved his hands over ink, so much fucking ink. Over painted skin and hard muscle, over broad
shoulders and under Nic's body, bowing his back. Pulling Nic closer, needing him skin to skin, as their hips
ground together, pounding toward the edge.

Nic hitched his knees higher, ankles crossed behind
Cam's back, heels digging into his ass, as he urged him
to thrust deeper, whispering, "More, Boston," in his
ear. That unaccented California voice, rough with sex
and the screaming Cam had drawn out of him earlier,
begged and moaned, "Harder, please."

Cam angled his face in, chasing the lips he couldn't
get enough of, the taste he'd dreamt about for months.

And woke with a mouth full of pillow.

Groaning, not the good kind, Cam pushed himself
out of the mound of pillows and flopped onto his back,
staring at the ceiling. Gripping either side of the bed, he
held himself back from the call of his cock, which had
made a fort of its own over his lap. Nic was at least two
dozen city blocks from the condo Becca had led them
back to last night, and yet he was everywhere inside
Cam's head and body.

Not that he didn't want or need Nic there, at minimum
occupying the spot in his brain stamped Agent Byrne.
Cracking the security systems last night had sent adrenaline racing up Cam's spine, a thrill at putting the forgot-
ten talent back to use. He'd channeled that adrenaline
more constructively, more legally, the past two decades,
but last night he'd been reminded of its original purpose.

Nic's voice in his head, and the card in his wallet, had reminded him to connect the two, to make the original purpose constructive.

For the mission.

Rolling his head on the fluffy down pillow, Cam squinted out the floor-to-ceiling windows. Forty-five floors up, nothing blocked his view of the midmorning sun shining over the Bay. It was a beautiful, breathtaking sight, bright sun over glistening water, the suspended span of the Bay Bridge, and the busy Embarcadero below.

Hand in the mattress, he shoved himself up and rested back against the padded headboard, surveying the bedroom. The view inside was breathtaking too. Plush white linens, ebony furniture, an ebony wall hanging with the San Francisco cityscape carved in gold flake. All of it was too neat, too much like a hotel room; not a condo someone actually lived in. And definitely not befitting Becca's punk rock aesthetic. A rental, then? Whoever was bankrolling this heist had shelled out a pretty penny, if this was their base of operations. That said, Cam had been in the Bay Area long enough to hear this building referred to as the Leaning Tower of Frisco, so maybe Deep Pockets got a good deal on it.

The slight lean helped as he reached for his phone on the bedside table. He should check in. Text Lauren at the untraceable number he'd memorized before leaving the office yesterday. He stopped midreach, however, catching sight of his jeans on the floor. That's where he'd left his phone. In his pants pocket with his wallet; not on the table beside the bed.

Someone had checked it. Maybe—probably—also tampered with it.

Was his wallet still even in his pants? Had they rifled through it too?

Without warning, the door swung open, and Cam retracted his hand, leaving the phone where it lay. Becca sauntered in, Abby tucked under an arm against her side. In the light of day, the coziness between the two gave him greater pause. Same purple dye streaking their dark hair, though Becca's was long and straight compared to Abby's curls. Same leather, denim, and lace punk attire. Fresh kiss bruises on each of their necks. He wondered again about their CI, whose eyes were skipping around the room, searching, assessing. She was still playing both sides against the middle, where her sister stood.

Becca perched on the side of the bed, her hip next to his. She propped a booted foot on the bed rail and hauled Abby into the V of her thighs, the both of them angled toward him. "You passed out on us last night, Hot Stuff."

He'd put on a show after they'd returned. Pretended the multiple Irish car bombs he'd partaken in at the bar downstairs had done him in. Please, he was Irish, from Boston. It took a lot more than a few beers and whiskey shots to knock him on his ass, but the lie had kept him out of Becca's clutches. The multiple days with little sleep were what had actually knocked him out, hard enough that someone had managed to enter his room and tinker with his phone without him waking.

"Long day and night," he said, running a hand through his hair. "But profitable."

Becca's eyes zeroed in on his chest again, then drifted down to his abs. She traced a similar path with her nail. "At least you lived up to that hype." Her nail dipped farther, trailing along the top of the sheet bunched around his waist. "Someone seems hyped this morning too."

Damn Nic-fueled morning wood. And damn dick with a mind of its own, even if Cam's heart and mind weren't interested.

"Thought you had a girlfriend," he said, gaze shifting meaningfully between Becca and Abby.

Becca paid him no mind, inching the sheet down so she could trace the sex lines on his hips. He fought not to shiver, a potent mix of mental disgust and bodily desire.

"We're not opposed to a third, and I think my girl likes you." She dropped the hand on Abby's waist to her ass, squeezing and tugging her closer. Bringing them closer. "She can't stop talking about you."

Cam's eyes darted back to Abby, worried she'd given too much away, but her eyes weren't skeptically assessing any longer. She seemed interested, for real. He had to put a stop to this seduction, now. "We should save it for the victory celebration," he suggested.

"But we have a day off." Becca palmed him through the sheet, and Cam dug his teeth into his bottom lip, biting back a curse. "And I'm not a fan of delayed gratification." Neither was his dick, apparently.

She lifted her hand, and he could breathe again, but only a minute, until she pried his lip free from his teeth and caught it between her own, drawing him into a kiss.

His insides churned, caught between his body's wants, his heart's desires, and his head pulling two different directions. Railing that this was a betrayal, while screaming back, in Nic's voice, of all people, that he should use it for his cover. He took a breath, ignored the scent of Becca's perfume, and separated mind from body, focusing the former on finding an excuse out of this. He caught a lucky break when a knock sounded against the door, giving him a momentary reprieve.

One of the bruisers, Jared, leaned his head in. "Call for you, Bex."

"I'll call them back." She pushed Abby closer to Cam. "Your turn, baby."

Abby looked ready to take her up on the offer, and if kissing Becca had caused Cam a near white-out of cognitive dissonance, it'd be worse with Abby, their CI. This was the job, but it felt like betrayal on a whole other plane. Did Abby really want to do this or was she playing a role, like him?

And if Becca didn't stop stroking him through the damn sheet, his body was going to put up a louder argument than everyone involved.

Another knock at the door, thank God. "He won't wait," Jared said.

Sighing, Becca held out her hand.

"Don't you want to take it out here?" Jared said, scowling at Cam with thinly veiled hostility. And suspicion.

Becca snapped her fingers. "Give me the damn phone."

Reluctantly, he handed it over and Becca shooed him to the door. She waited for him to pull it shut, then brought the phone to her ear. "Yeah?"

Cam couldn't hear the voice on the other end, but whatever the speaker said, caused Becca to straighten and remove her hand from his crotch. Playtime was over, thank fuck.

"We weren't planning to move until tomorrow night, after the soft opening like we'd discussed." Another pause, forehead wrinkling. "Yes, we know the museum layout but we just brought in a new B&E guy." Her eyes cut to Cam, staying there as she spoke. "Double my fee.

Half now, half on delivery." After a couple seconds, her mouth stretched into a satisfied smile. "Tonight it is."

She ended the call and pocketed the phone.

"No day off, then?" Cam said, thankful for the extended reprieve. It didn't last long, Becca kissing him hard. "I'll be holding you to that victory celebration," she said, once she pulled back.

"And I'll be expecting a similar deal. Up my fee, half now."

She considered him, eyes searching, then believing whatever she saw. She nodded and stood, drawing Abby toward the door with her. "You drive a hard bargain, Brady." She eyed his still interested cock. "Will expect you to drive something else hard tonight."

She pulled the door closed, with a wink and "Downstairs in ten," and Cam fell sideways onto the mattress, muffling his frustrated groan in the pillows. At least this would be over tonight. Much longer, and he was afraid even Nic wouldn't be able to pull him back over his line.

Line.

He needed to let the team know the estimated timeline had been accelerated, and that Becca was definitely taking orders from someone. He grabbed his wallet first, though. Everything was in its place, just as he'd left it. More likely than not, his cover held. Snagging his phone next, he turned it on, and the picture on the screen flickered, like it was shorting out. Maybe Brady Campbell wouldn't know what that meant, but Agent Cameron Byrne, best friend of former Cyber agent and hacker, Jameson Walker, knew exactly what that brief interruption meant. He'd make no calls and send no texts, messages, or emails from that phone.

He had to trust Lauren to see the extra deposit, coming sooner than anticipated. To tell Nic and Aidan and for them to realize the robbery was going down, tonight.

Chapter Thirteen

"Motion denied."

The judge's gavel fell, smashing some of Nic's confidence with it.

All he'd asked was to push the preliminary hearing from Monday to Friday. A routine motion, uncontested by the attorneys representing Mike and Scott. After a week of questioning and plea negotiations, it'd become clear their clients weren't talking because they didn't know jack shit. Becca was the crew's mastermind, not Scott, who was as surprised as them when she'd turned. As such, they and their attorneys were on board with more time for the FBI to prove they hadn't called the shots, especially the one that had killed Anica Kristić.

The motion should have been granted, given the circumstances. Their star witness was MIA, on the government's behalf, in what, if things went according to plan, was a sting that would wrap this case up tight, with all the suspects and players in custody. But according to the judge, those circumstances were outweighed by others.

A development Nic hadn't foreseen. Hadn't had any warning about. And not even questioning Harris or Percy earlier in the week had prepared him for this.

Fuming, he waited for the judge and bailiff to exit, for

Scott and Mike to be led out, and for their attorneys to follow, scurrying to their next hearings, before he drove his hand into his pocket for his phone.

"No need, Price," came a voice behind him.

Nic spun, finding Aidan at the back of the magistrate's courtroom where they were hiding again from the hounding press. Nic pushed through the swinging galley door and charged between the rows. "Did you know about that?"

"I got a call fifteen minutes ago. I sprinted up the stairs to tell you, but the judge had started early."

"Kristić's doctors cleared him to travel?"

Aidan shook his head. "Against medical advice."

The judge's ass had barely hit the chair when he'd been handed a statement from the clerk. From the Serbian embassy, on behalf of its citizen Stefan Kristić, the letter stated that Kristić would present himself for testimony and questioning on Monday, as scheduled, but a matter of state and personal security required him to fly home that same evening.

Nic had countered, but his argument had been a thin one. They had no basis to keep Kristić here. He wasn't a suspect or person of interest, merely a witness, who could provide a written statement, if he didn't want to testify. They could try to compel him, hold him in contempt of court, but he was a grieving widower who wanted to take his wife's body home. He wanted to do right by her memory—have the show and the fundraiser, which was a special cause to her—then he wanted to be on his way. How would throwing him in contempt look in the court of public opinion? Bowers would have Nic's ass. Hell, they were lucky Kristić was sticking around at all. So when the judge had given him the option of Kristić's testimony Monday or no chance to question him at all, Nic had to take the opportunity, which meant he had to keep the prelim scheduled for Monday.

Which meant even more pressure on Cam to get them what they needed, to make the bust, this weekend.

The one thing Nic could do to help Cam, to take some of that pressure off and protect his family, and he'd failed.

"He's going to leave, with the artifacts?" Nic said, still disbelieving. "Does he realize they may be at greater risk back in Serbia?"

"According to the person I spoke to at the embassy, Kristić thinks he and the artifacts are at greater risk *here*."

"Maybe not greater," Nic half conceded. If someone in Serbia was bankrolling this, they'd be in jeopardy there too. But here, someone *was* actively trying to steal them. "Does he know the payoff came from Serbia?"

"Still safer at home, they think."

"Can we use the secure line to get word to—" Nic cut himself off as the courtroom door swung open. Turned out he didn't need to.

"No," Lauren said, blustering in. "His phone's been jacked. The alert was waiting for me when I got in this morning. Doesn't matter anyways."

Nic scoffed. "Doesn't matter?"

"Cam probably already knows something is up."

"Get to the punchline, Hall," Aidan said, voicing Nic's frustration. As much as he valued Lauren, she had an infuriating tendency to hide the ball behind a ramble.

"Another deposit just hit Becca's account. Double the first one. And part of it's already been transferred to Brady's."

"They know the schedule's been accelerated too," Nic reasoned.

Aidan nodded. "I'm betting they make another attempt tonight."

"Good," Lauren said, and when both their faces whipped her way, she added, "Already called in tactical teams for a brief in thirty."

"Pull Cam's rescue plan and disseminate it."

"Rescue plan?" Nic said.

"This is his specialty," Aidan said. "He gave us a few scenarios to work with it."

"What about Bowers? Finding out who's really pulling the strings?"

"Fuck him," Aidan bit out harshly. "This is about closing our case and getting our people out. Now. We can make one bust, protect the artifacts, and keep Kristić, Cam, and Abby safe. I won't compromise all that for your boss's ego."

"All right, Counselor," Nic said, breathing a little easier. "Not gonna fight you on this motion."

Aidan smirked. "Figured you wouldn't."

In his father's home office, Nic pawed through desk drawers, looking for anything that might give him a better picture of Curtis's financial situation. He needed a distraction from worrying over Cam, and after two, maybe three attempts on his person, he needed more information about his father's debts. What little he'd gleaned so far was from Vaughn's goons, his conversation with Harris, and the mail he'd flipped through with Harris in the office. And from the angry lender voice mails left on the family office number. Harris had replayed all of those for Nic too. While Duncan had the most might, he wasn't Curtis's only lender.

If his father's in-town office hadn't been locked the other day, finding a laptop inside would have been Nic's primary objective. Copy its contents or swipe it for Lauren to hack. Lock notwithstanding, Harris hadn't thought it would be there. Curtis usually carried it on him. And it wasn't here at home now either, consistent with Harris's assertion. Neither were the financial documents Curtis had supposedly relocated. Nic hadn't found them anywhere. Built in the 1920s, the Hillsborough estate house was huge, with plenty of hiding places. Curtis could have stashed the documents in any of them. But Mary, the last of his father's household staff, who'd all but raised Nic, didn't recall seeing boxes of documents ever come home. Was Harris lying, or had Curtis stored or ditched them elsewhere?

If they did exist, Nic could use them for his case. Could maybe even get some of the pressure off his father. Until recently, Nic hadn't wanted to concern himself with any of this. A big part of him still didn't. Didn't want to know how bad the situation really was, and didn't want to involve himself in his father's life any more than he had to. Vaughn, however, wasn't giving him a choice. How much longer before someone else his father was in debt to exerted pressure? Came after Nic with that same pressure? Or after his new family, as improbable as that still seemed?

A loud crash, followed by Mary's hollered curse, shattered the silence. Sound carried under the high-pitched roof of the big old house. Nic barely flinched at the ruckus, accustomed to those sorts of sounds here. He did, however, act swiftly, something he'd been unable to do as a frightened kid. Bolting out of the study, he ran the length of the long back hallway—past the master suite, through the cavernous, empty living room, most of the furnishings sold off, according to Mary, through the conservatory full of drafty windows, several of the panes cracked, to the kitchen with its outdated tile countertops and white plastic appliances.

Nic skidded into the room through the open door, barely avoiding the shards of glass on the floor, just as his father bellowed, "Why the hell did you let him in?" and threw his coat the direction of the table, knocking over more crystal. Another pile of shattered glass joined the other on the floor, together with his briefcase, which must have caused the first crash.

Curtis moved Mary's direction, and Nic stepped into his path, blocking his advance. "That's enough!"

Dressed in a suit that had fit twenty-lost-pounds ago, with his blue eyes dull and his thinning blond hair gone white, Nic's once regal, terrifying father looked like a fuming bag of bones. "This is my house. I'm in charge here. She had no right to let you in."

To her credit, Mary didn't flinch either. "Mr. Dominic asked nicely, and I keep your house, so I let him in. I wanted to see him."

"You work for me!"

"For how many years, Mary?" Nic asked, without taking his eyes off Curtis, ready to divert any further advance.

"Since you were six, Mr. Dominic."

Four months, two weeks, and fifteen days after his mother had died, to be exact. Ninety-one days until his father had decided a potential investment in Wine Country was more important than parenting his confused, grieving child. She'd found him in the backyard, crying beneath the cypress trees. It was only supposed to be temporary, but she'd lasted when no one else had, mostly, Nic suspected, for him.

"She's right," Nic said. "She runs this house, has for years when no one else would, especially not you. She deserves your respect."

"Respect," his father muttered. "Like you'd know anything about that. Twenty-seven years, not a word, and the first thing you do is come in here and try to give me orders. No respect."

One eye remaining on his father, Nic angled toward Mary. "Would you give us a moment?" He didn't want to have this conversation with an audience.

"I'll go get a broom and dustpan," she said.

"Leave it outside the door. I'll clean it up when we're done."

"You don't—"

Nic held up a hand. "Please, Mary, let me take care of it."

He waited for her to exit and pull the kitchen door shut, before rotating back to Curtis.

"You were always too soft," his father chided.

Too soft.

He'd said those same words the day Nic had stepped between Curtis's fist and another good woman's face. He wouldn't let her take another hit for him. Eighteen and scrawny, still in his graduation gown, he'd gone to the ground, the punch nearly breaking his jaw. *Too soft*, his father had said. *Too soft*, he'd said again, after Nic, trying to distract his father long enough for them to get away, had confessed he was gay. The second punch his father landed had broken his jaw, and Mary had had to take him to the hospital. But it'd worked. And Nic had sworn away *soft* the next day.

Twenty years in the Navy—seven of them in combat, five as a SEAL sniper, before injury sidelined him. Instead of taking a discharge, he'd spent the next thirteen years as the JAG officer with the best courtroom record. Seven years after military retirement, he'd climbed to second-in-command of the USAO and become the FBI's go-to prosecutor. He also brewed beer and moved around boxes and barrels for a second fucking living. He was a long fucking way from *soft*, and his hand closed into a fist, wanting to prove just how far to his father. But if he raised that fist, if he hit a defenseless old man, Nic would be no better than the devil himself.

He uncurled his fingers and walked slowly over to the table, gathering his patience as he picked up his father's briefcase. "I'm not *trying* to give you orders," he said. "I *am* giving them. You will not disrespect Mary or anyone else helping you, including Harris Kincaid."

"I'll do whatever I want in my own goddamn house."

"Is it, still? Or have you mortgaged it to the hilt as well?"

His father glared, but no denial accompanied the milky-blue stare. Heat prickled over Nic's skin, his mouth going dry. He'd counted on at least some equity in the house to pay off Vaughn. It was worth nearly ten million, and unlike the commercial properties, there were no recorded liens filed against it—he'd checked—but that didn't mean Curtis hadn't used it for collateral elsewhere. Off the books. Which is what Nic had been looking for in the office. Seems he had his answer now. "Did you promise it to Duncan Vaughn? Or someone else?"

"You stay out of my business."

Nic talked over him. "I need to know what I'm dealing with, because if there's nothing but debts, it's only a matter of time before Vaughn kicks you out or burns it to the ground for the insurance proceeds."

"What did that little shit Kincaid tell you?"

"He didn't have to tell me anything. I'm smart. I figured it out myself, after Vaughn's goons tried to attack me."

His father turned his face away, staring out the opposite window. "I'm handling it." Still lording over his crumbling kingdom, stubborn to a fault, something Nic had admittedly inherited.

"You're not handling it well," Nic said. "I can help you."

Curtis's interest in the backyard didn't waver. "With that fancy legal degree of yours?"

Fancy, in the deriding tone Nic had heard every day for so many years, but a picture from his JAG commissioning was one of those in Curtis's office, according to Harris. Which meant Curtis had either been there, or gone through the trouble of calling the Navy's office to get it. "Yeah, with my fancy legal degree, if you'll let me help you." Nic stepped to his father's side. "But that's not all. I laid out two of his goons already, and I'll do the same if he or your other *creditors* send more. You be sure to tell them that."

His father's gaze swung back to him. "Hardened up, huh? See, I did do something good for you after all."

"You didn't do shit," Nic said, taking no small amount of satisfaction that Curtis shrank back a step. "I made me the man I am. And I won't let your mistakes jeopardize everything I've worked for."

Chapter Fourteen

The area around San Francisco's Museum of Modern Art was dotted with galleries and museums, a culture cluster as Becca had described it. Bars and restaurants also filled the bottom floors of the skyscrapers, making the live-work-party area not altogether deserted on a Friday night. Or rather, Saturday morning. Just past last call, they weren't the only ones skulking about the streets. Dressed as they were, mostly in black, a group of punk-looking thirtysomethings hanging on to each other, they blended in with the rest of the staggering bar hoppers and club-goers.

Except they weren't drunk and they were far more aware of their surroundings than they appeared. Hopefully not too observant, Cam prayed, as they passed a familiar red Mini and a Dodge Ram with a Boston Red Sox cap on the dash. It must have killed Nic to put it there, but it was the sign Cam needed. His team had followed the deposits, realized the schedule had been accelerated, and were in position.

Good thing too, as something felt off. The expedited schedule, the too-easy flow of funds, the tingling at the back of his skull that set his teeth to grinding and kicked his senses into overdrive.

Reaching the museum building, they darted down a side street, and the staggering-friends facade fell away as they pulled ski masks down over their faces. Jared took point, Cam, Becca, and Abby the middle, and Russ, Becca's other bruiser, brought up the rear.

Jared halted at the building corner, checking the back alley, then waved them around, their group gathering at the museum back door. "You're up, Brady," Jared said.

Cam pushed to the front, checking out the dual security system. Electronic keypad by the door, state-of-the-art locking mechanism on it. With Jared shining a penlight for him, Cam pushed up the sleeves of his camo jacket and went to work on the keypad first. No card to swipe or insert so he'd have to do it the old-fashioned way—pop the cover and cut the right wire before the open cover triggered a silent alarm. Wire cutters in his mouth, he used his multipurpose knife to unscrew the cover, then with the flat end of the wrench from the lock-pick set, popped the cover the rest of the way off, right into Jared's waiting hands. Wire-work already in mind, Cam dropped the cutters out of his mouth, into his gloved hand, and aimed for the wire. Sniping the right wire, the blinking yellow alarm light died, and after a few crossed wires, relit green.

"That's one layer down," Cam said.

He dropped to a knee in front of the door lock, was about to call Jared lower with his penlight, when scratches on the lock, rough beneath his thumb, made him pause. The lock had already been tampered with. He ran his thumb over it again, but with gloves on, he couldn't tell if the damage was fresh or if it'd been there a while. He glanced down, subtly checking the ground. No metal fibers reflecting in the moonlight.

Why would the FBI need to pick the lock? If they were inside already, they wouldn't have needed to, and if they did, they wouldn't have made such a sloppy job of it. Neither Danny nor Aidan, who'd taught Danny to pick locks, would leave that kind of mess. Was a third party on-site? Another third-party rip-off in the making?

"Problem, Hot Stuff?" Becca asked behind him.

"Nope, just getting a feel of things." He didn't mention the lock damage, in case he needed to use it, or what it might mean, to his advantage.

Inserting the wrench, he tested left and right for tension—right—then withdrew the other two lock-pick tools. He swept the rake across the inner pins and found the binding pin. He traded rake for pick, set the binding pin, then reinserted the rake, ticking off the other pins in the order he'd earlier assessed. On the third pass of the rake, the lock disengaged and he nudged the wrench right.

The door opened.

Grinning, he stood and tucked his tools back in their pouch. "And that's what you pay me the big bucks for."

Jared entered first, gun drawn. Becca pushed Abby over the threshold next, then waited for Cam to step forward. "Don't get cocky." She palmed him through his jeans. "Yet." She followed Abby inside, and Russ waved him on through, pulling the door shut behind them.

They crept along the inside of the outer wall, avoiding the infrared security around each exhibit block in the open space. Cam watched for any sign of movement, feds or otherwise, as he asked Becca the question that'd been nagging him since she'd laid out their plan for this heist. "You mentioned earlier that the vault is like a Russian nesting doll. Multiple layers. The dual system on the exterior entry. The vault door. Then, inside the vault, the voice-activated safe."

"That's right."

"For the last, you need two voices. Abby's got the wife's. What about the husband's? Who's going to mimic his voice?" There was no way he could pull off a Serbian accent, and he'd be shocked as shit if Jared or Russ were hiding that in their bag of thug tricks.

Becca shot him a sly grin. "Don't you worry about that," she said, as they approached the in-wall vault door. "You worry about this instead."

Cam continued to work over her answer as he worked over the vault door, first, hacking the electronic lock, then pulling the tools he needed out of his bag and getting back on the bike for the physical bolt. Same as last night, a thrill ran up his spine, a rush of adrenaline pumping blood and excitement through his veins. He came up on his line in the sand fast and slammed his eyes shut, bringing to mind the smiles and voices of his older, wiser brother, his nieces and nephews, his friends who'd become his family here. The library card in his pocket. The ball cap on the Dodge's dash, the taste of his new favorite stout, magnificent ink over hard muscle and pale skin.

Nic. His here and now.

Using the thrill—not letting it use him—Cam channeled the energy into his hands cracking the safe and into Agent Byrne hovering just beneath Brady Campbell's skin.

After another minute's steady work, the lock on the vault door disengaged. He stepped back, pulling the reinforced steel door open for Becca and Abby. "I believe you're up now."

"You remember the script, baby," Becca said to Abby.

She nodded, and they approached the voice-activated safe together, Becca texting someone on her phone. It vibrated in her hand a moment later. Becca brought it to her ear. "We're ready," she said, as she entered an unlock code to start the process. It signaled for the voice-activated commands, and Abby spoke first in a dialect unlike anything Cam had ever heard.

One light turned green.

Becca hit speakerphone and the next instant, a man's voice filled the room, in what Cam vaguely did recognize as Serbian. Spoken clearly, assertively, like someone well-educated and powerful, and somehow also familiar, even though Cam didn't understand the words.

The second light turned green.

Who'd called Becca? From where Cam stood, he couldn't see her phone screen, but he'd bet it was a random number. He'd also bet his team was right. A native Serb, or someone who'd spent enough time there to speak like a native, was bankrolling this venture.

And Cam had a pretty good idea who that person was now.

The bright glare from Jared's penlight shining on glittering objects drew Cam's attention back to where they were pulling a shelf from the safe.

Then to where a red light suddenly appeared, aimed right at Becca's head.

"Gun, get down!" Cam shouted, as shots rent the air.

Becca yanked Abby to the ground, while Jared and Russ crowded on either side of the vault doorway, returning fire at the rafters.

"Who the fuck is shooting at us?" Becca hollered

over the *ping* of bullets on metal and the *pop* and *crash* of shattering glass.

For a second Cam had thought it was his people, but no one on his team, not even Bowers, would have given the order to take Becca out. They needed her. Someone else, the person or team who'd tampered with the lock, was in here with them.

He ran back over to the safe, shoved the tray inside, and slammed the safe door shut.

"What the fuck did you do that for?" Becca demanded.

"Because a third party is not getting their hands on our prize."

"Shit!" Becca cursed. "Someone else must have gotten wind of it."

"Or your boss doesn't trust you to get the job done either."

Becca gave him a look, affronted, but not totally surprised.

"We need to get the fuck out of here. Jared," Cam hollered ahead of him. "Clear us a path. Russ, close the vault door behind us. We can't let them in here."

The bruisers nodded, then sprang into motion, and Cam covered Becca and Abby between them. "Go! Go! Go!" he shouted, as shots continued to pound the ground and walls around them, one slicing a gash across his outer arm. "Fuck!"

Adding to the chaos, glass shattered at the front of the museum and shouts of "FBI!" rang through the open space. The cavalry had arrived, clearly getting the picture that all was not right inside.

Cam had a split second to decide. End this now, or find out who was on that call with Becca? If his suspicion was correct, there was only one choice to make. "Head for the back!" he shouted, while Jared and Russ laid down more cover fire. Finally, they made it out the back door and bolted down the alley. At the next intersection, Cam hauled Abby to his side. "We have to split up and divide their efforts. Becca, take Jared and Russ. I've got Abby. We'll meet back at the condo."

Becca protested, even as Russ began to drag her the opposite direction. "I'm the one calling the shots here."

"The two voices needed for the safe can't be in the same location," he explained. "You've got access to one. I've got the other."

She pressed her lips together, stymied. "Fine, go! We'll meet back up at the condo."

Cam grabbed Abby's hand and off they ran, around another building and past more alleys. "What the hell is going on?" Abby panted behind him. "Are you on Becca's side now?"

"I need to know who Becca's working for. But first, I need to get you safe." He glanced down the next alley, toward the main street. *Bingo!*

He charged forward, dragging Abby behind him, until they hit the main drag. Right in front of Nic's truck. After cracking through two vault-level doors, the lock on the truck's door was a piece of cake.

He jimmied it open and hoisted Abby into the cab, with a "Stay down."

Ripping off his mask, he circled around front to the driver's side, and Abby leaned over, popping the lock for him. She fell back into the passenger seat as he climbed in. "Where are we going?"

"Safe house." He reached under the dash, grabbing

the two wires he needed to spark a hotwire. Thank God Nic still drove an older model.

Next to him, Abby turned in her seat to sneak a peek out the back window. "Someone's coming!"

The hotwire sparked, the truck roaring to life. Cam righted himself, grabbed the ball cap off the dash, and yanked it down on his head.

As he peeled away from the curb, he caught a fleeting glimpse of Nic's blue eyes glowing in the moonlight. Cam hoped he'd read the message in his actions for what they were.

Chapter Fifteen

The dim cone of light at Nic's feet wobbled, as did the man holding its source, Aidan's curses coming in a steady stream of Gaelic.

"We're almost at the top," Nic said. He'd taken the lead, knowing the path well and used to scaling mounds of sand. He didn't need the phone light, or even the weathered wood steps, to make his way up to the cliff-side patio. But Aidan and Lauren did.

"Are you sure this is where they went?" Aidan huffed.

"According to my truck's GPS."

"Someone else could have stolen the truck."

"And come here? I told Cam to use this place as a safe house."

Lauren piped up from between them. "Then why are we scaling this fucking cliff? I'm a fan of *Lord of the Rings* and all but screw this many-steps shit. I don't want to live it."

Chuckling improbably, Nic crested the last step onto the stone patio and held out a hand to Lauren, helping her the rest of the way up. "We came this way because we don't know who's with Cam." He'd recognized Cam in the truck, met his dark eyes in the mirror and watched him don that fucking BoSox cap, but in the dark, he hadn't been able tell if the woman with him, in a ski mask, was Becca or Abby.

"Oh, I think we do," Lauren said.

Nic whipped his head around, from where Aidan was throwing a leg over the patio ledge, to the big bay window of Eddie's house perched above the patio at the top of the cliff. Backlit by the glow of house lights, Cam sat shirtless at the kitchen table. Abby stood close to his side, wrapping a bandage around his upper arm.

A low burn simmered in Nic's gut. It kicked up to boiling when Abby leaned in, kissing Cam's shoulder, then his neck, then his lips.

Cam lifted a hand, resting it on her waist. Maybe he was holding her back, but he sure as fuck wasn't pushing her away.

"This was the other reason he was perfect for the job," Aidan said, knocking the sand off his shoes.

"Because he's hot," Lauren replied, and Nic shot her a deadly glare.

Aidan, thankfully, didn't notice the exchange. "According to Jamie, he was a legend at BC, in both the frat and sorority houses."

"Really?" Lauren said, surprised. "He's generally so by-the-rules at work."

"Not outside of it."

"So, what, you want him to fuck his way onto the crew too?" Nic barked at Aidan.

Aidan did notice that remark, and the tone. "If he needs to, yes. Or he can just steal more of my chocolate for bribes."

Rolling his eyes, Nic glanced again at the house. Cam had leaned away from Abby. She nodded at something he said, then with a tired smile and another lingering kiss to his shoulder, disappeared from view. A few seconds later, the lights a floor down, where the bedrooms were, clicked on and Abby moved around, getting ready for sleep.

Upstairs, Cam slid off the stool, walking back into the kitchen and lifting the phone receiver off the wall. Nic had his phone in his hand when it buzzed.

"Boston," he answered, voice clipped, quiet.

"Where are you?"

"Back patio."

Cam spun around, staring out the window.

Nic held up his phone, the light from the screen letting Cam know exactly where they were. "Get down here. Leave the spotlights off."

"On my way."

"We're not going up?" Lauren asked.

"Not until we get a read on the situation," Nic said, glancing to Aidan, who nodded.

They crossed the patio to the tiny writer's cottage tucked into the hill at the corner of the property. Nic flipped the lights on and gestured to the desk for Lauren to set up. Dropping into the chair, she booted up her computer, while Nic and Aidan pushed the other furniture to the outer walls, making room. The space was meant as a retreat for one. Four was going to be tight.

Tighter than anticipated when Cam entered, puffed up and full of something Nic couldn't read. Leaning back against a bookshelf, Nic held his tongue, not wanting to say something he'd regret, one way or the other, especially in front of Aidan and Lauren.

Aidan rested on the arm of a chair and nodded at Cam's arm. "You okay?"

"Just a graze."

"Need stitches?" Aidan asked.

Cam shook his head. "Couple of butterfly bandages under the wrap. What's the latest from the scene?"

"We cleared out about an hour ago. One suspect from the other crew is in custody. The museum's security personnel are on-site now."

"Did anyone else get into the safe?"

"Nope," Lauren said. "The other crew scattered when Becca's did."

"Becca back at the condo?"

"Don't know," Aidan said. "Tracker went offline, and she and her two bruisers are off the grid."

"Could she have traced the truck's GPS, if she saw us get into it?"

"Negative, I'm jamming it." Lauren brandished her phone before turning back to her computer.

"Anything out of the suspect you did catch?"

"Nothing, yet," Aidan answered. "I'll question him again in the morning. We do have an ID, and we're tracing his accounts. What the fuck happened? Who was the other crew?"

Cam flopped into the other chair and propped his elbows on his knees, running his fingers through his blue-tipped hair. It looked so out of place on him, especially in this conversation, but Nic couldn't deny he liked it. Which only pissed him off more in his current pissed-off state.

"One of three scenarios," Cam said, and Nic checked back into the conversation. "Someone else got wind of the heist, and it was a pure third-party rip-off."

"Or?" Aidan prompted.

"Whomever Becca's working for, and she is working for someone, which I'll get to in a minute—" he split a glance between them "——either didn't trust her to get the job done or didn't want to pay her the rest of her fee."

"Contingencies," Aidan said, as he hitched a foot up.

Cam nodded. "And to protect his identity."

Death would be the only surefire way to protect that, Nic thought, as Aidan asked, "The ringleader's a 'he'?"

"Stefan Kristić," Cam said.

Aidan's foot slipped off the seat cushion and hit the floor. Lauren's *tap-tap-tap* likewise abruptly ceased. And Nic sucked in a breath, awaiting the rest of Cam's reasoning, even as his own brain fast-forwarded, putting together pieces. Kristić's unavailability for an interview. His emergency need to flee. "Interrupting" the initial raid, which had led to his wife's death. *Asshole husbands strike again.* Nic forced himself to remain still, grinding his teeth against his own instinct to rage.

"Becca had someone on the phone," Cam explained. "A male voice to read the male part. I'd bet every cent to my name, which granted isn't much, that it was Kristić."

"Was there any unusual activity on his accounts?" Aidan asked Lauren.

"None, and I checked it for connections to Rebecca Monroe too."

"What about the deposits to Monroe?" Cam asked. "Where are we on that trace?"

"Brick wall. I can't get through, and the bankers won't talk either."

"Because he's an oligarch in the new Serbia," Nic said, finally breaking his silence. "I've seen this on Russian cases. Check all of his companies, particularly the ones that do business in the States. We have legal standing to get access to those records. If we can find a matching outlay, that's how we usually nail them."

"We only have the weekend to do it," Aidan said.

"You didn't get the continuance?" Cam said, eyes on Nic.

"Kristić's flying back Monday," he said, "after giving his testimony."

"Getting clear with the artifacts more likely."

"I don't get it," Lauren said, twisting in her chair. "He's got the artifacts. He's the dignitary overseeing their transport."

"But who actually owns them?" Nic said. "His deceased wife? Her heirs? The government? I'm guessing not him. We need to see the bill of lading on those pieces, and the wife's will."

"What's his end game?" Cam said. "Sell them on the black market?"

Nic nodded, as Aidan added, "Something tells me his flight plan will change Monday."

"After he kills or puts away the people who worked for him," Cam said, and Nic didn't like that determined glint in his eye one bit. "I'm going back in."

"No," Nic snapped, pushing up off the wall. Two steps and he was standing right in front of Cam. "You're safe, here, now." He glanced out the window, toward the house. "And so is Abby."

"He'll make another run at the artifacts, probably at the show tonight or Sunday. We can't risk more people getting hurt."

Desert sand and heat settled in Nic's gut, suffocating and uncomfortable. "So we risk you instead?"

Cam shot to his feet, the space between them narrowing more. "This is my job, Price."

"And your case is circumstantial, prosecutor," Aidan added from his spot on the other armchair. Fucking traitor. "If Cam can get direct evidence that it's Kristić pulling the strings…"

Cam glanced over at him. "I can get it."

"Kristić knows who you are," Nic reminded him.

Cam had taken off his mask and helmet in the penthouse after the heist that started all this. And he'd been in Kristić's hospital room after.

"*If* he ever shows his face," Cam said, "I'll convince him Abby turned me. That I've gone rogue."

"That why you kissed her?" The words were out before Nic could stop himself.

Aidan cut in before the argument could go further. "She'll have to go back in with you."

"I'll protect her."

Of course he would.

"This is a fucking suicide mission," Nic gritted out.

"What was it last week when you jumped out of the van and ran toward the Kristićs' building?" Cam replied. "Or when you ran out of Mel and Danny's condo the other night, charging for the park?"

Effectively silenced, Nic scoffed and turned away, hands braced on either side of the window frame, glaring out at the ocean.

"I can do this," Cam said to Aidan behind him. "I can close this case."

And he'd try not to get himself killed in the fucking process.

Chapter Sixteen

After seeing Lauren and Aidan out, Cam made his way back across the patio to where Nic waited inside the warmly lit cottage. He'd claimed he was staying behind to take back his truck. Cam figured he wanted one more chance to plead his case. Not that it would change Cam's mind. He knew what he needed to do.

About Nic too.

Bucking up his resolve, he entered the cottage and closed the door behind him. Nic didn't flinch, arms still spread on either side of the window, his back to the room. Sleeves rucked up to his elbows, Nic's toned forearms were on display, as was the perfect V of his torso. Broad shoulders that led down to a trim waist and a firm, round ass. Cam's pulse ticked up, remembering the tattoos on Nic's chest, imagining the JAG emblem on his hip, wondering about the ink on his back. Something was definitely there, the spindly ends of it had been visible on Nic's shoulders and sides the other night, but Cam hadn't gotten a look before they'd been interrupted. He wanted to see it now.

But he needed to set something else straight first.

Nic, however, as Cam anticipated, wasn't ready to let

go of their earlier argument. "I don't like this plan," he said, still glaring out at the ocean.

"Of course you don't."

"We have no idea who is playing who here."

Not exactly true. "Kristić's at the top."

Nic spun, blue eyes flashing. "You *think* Kristić's at the top but you don't *know*. Either way, there are two crews working every heist, and you want to walk right back into the crosshairs."

"Says the ex-SEAL." Cam took two steps forward, bringing them face-to-face. "This is my job."

"Do you often do your job with this many unknown variables?"

"Not if I can help it, but it's not unheard of." He'd gone on less before. Nic had too. "Shouldn't be hard for an ex-SEAL and prosecutor to grasp."

Nic threw a hand out toward the house. "We don't even know if our own CI is still on our side."

Now they'd reached the conversation Cam wanted to have. "You haven't doubted Abby before. Granted, I've had mine, but evidence indicates you were right. She's an unwilling participant, one way or the other."

"Unwilling." Nic scoffed, turning back to the window.

Cam fought not to smile. He really shouldn't take any delight in this, but Nic was playing right into his hands. "What's really going on, Price?"

"You know damn well what's going on."

Laying his hands on either side of Nic's spine, Cam slowly glided them up his back, drawing out a tremble. "Then why won't you turn around and kiss me?"

The tremble gave way to a jolt, then a harshly bit out, "After you just kissed her?"

"*I* didn't kiss her. Brady kissed her."

"Semantics."

"Says the lawyer." Cam was intentionally needling him, using Nic's own tactics against him as he poked holes in the prosecutor's argument.

In his protective outer layer.

"She knows who you are, Boston."

Cam coasted his hands over the packed muscles of Nic's stiff shoulders. "It's still a cover. While evidence points to her being cooperative, if Abby decides Becca's a better bet than us, I'm gonna need to convince her I've gone rogue so I can stay close and protect her. That's what you want, isn't it?"

Nic was silent a long minute, the building tension heavy in the small space. "This is why you're not sup-posed to get involved with colleagues."

Finally, an opening. Cam closed the distance between them, winding his arms around Nic and hugging him from behind. Body warm, despite the cool night, Cam wanted to get even closer to it. They might both get burned, but he was done watching the fire from a dis-tance, holding himself back from the heat.

"Technically, we're not," he said.

"You have an answer for everything, don't you?"

"If it wins the argument with you, yes."

Nic chuckled, hanging his head, and Cam skirted his nose and lips along the nape of his neck. Nic's quiet laughter died on a breathy gasp.

"Turn around, baby," Cam whispered. He stepped back, only far enough for Nic to rotate, then pulled him close again. "We've been dancing around this for months," he said, walking them back toward the desk, Nic bumping up against it. "You want this as much as I do, if the two kisses we've shared are any sign. Unless I read them wrong?"

Chin down, Nic glided his hands up the outsides of Cam's arms and over his shoulders, leaving a trail of goose bumps in their wake. "You're not wrong."

It was a miracle Cam had held out this long. This close to what he'd desired for months, the wild part of him desperately wanted to break free, wanted to play rough and hard with Nic. "Then what's the problem?" he asked. "You came to my place the other night. You made that move."

"A lot can change in forty-eight hours," Nic said, angling his face away.

Cam didn't let him get away with it, trapping Nic's chin between his thumb and forefinger and righting his gaze. "The way you feel about me?"

"This is messy, Boston, for a number of reasons, the least of which is you could get killed tomorrow."

Nic's blue eyes swirled with a stormy mix of lust and hesitation, the former on the cusp of winning out. Cam just needed to push a little harder. Hands traveling north, he tangled them in Nic's hair and tilted his head back, exposing his neck for Cam's mouth. "The last thing I want to do," he said between kisses there, "is get killed before I get my dick in you."

A deep groan rumbled against Cam's lips. Nic clutched his waist, holding him close. And tight.

"That's what you like, isn't it?" Cam taunted, kissing a path up the column of Nic's throat. He wedged a knee between Nic's thighs, as he'd done the other night, and pressed his own need into Nic's hip. No hiding that, or the way Nic ground an equally hard cock against his couldn't wait to ride it, but tonight, he'd be the one riding. "Please tell me Eddie's got condoms and lube in here somewhere."

"One thing you can always count on with Eddie…" Nic leaned to the side, opened a desk drawer, and pulled out two foil packets. "He stashes this shit everywhere."

"Good friend." Cam grinned, snatching the packets from his hand, and while Nic seemed momentarily blinded by the smile, flipped their positions again, manhandling Nic around so he was chest down on the desk, Cam's hand planted in the center of his back.

His eyes went first to the JAG tattoo on Nic's hip, as striking as Cam had fantasized. But it was nothing compared to the single tattoo spanning Nic's back. Cam was struck speechless, a curse too crass for this kind of beauty and a prayer not holy enough. Tossing the packets on the desk, he brought his hands back together at the small of Nic's back, then repeating his earlier motion, coasted them up his spine, tracing the trunk of a giant cypress tree. At Nic's shoulders, Cam's hands separated, following the limbs out, his fingers feathering along the twigs and branches that crept over his shoulders and down his biceps. Now he knew what was peeking out from under Nic's sleeves and collars. The artwork was so delicate and precise, the opposite of the beautiful yet stark symbols inked elsewhere.

"My God, Nic, this is incredible."

Nic trembled beneath him again, his breath coming in shorter pants as Cam traced the most striking feature of all. Initials carved into the trunk of the tree. Worked into the knots of the wood, Cam hadn't seen them at first but now they seemed the most obvious and important part.

"Who's GS?"

thigh. Cam trailed his open mouth along Nic's stubbled jaw and up to his ear.

"Boston…" A warning wrapped in so much desire it might as well have been a plea.

"You're standing here, jealous and angry my cover kissed someone else." Cam brushed his lips over the hinge of Nic's clenched jaw. "Worried about my safety and about what our friends will say." Nic opened his mouth to protest, and Cam pressed his lips to Nic's chin, forcing it closed. "Don't deny it." He dipped down, suckling the other man's bobbing Adam's apple. "It's part of what's kept you away all these months. Me too." Then back up, a peck in the hollow of Nic's cheek, before Cam dragged his lips back to Nic's ear. "But most of all, you're turned way the fuck on and ready to bend over this desk for me." He punctuated his assertion with a roll of his hips. "Have been for months." Nic's hands slipped from his waist, onto his ass, and hauled him closer, so close to conceding the argument. Cam ground against him. "Stop pretending the mess doesn't already exist."

Cam was surprised when Nic's hands left his ass to grip the sides of his face, Nic forcing him back enough for their eyes to lock. "Is this going to push you over the line? Break one rule, break them all?"

Cam's heart stuttered in his chest. Nic was hesitating out of worry for him, over what he'd said the other night at the house. Cam was nowhere near good enough for this man, probably never would be, as dirt-broke and as screwed up as his past had been, but fuck if he could hold himself back now, the chemistry between them winning out over good sense.

"I broke the rules the minute I laid eyes on you, Dominic Price." Shaking off the hold, Cam leaned forward, brushing his lips against Nic's. "Now you're the fuck-ing rope keeping me tethered to shore."

As if a judge's gavel had fallen, Nic came after him, hard and fast. Clutching his ass in one hand, the back of his head in the other, Nic hauled him into a kiss that had blood roaring in Cam's ears, loud enough to drown out the crashing waves.

Case closed.

Finally.

Onto a more pleasurable argument, which Nic was already winning. Hands beneath the hem of Cam's shirt, he forced it up and their lips apart long enough to tear it off Cam's head. They fought for whose lips would hit whose neck first, and Nic won, biting and suckling a path over the temporary tattoo. "I like the ink, even if it is decades out of style."

Cam laughed. "Good thing it's not permanent." Head tilted back, he struggled blindly against Nic's buttons, too many valuable seconds passing before he reached warm and hard skin, searing against his palms. "Doesn't hide as well as yours." He tried to look down, to the ink that still surprised him and turned him on to no end, but Nic had other ideas.

Long fingers tunneling through his hair, Nic tilted his head back even farther. "Like the hair too," he said, before licking into the hollow of his throat.

Knees going weak, Cam flipped their positions while he still could, resting back against the desk. "Reminded me of you."

"I'll give you something else to remember," Nic mum-bled, before dropping to his knees and giving Cam's belly button the same attention he'd bestowed on his neck, and fuck if that didn't have Cam gasping toward

the ceiling. If Nic's hands weren't already working on his zipper, his hips would have been off the desk, dick begging for attention.

As it were, Cam lifted them the instant he heard the zipper *rip*, helping Nic get his jeans and briefs down, but after that, once Nic circled the tip of his cock with this tongue then swallowed him whole, the most Cam could manage was flailing.

"Holy hell," he cursed, the arm braced behind him giving way. Lie back or watch the show? No question. He curled forward, hands diving into Nic's hair and down his neck, creating a cocoon while he watched Nic blow him. "Oh, fuck yeah." He babbled, all manner of curses and Hail Marys, as Nic worked him over. Long pulls, suction like Cam had never felt, and a tongue teasing with each wet slide down his cock. Over and over. Cam dug his fingers into Nic's shoulders, leaving bruises. Maybe even breaking the skin as Nic ventured off his dick and to his balls, one then the other in his mouth, before aiming lower still.

If Cam let him go on, it'd be sentencing over in no time flat. And Cam wanted more. He hadn't been lying before when he'd said he wanted his dick inside Nic be-fore walking back into the line of fire tomorrow.

Hands drifting back up, weaving again through Nic's hair, he pulled him off his cock, and with a foot beneath Nic's balls, forced him up.

"My turn." He yanked Nic into another kiss, their tongues battling, as Cam kicked his pants and boxers off and went to work on ridding Nic of his, satisfied when the metal belt buckle hit the floor, taking pants and briefs with it. He wrapped his hands around Nic's cock, groaning to find it hard and dripping already. He

Nic stilled, completely, and when he spoke, Cam could barely hear him. "The worst mess I ever made."

The agent part of Cam's brain went into overdrive, wanting to know more, to know everything, but with Nic stretched out under him, just as they were getting this thing between them going, just as it could possibly end tomorrow, now wasn't the time.

He ran his hands the rest of the way up Nic's back again, then out over his arms, blanketing him and nestling his aching cock between those firm, round ass cheeks that had tempted him for months. He dropped a kiss on Nic's shoulder. "I knew there was a body under that suit, but this." He traced his tongue along the branch that disappeared over Nic's shoulder. "*This*, Dominic, fuck." He thrust against Nic's backside. "Can you feel what it does to me?"

Nic reared up to his elbows, tried to reach a hand down and around his cock, but Cam caught his wrist, pinning it to the desk and keeping him spread. "Nuh uh-uh."

Countering, Nic pushed his ass back against Cam. "Don't forget, Boston. I argue for a fucking living."

"You want to talk *fucking*?" Cam sucked three fingers into his mouth, wetting them good, then backed off enough to tease Nic's rim. "Try that power bottom shit all you want, but I will win this argument, Counselor."

Groaning, Nic squirmed and chased after the touch. "Jesus Christ, need you to fuck me, now."

Cam pushed a finger past Nic's rim, eliciting a strangled moan. "What was that?"

"With your dick, for fuck's sake."

"I don't know." He inserted a second finger, spreading Nic open. "I'm enjoying myself here." And a third, pumping.

Nic rode back on his fingers, panting. "Not the time to argue."

Leaning over him, Cam nipped the back of his neck. "Thought you said you could play this game."

"Prosecution rests." His braced arm gave out and he sank, lying flat out on the desk again. "Please, Boston…"

Cam couldn't get the condom on and his dick lubed up fast enough. "I got you, baby," he whispered, as he lined up and slowly pushed in. Groaning, he filled up every inch, and once fully seated, bowed over Nic's back and rested his forehead against his shoulder. "Fuck, you feel good."

Did this feel better than any other time he'd been with someone, or had it just been too long? Everything fit and moved just right, his cock inside Nic's tight, hot ass, his body stretched over that amazing body, they're breaths heaving and hips rocking as one, neither of them having to think about it. Just doing it. Presenting the argument together, like they had been the entire time on this case.

Nic pushed up to his elbows, bringing their bodies closer, and Cam kicked his legs farther apart, changing the angle, the both of them strangling their screams as Cam slid in deeper, pounding Nic's prostate. Nic forced them another degree upright, enough for Cam to get one hand around his chest and the other around his dick, jerking him off in time with the thrusts of their hips and the thrust of their tongues, mouths meeting over Nic's shoulder.

Cam barely won the argument, Nic crying out as he came first, coating Cam's hand. The warmth of his re-lease, combined with the tight clamp on Cam's cock, gave Nic the final word. Cam followed him over the edge, falling further than he thought possible.

Case closed, sentenced to life.

Chapter Seventeen

Cam did a double take as Abby punched the elevator button for the fortieth floor. "Aren't we on forty-five?" He'd only been to Becca's base of operations once, but he distinctly remembered being forty-five floors up.

"Becca's text said Unit 4042. That's floor forty."

It was the right move. Change locations after another near bust but stay close to their target. There were fiftysomething other floors in this building to choose from. Becca's crew wasn't one of the best for no reason. Granted, things had gone sideways on this particular job, but Cam attributed that to his agency's interference and Kristić. Man clearly had trust issues.

Abby clicking her rings dragged Cam out of his thoughts. She stood in the far corner, jittery and nervous. "Hey," Cam said, sliding along the rail over next to her. "I can push the red button right now, call security, and have them turn this cab around. I'll tell Becca I lost you last night and I sent that text from your phone. You don't have to do this."

He'd laid out the game plan to Abby this morning, carefully stepping around his rogue contingency and his suspicion about Kristić. He needed both to register as real surprise with Abby, if he had to use them.

He'd given her the option to bail, multiple times, but she wanted to see this through. He wasn't surprised she hesitated now; most sane people would.

"I do," she said quietly. "A woman died."

Cam laid a hand over hers, stopping their restless motion. "*You* tried to stop that. You went to Nic."

She sucked in a deep breath, then lifted her chin, meeting his gaze. "I don't want anyone else to die. That's why I have to do this."

Under different circumstances, if Abby weren't a source, if she weren't the kidnap victim he was sent to rescue, and if Cam had never met Dominic Price, he'd probably try to charm a date out of her. He liked Abby. She had spunk, a good heart, and no denying she was beautiful. Even more so as she straightened her spine, let loose her hair, and fluffed out her curls.

Game face on, she gave him a nod, as the elevator doors opened. "After you." He followed her out, she hooked her elbow around his, and they walked arm-and-arm to Unit 4042. Abby knocked on the door, a pattern of short and long raps to announce her arrival. The peephole darkened, someone peering through it, then after several clicks of a lock, Russ opened the door. The bruiser stopped them in the shadowed foyer for pat downs, checking for any weapons or wires.

"I take it we're in the right place," Cam said.

Ignoring him, Russ called, "They're clear," over his shoulder, and Becca replied with an "In here" from around the corner. If the layout was the same as the condo upstairs, the foyer led to a parlor of sorts with a grand view of the Bay. To the parlor's left was an open-plan kitchen and living area, and to the right, a hallway to bedrooms and bathrooms.

Cam and Abby started forward, Cam's hand at her lower back. As soon as they hit the opening of the foyer, they were separated. Abby was pushed forward, yelping, while Jared jumped him, wrenching his right arm back and forcing him down. Russ was on him the next instant, knee to his back. Despite the blinding pain in his arm, the same one grazed last night, Cam could have thrown them off. Scrapping had never been a problem for him, even less so once he'd been professionally trained, but Becca's gun trained on a shaking Abby guaranteed his compliance.

"You're going to answer my questions," Becca said. "And you're going to tell me the truth or I'll put a bullet in her head."

"She's your girlfriend," he replied, appealing to that part of Becca he thought might have genuine feelings for the other woman.

Becca ignored the comment; maybe she didn't after all. "Near as I can tell, things started to go sideways when *you* entered the picture."

"Hey, I replaced your old B&E guy. Near as I can tell, things were fucked before I got here."

"Maybe you're right." Becca pressed the gun's muzzle against Abby's temple. "Maybe *she's* the one throwing curveballs."

"Or your boss," Cam countered. "Was that him you called from the museum?"

She dodged his question, asking Abby, "Where'd you go last night?"

"A house on the coast," Abby replied, voice trembling yet dry-eyed, doing her damnedest to hold it together despite the betrayal that had to be coursing through her.

"A buddy of mine's place in Half Moon Bay," Cam

said, trying to draw Becca's attention off Abby. "He was out of town. No one saw us."

"How'd you get back here?"

"Boosted a car."

"The same one from last night?"

"I'm not a fucking amateur," he sniped back. "I ditched the one from the City in San Mateo. Boosted a second and drove over the mountain to the beach. Ditched that one and stole a third this morning."

"Describe them," she demanded, as they moved into the living area.

He rattled off specs, ones he pulled from his memory as easily as he put one foot in front of the other. Convinced, for now, Becca nodded and the bruisers let him up. Becca dropped her arm, and Abby bolted over to him.

"Ooh," Becca said, voice dropping into a lower register. Less severe, more interested. "Did someone have fun last night? You're supposed to share, baby."

"What's the plan now?" Cam said, redirecting the conversation again.

Becca grabbed a still smoking joint from an ashtray and tucked herself into the far corner of a sectional. She waved Abby over, took a long draw on the joint, then held it out, waiting for Abby to take a drag. Becca beckoned him to the cushion on her other side. "You're going to prove who you are."

He relied on his charm, hoping to avoid crime. "What is it you want me to do, sweetheart?" He reached for the joint, but Becca offered him her mouth instead, inviting him to shotgun the hit. Smoke seeped out from between their lips as they kissed, and there was nothing sweet about the pungent smell. It reeked, made his stomach churn with disgust, an accurate reflection of his tortured conscience. Yes, this was still his cover, but after sharing last night with Nic, everything about this felt wrong. He clutched at that feeling, at the rope keeping him tied to Nic and Agent Byrne, even as Becca pulled Abby onto her lap, shotgunning another drag with her, then waiting for Cam and Abby to do the same. Cam clawed at the rope tighter. He hated using Abby like this, hated manipulating the genuine interest he felt in her kiss and in her gentle hands last night.

"You got some of that last night?" Becca asked when they parted.

"Not enough," Abby said, her eyes dark green.

"You'll have to wait for more." She shifted Abby off her lap, back to her other side. "Brady, here, has a safe to break into first."

Crime it was, then. "Didn't I already pass your trial run?" he asked, stalling. Not because he didn't want to do it. Charm had been leading him down a worse path. No, he stalled because if he were in Becca's position, he'd demand a reaffirmation of loyalty too.

"I want to know if you're willing to steal from the FBI."

He forced himself not to jerk. "The FBI?"

She nodded toward the bedrooms down the hall. "Assistant Director Moore's safe is in the master."

He snagged the joint from her, taking another drag to hide his surprise. "This is his place?" Swanky local digs for their regional assistant director who hopped between here, Sacramento, and the North Coast.

"Nice work getting in here," he said, assuming Moore had better than decent security.

"Know the building manager," Becca said with a wink.

"Cheater," he winked back. Standing, he retrieved the bag he'd dropped on his way in and headed down the hallway, Jared and Russ on his heels. He found the relatively basic safe in the master and knelt in front of the lock, getting it open in short order. He'd have to talk to Moore about that next time the AD was in the office.

He reached inside, expecting stacks of cash or jewelry, something a high-profile heist crew would be after, and drew out three flash drives instead. He palmed the plastic and returned to the living room, flopping down on the couch. "Flash drives?" he said, handing them to Becca.

"That's what my client was after."

Not Kristić, Cam realized. "Don't put all your eggs in one basket. Smart."

He reached for the joint again, but Becca held it out of reach. "Also smart because I like to know who's working for me."

Cam's stomach sank, another realization dawning. Becca knew.

"Yes," came a polished, assertive Serbian voice from down the bedroom hallway.

A voice Cam recognized, from last night and a week ago. Whipping around, his suspicions were confirmed, Stefan Kristić standing in the parlor.

"Tell us, Agent Byrne. How far is an FBI agent willing to go?"

There was no time for surprise, no time for panic. Cam had to put his contingency plan into play, right this instant. He leaned back into the cushions, playing it cool. "What is it you think you know about me?"

"Cameron Patrick Byrne. Assistant Special Agent-in-Charge of the San Francisco FBI field office," Kristić rattled off, and Becca's eyes grew wide. He must not have told her everything. "One of the Bureau's best kidnap and rescue agents."

"*The* best," he corrected, which was why he'd do everything he could to get Abby out of this alive, including playing the turncoat.

"Recently moved to the Bay Area from Boston for the ASAC job, working with his best friend's husband," Kristić carried on. "Big Irish family back in Boston."

Cam glanced over his shoulder at Becca. "Didn't lie about that one."

"Three brothers," Kristić said.

Cam swung his gaze back around. "And a sister." Kristić paused, tilting his head. "Didn't look back far enough, did you?"

"I only just realized it was you who was Brady last night."

"Well, then, I'm guessing your quick-take research didn't yield that Brady Campbell's backstory isn't made up. It's mine." Most of it anyway.

Becca arched one of her dark brows. "And the FBI still let you in?"

"They offered me something I couldn't get elsewhere."

"What's that?"

"Doesn't matter," Cam said, gut burning at the memory of his greatest failure, preserved on his sister's laminated library card in his wallet. The one case that still eluded him and continued to cast a gray cloud over his family. "They couldn't deliver." Neither could he.

"And now?" Kristić said, drawing him back to the present.

"And now they offer nothing," Cam said, throwing his

booted feet up on the glass coffee table. "If you haven't checked my real bank account yet, let me go ahead and tell you the balance. Two hundred fifty-three dollars and twenty-four cents. I'm tired of being a broke-ass government servant, especially living here."

"So, it's about the money?"

"Isn't that what all of you are in it for?"

"I'm in to get what's rightfully mine," Kristić said.

"The artifacts?"

"They belong to me. Not the government."

Cam would lay odds they'd actually belonged to his wife. He prayed Lauren was getting him the goods to back up that hunch, because this asshole had to go.

"Tell me," Cam said, deflecting, but also getting at something else that had to be addressed. "How are we supposed to trust you? You've tried to rip off your own heist, twice. They were shooting to kill in the museum."

"Because I didn't trust all the players." He looked over to Becca, saying "I do now," before glaring back at Cam, "Except you."

Cam figured it had more to do with protecting his identity and killing all the players to keep the money for himself. And Becca had been paid enough to be fooled those weren't still Kristić's objectives.

"I don't believe you're in it just for the cash," Becca said. "You entered the FBI for something more. A guy like you, you're leaving for a reason too."

"My partner, my boss, my best friend's husband you mentioned…he slept with the guy I'm fucking." Not exactly, but if it sold the story, he'd use it.

Becca bought it. "Oh-ho, so that's why you were reluctant to have fun with us?" She clutched Abby to her side. "Like the men, do you?"

"I like men and women, for what it's worth." Becca's eyes lit, until he shut her down. "I just decided not to get in the middle again."

Becca seemed to understand, lifting a hand and backing off, but at her side, Abby looked utterly shocked. And that, more than anything, sold his story.

For everyone except Kristić. "I'll decide if you're lying, after I have the artifacts."

Nic sat at the conference table in his war room, thumbing through Anica Kristić's will. Across from him, Aidan sifted through customs forms, looking for the one documenting the artifacts' entry into the county. He looked about as happy with his stack as Nic was with his.

The will had been poorly and hastily translated from Serbian, and Nic was having to look up every third word with regard to certain items that didn't have a direct English translation. Didn't help that every other minute his mind flashed back to last night. To the way Cam had felt inside him, over him, blanketing him in everything he'd wanted for months. It was messy, in part because of the man across from him and his husband, and in part because of Nic's own screwed-up family and past, the tattoo on his back the epitome of all that'd gone wrong before, but Christ, last night with Cam had been perfect.

Wanting it again, Nic rode the roller coaster of desire and worry. Cam was playing a dangerous game, undercover with Becca's crew. The sooner he and Aidan found evidence that Stefan Kristić was behind the heists, the sooner they could get Cam and Abby out of there.

"Any luck?" he asked Aidan.

"It's like looking for a needle in a fucking haystack." The SAC pitched another customs form into the discard box on the floor and tilted back in his chair, guzzling his third coffee of the morning. "It should be easy. The Kristićs and their belongings came in on a diplomatic visa, but do you have any idea how many diplomatic visas clear SFO daily?"

"More than a few?"

"More than a few," Aidan said with a nod. "Any luck there?"

"We need someone who speaks Serbian," he said. "And someone who understands wills and trusts better than me." He had a working knowledge from the occasional case, but it wasn't his specialty.

"Switch," Aidan said, pushing his remaining stack across the table. "I used to help with the estate docs for the family, before it got too damn big. I'll at least know where to look."

Nic welcomed the change, for twenty minutes or so, before his eyes started to glaze over.

"Hold on a sec," Aidan mumbled from across the table, intent on a page midway through the will. "I think—"

"You want to know what I think," an angry voice interrupted. Nic looked up to find Bowers in the doorway, his beady eyes intent on Aidan. "I think your boy's gone rogue."

Aidan lifted his coffee cup like he was looking for patience and salvation at the bottom of it, then glared when he realized it was empty. He turned his glare on Bowers. "That was the plan. To make the crew think that."

"Is that why he robbed Elton Moore this morning?"

Nic startled, but Bowers was too focused on Aidan to notice.

"It's part of the cover," Aidan said, not an ounce of

surprise in his voice or on his face. Nic could see why
the other man had been so damn good at undercover
work before he took the desk job. Or maybe Aidan had
been privy to the information, in which case, why the
fuck hadn't he told him?

"To rob an FBI Assistant Director?" Bowers
squawked.

"One, Moore knows, I talked to him already." Well,
that answered that question, but again, why the fuck
hadn't Aidan told him? A question for another time.
"We'll recover the flash drives that were stolen when we
take down the crew," Aidan continued. "Moore doesn't
think the encryption on them can be cracked before then.
Two, Cam and Abby were off the grid for hours last
night, and Abby's already been in custody once. They
had to prove themselves loyal to Becca, not us."

"Or Byrne's gone rogue," Bowers insisted.

"We met with him last night and discussed this plan,"
Nic said. "It's an act. He's not gone rogue."

"You sure about that?" Bowers threw down a file, a
photo sliding out.

A younger Cam with dark hair and dark eyes grinned
up at Nic from the picture, the overall look remark-
ably like Brady Campbell, right down to the same camo
jacket.

Aidan grabbed the rest of the file, flipping through
it. From the markings on the outside of the folder, Nic
could tell it was an FBI personnel file. Agent Cameron
Byrne's.

"How the hell did you get this?" Aidan growled.

"I'm DOJ too."

Except when it came to personnel files—even Nic
knew they were supposed to be kept separate to, among

other reasons, avoid any conflicts of interest. The only time he'd ever delved into FBI personnel files was when he had an agent testifying in a high-stakes case and he needed to assess his expert's credibility. Before doing so, Nic had always gotten the sitting SAC's or AD's permission. There was no way he'd release any of his people's files without the same courtesy. What other files had Bowers gotten access to?

"Breaking and entering. Grand theft auto. Larceny," Bowers rattled off, a more extensive list than even Nic knew about.

"He was never charged." Aidan stood, hands braced on his desk. "And those are exactly the reasons we sent him under on this case. He can do the job."

Despite his head still spinning, Nic added his two cents. "Cam's using all that to infiltrate Becca's crew and find out who's in charge, which is what *you* wanted."

"If we don't have that person in custody by Monday," Bowers said, "I'm bringing charges against Byrne. DOJ's orders."

Bowers stormed out, not giving them time to object or to tell him they had a lead. Nic, however, wasn't sure he wanted to tell Bowers about Kristić yet. His boss's current bone had Cam's name on it. No telling what he'd do given another. Hell, he'd probably try to argue Cam and Kristić had been working together all along.

"Is it just us he hates?" Aidan asked. "Or is he this way to everyone?"

"He's generally not pleasant," Nic replied. "But it's worse with this case. And us."

"Politics?"

"Maybe," Nic said, contemplating again why this case in particular had dinged Bowers's radar so hotly. DOJ was in turmoil, from the top down, and dead diplomats would bring State down on them too, but Bowers's vehemence was enough to scratch a mental note to have Mel check his bank accounts too.

"I'll be ready for you to inherit," Aidan said, jarring Nic out of his thoughts.

Nic shook his head. "Don't get your hopes up. And the far off, unlikely future is not my concern right now."

"Later," Aidan grumbled. "In any event, Bowers doesn't have a leg to stand on."

"Technically, he does," Nic said. Legally speaking, crimes had been committed, including by Cam. "But if we get this closed, and Kristić in custody, it'll be gone."

"We need answers," Aidan said. "And I know where to get them." He shoved the will and remaining customs forms into a folder and headed for the stairs at the back of the office. Nic followed him up two flights to the FBI's floor, then around the corner into "the cave," the interior boardroom that'd been converted to the Cyber agent bullpen.

Through the stacks they found Lauren hunched behind three open laptops, at least one unofficial. "Agent Hall," Aidan said, announcing their presence.

Her head bobbed up, blue eyes wide. "How'd you find me?"

Aidan dropped into a visitor chair. "What would Whiskey do?"

Lauren clapped, absurdly loud in the otherwise deserted room. "Oh! We should get W-W-W-D bracelets!"

"No," he and Aidan said together.

She stuck out her bottom lip in a pout. "I'm going to grow a sense of humor tree in the corner."

"In the cave?" Aidan said, gesturing at the window-less room they occupied.

"Touché," she conceded. "A girl can dream."

Nic claimed the other visitor chair. "Can a lady tell us what she's found so far?"

She shot him a sly grin. "You're picking up his habits." She was perceptive as hell, an analyst first, specializing in human behavior before she'd become an agent. She must have also read his hesitance to say anything about it, or Cam, in front of Aidan, because she mimed sealing her lips and launched into her findings.

"We have an answer on Kristić," she said. "He's definitely the one behind it."

"Freeze all of his finances and travel," Aidan ordered. "He may think he's leaving Monday, but not if he's officially under suspicion."

"Already made the requests," Lauren said. "But it's the weekend. It might not trickle down to some agencies until Monday."

"Fuck," Aidan cursed.

"And if there's anyone at the bank I just tapped who's friendly with Kristić, they'll tip him off."

"Where is he?" Aidan said. "I'm assuming not in the hospital."

"Checked himself out, against medical advice," she confirmed.

"When you came in, you said it was Kristić, for sure," Nic said. "What else do you have on him?"

Lauren spoke as she rotated one of her laptops toward them. "Going on what you said last night, or rather this morning, I found the deposits to Rebecca Monroe." She struck a few keys, highlighting deposits. "Account numbers match."

"And this one's Kristić's?" Nic said, pointing at the sender account number.

More keystrokes and more account records populated the screen. "One of his shell companies, emphasis on *his*."

"Meaning?" Aidan said.

"Kristić set this company up, personally. He signed all the paperwork, and it's three affiliates deep behind one of his US registered companies. It's also not tied to any accounts he shared with his wife. She didn't have access."

"She probably didn't even know about it," Nic reasoned. "Do we know why?"

Lauren spun one of the other laptops around, browser windows open. On one, the museum's page with details on tonight's exhibit opening and the artifacts on display. The other, a Wiki page on the Kosovar Romani displaced in Serbia during the Balkan War. "He was trying to steal her heritage."

"I thought the artifacts were Serbian, same as Kristić," Nic said.

"No," Aidan said. "They're Romani." He grabbed the folder off the floor, yanked out the will, and rifled through its pages, finger eventually jabbing at one in particular. "They go back to her people after her death, a heritage museum in Kosovo."

He shoved the page under Nic's nose, and now some of the Serbian-Not-Serbian made sense. "They were never going to him," Nic said. "How much are they worth?"

"Exactly the right question, Attorney Price." Lauren pulled up another screen. "The last assessment, from the insurance forms they updated before traveling."

The number on-screen boggled Nic's mind. "He can't just take them either," Nic said. "It has to look like a robbery, unconnected to him."

"Which they could do under the cover of the gala opening, tonight." Aidan was up and already moving toward the exit. "Briefing in thirty."

Nic shot out of his seat and grabbed him by the arm. In the excitement over Kristić, they'd lost focus on one critical element, the most important person, to him. "Cam—"

"Is undercover for the FBI," Aidan said, not missing a beat. "He's one of the best agents I've worked with, and I trust him completely. More importantly, he's family. I won't leave him behind."

Words Nic's SEAL brain could understand, even if his insides still tossed and turned with worry.

Chapter Eighteen

Cam had barely stepped out of the bathroom when fingernails dug into his arm, Abby yanking him out into the hallway.

"What the hell is going on?" she hissed. Every bit of control and obedience she'd fronted for Becca was gone. Eyes wide, her breath came in short bursts and her grip on his arm, while strong, still trembled.

He had to make a decision. Keep up the ruse that he'd gone rogue, or put it all out there, let Abby in on the bluff, and hope he'd done enough to earn Abby's trust, to convince her he was her best shot, not Becca. Weighing in favor of trust was her sincerity and remorse in the elevator. Cam didn't think she could fake that, and there'd only be more of that in Becca's column.

He made his decision. Backing her against the wall, he stepped close and whispered low. "I'm trying to keep us alive."

"So all that out there—" she threw an arm out toward the living area "—was a lie?"

He wished. "Not all of it."

A shadow fell across the mouth of the hallway, and Cam crowded into Abby's space, a forearm braced on the wall blocking their faces, pretending he was going in for a kiss. Abby's lips brushed against the corner of his mouth, wanting a real one. He turned his chin instead, dodging and slipping past her cheek. Pretending to kiss her elsewhere for anyone who was looking. But really not.

Cam waited until Jared passed, on his way to the bathroom, then stepped back and hustled Abby into the bedroom across the hall, closing the door partway behind them.

Abby jerked out of his hold, halfway between seething and dejected. "So that kiss last night was a lie too?"

"I had to know whether *you* were lying. If you were still on Becca's side, for real, I had to sell the rogue cover. I need to stay close, if I'm going to get you and your sister out of this."

Sighing, she sank onto the end of the bed. "Who the fuck am I supposed to trust? How do I know you're not lying now? Becca's got me tied in knots and you just pulled a fucking one-eighty. Which end is up? Fuck, I just want to get me and my sister out of this alive."

The fact she was asking him those questions, telling him where she was at, was all Cam needed to know. There was more than a nugget of trust there he could expand on. "I believe you, Abby, and I need you to believe me." Cam knelt in front of her, a gentle hand over hers on her knee. This was what Cam did best—the rescue part of the equation—and he wouldn't fail Abby. He'd do what Nic said. Use all of his past, and all of his present, to do his job. "I won't lie. Right now, we're on a razor's edge. We have to play this very carefully, but this is what I do. Trust me, work with me, and I will get you and your sister clear. Can you do that?"

She looked up, eyes still wary, but after a deep inhale, nodded. "All right. What do we do?"

"Let's go put on a show." Standing, he held his hand out to her, and once she was steady on her feet, slung an arm over her shoulder. She circled his waist with her arm, but the hold, while convincing, was just shy of being with actual intent.

They strutted back out into the living room, together.

Becca grinned. "Not staying out of the middle any longer?"

He kissed Abby's temple. "Your girl convinced me otherwise."

Becca approached, trailing a nail down his chest over his T-shirt. "Maybe we can take a little break."

"On the contrary," Kristić said, reemerging from the kitchen. "Our timeline's been accelerated again. We're doing this tonight."

Abby's arm clenched around his waist. He held her tighter.

"I thought we were waiting for the public show tomorrow night? Or at least after the soft show tonight?" he asked. "Let the attention die down."

Kristić shook his head. "I'm not waiting. And doing it during tonight's show will provide distraction and cover."

The change in plans wasn't necessarily a bad thing, but would his team on the outside be ready? "Why the expedited schedule?" he asked.

"Because someone just pinged my bank accounts."

A five-foot-nothing someone who was as accurate with a computer as she was at the firing range. Cam bit the inside of his cheek, hiding a smile. His team knew all right.

* * *

Cam hated wearing a tux. At least this jacket didn't have fucking tails, but the stiff fabric and bowtie still made him feeling unnecessarily contained.

Caged.

He was restless enough as it was, eyes roving the museum floor as he followed Kristić and Abby. Kristić shook hands like the consummate dignitary he was and accepted condolences like the grieving husband he should have been, near tears and with a choked voice he effortlessly affected. Acting as translator, Abby, dressed in a stylish silver gown with her hair pulled back in a bun, played the part well. In front of them, Becca, wearing a blond wig and black pantsuit, acted as security and cleared a path for them. Jared had hung back, an evil shadow on Cam's tail, while Russ waited outside in the car, ready for a quick getaway.

Observing the situation around him, Cam counted guests and security personnel. It didn't look like any more force than usual for one of these events, not that he'd been to that many to know, but this was what he'd expected. Maybe a few more guards were on hand than would normally be for a soft opening, but not unexpected given the repeated theft attempts.

He was beginning to second-guess whether his team knew this was going down tonight when the crowd parted for a striking couple. The man, with bright blue eyes and light brown hair, was taller than everyone else in room and wore a tux better than everyone else too. And the woman... Well, if a certain prosecutor wasn't already in Cam's sights, and if the woman in red weren't married to his boss's brother and able to break his neck with her bare hands, Cam would have definitely asked for her number.

As it were, he already had it.

Jamie and Mel, clearly recruited for an assist, walked close and cozy, seemingly in their own little world. So much so that neither Becca nor Kristić gave them a second glance, their attention elsewhere as Jamie, passing by, dropped something into Cam's pocket. His best friend always did have a trick up his sleeve. By the slight weight of the object, Cam figured it for a flash drive or some sort of trigger.

After another few minutes of shaking hands, Kristić was interrupted by a museum docent. "Sir, if you'll come with me please, we need to finish preparing the exhibit." Meaning they needed him and Abby to open the safe.

It was the perfect setup. If Kristić got away with the artifacts, no one would be the wiser, their attention distracted by the crowd. If things went sideways, he'd play the hostage, taken by Becca's crew. Becca had realized she was the patsy as they'd gone over the plan earlier that day. Too far in to change course, she'd negotiated for more money instead. Kristić had given it to her, which made Cam wonder exactly how much those artifacts—and Kristić's ego—were worth, given the funds he'd expended to get them.

On the way to the vault, Kristić slowed, waiting for Cam to draw to his side. "There's more security on the floor than we accounted for."

Not as many as Cam would have liked, but Kristić had noticed. He'd missed the deadliest, though. The woman. Mel.

"Only a few extra," Cam said. "And not mine anymore."

"Good. Abigail, dear, wait a moment."

Abby halted a few steps ahead with Becca, and when Cam and Kristić approached, the other man lifted his hands. He appeared to be adjusting a cufflink, but in fact, he was showing Cam a hidden trigger. He tapped it once and a soft glow lit the pendant on the necklace he'd insisted Abby wear. "You're going to have to prove it, Agent Byrne, or two taps, and Miss Monroe will pay for your ruse."

Fuck, she was wired with some sort of explosive.

The light died in the necklace, explosive inactive since Kristić hadn't tapped the trigger a second time, but Abby remained deathly still, staring at Cam with unguarded terror in her eyes. He tried to impart in his stare that he wouldn't let her down, but she looked unconvinced. And absolutely repulsed when Kristić looped his arm through hers, tugging her along. She glanced back over her shoulder, and Cam mouthed, *It'll be okay.*

As they moved through the crowd toward the exhibit antechamber, Cam dipped a hand in his pocket, getting a better sense of what Jamie had dropped in there. A button of some sort. An SOS transmitter? A trigger to create a diversion? An EMP that would kill all the power? Maybe also kill the signal from Kristić's cufflink to the bomb around Abby's neck? He prayed for the latter, and prayed he'd be able to time it just right, if the moment presented itself. He still wanted to catch Kristić red-handed, to lock up Aidan and Nic's case airtight. He assumed that was why the FBI also hadn't moved in. They were letting him drive this, and he had to do so very carefully.

The docent led them into a private room that backed up to the wall where the artifacts would be displayed. Midway along the wall, there was a latch and a pass-through door, through which the artifacts would be transferred and arranged in a glass exhibit case on the other side. It'd make for a good reveal, if Kristić had any intention of actually revealing them. In the middle of the room, two rolling carts sat side by side, one prepped with a velvet display tray, the other transporting the voice-activated safe.

The docent held his hand out toward the safe. "Mr. Kristić, I understand your translator will be able to provide the necessary access."

Nodding, he approached the safe, went through the sequence to get to the voice prompt, then he and Abby spoke the unlock phrases in Serbian and Romani. The safe door opened.

"Very good, sir," the docent said.

Kristić drew out the tray of valuable items—the shining cloth and jewels bright, the papers carefully tucked in leather. Abby tried to step back, but Kristić tightened his arm, still in the curve of hers. The first sign things were about to go sideways. As they'd sketched out the plan this morning, they would wait for the docent to turn his back, to roll the cart over to the display case, and then Becca would knock him out.

Instead, he'd put out his hand for the tray, and Becca, who'd circled behind him, shot the docent in the back. The other cart broke his fall, but in doing so, the racket drew another docent through the door.

Jared shot him in the chest.

"I said no shots!" Cam shouted low, crouching next to one, then the other docent's body, feeling for a pulse. He felt that, and the rough edge of Kevlar vests, on both. He patted once, signaling them to stay down. "They're dead," he said, standing again, then to Becca and Jared, who was handing a spare gun to Kristić, "No more shots, or you'll draw more men down on us."

"They're already here," Kristić said, as voices and the thunder of foot traffic approached from the back of the museum. "We need to get out of here," he said, folding the fabrics around the leather binders and placing them and the jewels into a satchel he'd pulled from inside the safe. "Becca, let's go!"

She grabbed him by the arm, gun in her other hand, positioning them to look like hostage and hostage-taker once they opened the door to the main gallery.

"Give me Abby!" Cam demanded, determined to get her away from Kristić and get that bomb off her neck.

"I don't think so, Agent Byrne, and I say with complete certainty that you never went rogue. If I had to guess by the racket outside, the FBI's waiting for me on the other side of that door." Kristić dragged Abby closer. "She's my insurance for getting through them, and then she's going to bring this whole place down on top of everyone, including you."

No third party needed when Kristić could do the job himself.

"Let me go!" Abby struggled in his hold, trying to kick and claw her way free, but Kristić silenced her fight with a finger over his cufflink trigger. "Not another move. The door, Jared," he said with a nod.

Jared pushed open the door, exiting first.

A flash of red streaked by—the flutter of silk swirling around the wearer's lightning-fast combat moves, her arms and legs moving in precise, deadly fashion—and Jared collapsed onto the floor.

Becca charged out next, gun raised, her other arm around Kristić's chest, pretending to drag him and Abby.

"I've got Kristić and his translator!" she shouted. "Hold your fire or I'll shoot them."

In her haste, and perhaps shock at Mel's surprise attack, Becca had lost sight of Cam behind her. He kicked a leg up, hitting the pressure point at her wrist and knocking the gun free. He grabbed it out of the air and Mel grabbed Becca, tearing her from Kristić and tossing her to the floor next to Jared.

Kristić spun, clutching Abby in front of him, using her as a shield against Cam, who had his weapon trained on them, and a dozen other FBI agents also aiming guns at him. While they'd been in the antechamber, the patrons had been cleared out and the scene secured.

Kristić's number was up, and he knew it, his desperation escalating. "I have a bomb," he shouted, ripping off the cufflink and holding it up, exposing it as the trigger. He tapped it once and Abby's necklace glowed.

"Hold fire!" Aidan hollered from the rafters.

"You let me walk out of here with the artifacts and no one gets hurt."

That was a load of shit. Kristić had said as much to Cam seconds ago. He'd step one foot outside the door and blow this place to smithereens. Hoping his earlier prayers had been answered, Cam pulled the device from Jamie out of his pocket.

"I have a better idea," he said, mentally added another Hail Mary, and pressed the button.

The light in Abby's necklace clicked off.

"You're done, Kristić," Cam said.

"So you'll be a dead fed instead of a dead traitor." He yanked Jared's spare gun from his waistband and leveled it at Cam.

Then two things happened at once.

Abby slammed her heel into Kristić's instep, loosening his hold enough to slip away, and a shot rang out from above.

Kristić hit the ground, just as Abby slammed into Cam. He wrapped an arm around her shaking shoulders and hunched over, covering her in case of more gunfire. When none came, he straightened and looked up, following the trajectory of the shot that'd nailed Kristić.

The glare of a sniper's sight reflected light, then, once it was lowered, all Cam could see was the icy hot warmth of Nic's pale blue eyes.

Chapter Nineteen

Nic stepped off the elevator onto the FBI's floor, loaded down with coffee again. He'd snuck by his office for a quick shower and change of clothes, and when that hadn't chased away the fatigue, he'd diverted downstairs to the horribly hipster late-night coffee shop. Decades ago, when he was a young SEAL, he could have gone without sleep for days, but at forty-five, sleepless nights, no matter how enjoyable or action-packed, caught up with him. And if anyone tried to steal his coffee this time, they'd be in for a nasty surprise.

The FBI bullpen was busier than usual for Saturday at midnight—agents taking witness statements, giving their own, and processing paperwork for their suspects in custody. In Aidan's office at the far end, the SAC and Bowers were shouting, as they had been twenty minutes ago. Nic was no more ready now than he had been then to step into that ring. And what the fuck were they even arguing about at this point? Their suspects, *all of them*, were in custody.

He surveyed the bullpen again instead, searching for blue-tipped hair and finding none. He did, however, spy a messy topknot. Before he could take a step in Lauren's direction, though, a big hand clapped him on the shoulder.

"I owe you a thank-you," Jamie drawled.

Jacket and bowtie gone, sleeves pushed up, he still looked too handsome for his own good. Nic couldn't blame Aidan for falling head over heels for him.

"For bringing your husband coffee?" Nic said.

"Or tea?" Jamie nodded at the tea tag hanging out of one cup.

Nic jutted the tray at Jamie. "Hold this." He tucked the tag into the cardboard sleeve, hiding it. "If he takes a cup without asking again, then it's his own damn fault if he loses at caffeine roulette."

"Good." Jamie smirked, handing the tray back. "I like hearing him curse in Gaelic."

Nic chuckled, his first all night, and it finally hit him that this ordeal was over. And everyone he cared about was still standing. Uninjured even, save for Cam's grazed shoulder. When was the last time that had happened? He looked out over the bullpen again for the ASAC.

"That's why I owe you," Jamie said, quietly at his side. "Thank you, for saving my best friend's life."

Nic coughed, clearing his throat of the unexpected knot. "Thank the Navy for training me as a sniper."

"I don't just mean taking the shot. I mean never doubting him on this assignment. You know what all this has brought up for him?"

Nic nodded.

"Then thank you, for being on his side."

"Always."

Jamie's smile was a little too knowing for Nic's liking, so he moved the conversation on before questions could be asked or assumptions made. "You want to do the honors?" he said, turning the cardboard tray, and cup of tea, toward Jamie.

Jamie smiled wider as he tugged the cup free. "Go find Cam, and remind him we have a date on the court at noon."

"Will do," Nic said, even as he mentally rearranged Cam's schedule. If the day didn't involve them in bed for most of it, he was objecting.

Still probably wasn't the smartest move, but seeing a pistol aimed at Cam's head had muted many of the reasons for pushing him away.

He stopped by the bullpen desk where Lauren was sorting stacks of papers and transferring files between a flash drive and her computer, the light on the jump stick blinking. There were three others just like it on the desk. How she could tell them apart, he had no clue.

"Those the ones from AD Moore?"

"Yes and no." She held her free hand out, and Nic placed a coffee cup in it.

He lowered his voice. "Are you copying them?"

"Don't ask that question."

Plausible deniability seemed like a wise plan. "One of those also have what we need for Bowers?" he asked.

"Of course." She waved him off with her coffee, adding "Cam's in Holding Room Two, with Abby."

He crossed the bullpen to the holding rooms, knocking the door with his shoe. It opened to a dressed-down Cam, wearing those worn jeans and another gray FBI T-shirt. Between the tight tee and blue-tipped hair, if Abby weren't sitting right there, if a bullpen of agents weren't sitting right behind them, Nic would have dropped the tray of drinks and dropped to his knees.

Cam cleared his throat, and Nic's eyes shot up. Cam knew exactly what he was thinking, judging by his handsome smirk.

"Agent Byrne." Nic returned the knowing smile as he stepped past Cam into the room. "How you doing?" he asked Abby as he handed her a cup.

Dwarfed by Cam's tuxedo jacket, she looked drained, her eyes tired, curls limp, and shoulders hunched. She wrapped both hands around the coffee cup, absorbing the warmth. She was probably in shock too.

Noticing the direction of his gaze, Cam addressed his concern. "Already been checked out by medical," he said, as he took the chair next to Nic. He worked the last two mugs free from the tray, setting one in front of Nic and sipping from the other.

"Not my best day ever," Abby said with an ironic twist of her lips. "But Becca's behind bars and sis is safe."

Nic reached out a hand, covering hers. "Look at it this way... They can only get better from here."

"Holy shit!" Cam said, clutching his shoulder. "Is there an optimistic bone in that body after all?"

Nic side-eyed him. "Shut it, Boston."

Across from them, Abby laughed as she split a glance between them. "I'm guessing there was never a shot with either of you."

"How do you mean?" Cam said.

She waved a finger back and forth, the implication clear, but then her brow furrowed and her smile morphed into a frown. "Though, what you said—"

"Before, we were—" Cam waved a finger between them.

Nic had clearly missed a conversation somewhere. "Did Agent Byrne explain what happens now?"

She took a long swallow of her coffee. "Back to the safe house, then the preliminary hearing on Monday."

"We don't expect any blowback at this point, since all the players are in custody," Cam said. "The safe house should just be temporary."

"And I do expect the judge to take into consideration that you've helped us apprehend all the culprits," Nic added.

"What's that mean, exactly?" Abby asked.

"House arrest and community service is what I'll recommend."

"What about my sister?"

Cam shrugged one shoulder. "She's done nothing on our watch. The FBI's not launching an investigation."

"And the US Attorneys' Office won't be bringing charges at this time either. But she needs to keep her nose clean. You too."

"Thank you," Abby said, grateful but not as happy as Nic expected.

"Something wrong still?" he asked.

She stared down at her coffee, picking at the sleeve. "I feel like there's more I need to do…to atone for what happened to her."

She didn't have to name her for Nic to understand she still felt guilty over what had happened to Anica Kristić. "You couldn't have known how that was going to go down, that her own husband was willing to kill her for those artifacts. That wasn't your fault. *You* tried to prevent it."

A corner of her mouth twitched, her eyes darting to Cam. "That's what he said."

"For your community service," Nic said, "might I suggest a women's shelter, or RAINN?"

Her brow furrowed again. "Rain?"

"R-A-I-N-N. Rape, Abuse and Incest National Network. I've got some contacts there, and at the local shelters. I can put you in touch."

He ignored the slight intake of breath from Cam beside him, hoping he'd leave it alone. Just write off Nic's knowledge of those organizations as the natural byproduct of his casework, which if anyone looked closely, skewed more heavily toward prosecuting human traffickers, child pornographers, and other serial abusers than most AUSAs.

"Yeah," Abby said, after a deep breath. "That might be a good fit."

It might be a better fit for her than she realized, given how Becca had controlled and mentally—if not physically—abused her.

There was a knock on the door behind them, and Tony poked his head in the room. "Safe house is ready, boss."

"You're okay?" Abby said, brightening, as she stood.

"Yup, despite getting hit with enough tranqs to take down a horse."

Nic laughed, as he and Cam rose. "Because you're as big as a horse."

"I'm glad you're okay," Abby said, smiling wider, and Tony grinned back.

"Your chariot awaits, and by chariot, I mean a Ford Explorer."

As Abby twirled her hair on the way out, eyes checking out Tony's backside, Nic wondered how much longer the big man would be single.

He moved to follow them out and finally tackle the Talley-Bowers cage match. "You ready to face the music," he tossed over his shoulder, and barely finished his sentence, much less his step.

Hand around his upper arm, Cam jerked him back into the room, spun him so his back hit the wall, and swallowed his *oomph*, sealing their mouths in the kiss Nic had fantasized about minutes earlier and had intended to wait to claim until they were in private again.

Fuck it.

If Cam wanted to kiss him now—wanted to grind that hard body up against his, thrust a tongue through his lips, and groan his want down Nic's throat—Nic had no objections. Not after the week they'd had.

When Cam finally broke for breath, he rested his forehead against Nic's, nuzzling. "Thank you for saving me today."

Nic lifted his hands, framing the other man's face and leaning slightly back to meet his eyes. "I'm not risking you either." He drew Cam in for another kiss, taking control this time as he savored Cam safe and sound in his arms. He wove his hands through the dyed hair he liked too much, glided them over the broad shoulders and toned back that was warm through the thin T-shirt, and aimed them lower, on his way to grabbing two handfuls of denim-clad ass when a throat cleared beside them.

Cam didn't shoot out of his arms, probably because the person who'd walked through the door they'd stupidly left open was no longer FBI, and because they both knew she could keep a secret.

"Gentlemen," Mel said, not bothering to hide her smirk as they untangled themselves.

Cam found his voice first. "Thank you for the assist today."

"Glad I could help. Felt good to be back in the field."

"Don't get enough of that as TE's Chief of Security?"

Mel sashayed around the room, smirk still in place. "That job, no. The other…" Neither Cam nor Nic asked, not wanting the answer. Mel's bounty hunter business was booming, but they didn't need the details. "Is a solitary gig. Felt good having the team back together."

"That it did," Cam said, and Nic couldn't disagree.

She tossed her glittery purse on the table and took a seat, making herself at home. "Price, if you have a moment."

Cam looked back and forth between them.

"Why don't you go make sure Aidan hasn't killed my boss yet?" Nic suggested.

"He and Bowers were still shouting at each other when I passed by," Mel said. "Can't say I miss dealing with him."

"Which one?"

She laughed, and Cam did too as he drifted out of the room, the sound music to Nic's ears. The tune changed quickly though, as the smile dropped from Mel's face. She nodded at the door, and Nic closed it.

"I assume this is about the matter we discussed last week?" he asked, taking the seat across from her.

She opened her purse and pulled out a flash drive, TE branded, swiped from her day job. "Everything I could get on your father and his associates." She slid it across the table to him. "You need to be careful. These people are dangerous."

"How dangerous?"

"Yours wouldn't be the first blood they've spilled."

"Enough for a case?" Sure, he could take the shot when needed, but what he was really good at was building a case and putting bad people away, for good. That was how he needed to approach Vaughn, understanding it'd be one of—if not the—toughest cases of his career. He hadn't had a concrete place to start before. Now he did.

"You're the prosecutor. You're the one who determines if the evidence is sufficient." She stood, picking up her purse. "Good hunting."

If there was one thing the SEALs had taught him, it was that.

As he had been on Wednesday, Cam stood in the corner of the conference room, watching Aidan and Bowers square off.

"He's not a suspect!" Aidan shouted.

"He committed two robberies and helped perpetrate a near third one and the attempted murder of two law enforcement offers."

"He?" Nic said, as he followed Lauren in and closed the door behind them.

"That'd be me," Cam said, folding his arms. If he could burn a hole through Bowers's head, he would. Did the US Attorney not understand how undercover assignments worked? Or was he just looking for any excuse to tear apart their team? And why now that they'd bagged the case?

Nic stepped into the path of his imaginary laser beams. "Did any civilian, fed, or other LEOs on scene die today?" Nic asked Bowers.

"No, because they were wearing vests."

Cam stepped to Nic's side. "Which I knew, because it's protocol. My boss wouldn't send our people in without them."

"Your boss—" Bowers cut a glare to Aidan and back "—has a habit of breaking protocol."

"We handled the situation," Aidan replied, not deigning to address Bowers's accusation. "With zero loss of life."

"Kristić's not talking," Bowers said, changing the topic from a nonwinning argument to another one. The mastermind behind the heist was in the hospital again with another shoulder wound, Nic's aim perfect. "Neither is anyone else in the crew. How're we supposed to make a case?"

"Lauren," Nic said, with a nod to her.

She laid three flash drives down on the table. "AD Moore's."

Bowers reached for them; Aidan snatched them first. "FBI property." Before Bowers could object, Lauren laid down another. "Everything you need for the case against Kristić."

Bowers's gaze shot to Nic. "You were already building it?"

"Of course I was." He gestured around the room and took a step closer to Cam. "We were."

Bowers scowled at each of them, then scooped up the flash drive. "This better be enough."

"It is," Cam said.

Bowers's glower whipped to him. "And you're suspended."

Cam snapped, lurching forward, into Nic's outstretched arm. "You don't have the power to do that," Nic said.

"But I can ask DOJ to."

"Do you really want to go to war with me?" Aidan said. "Do you know how many of your cases I can tie up?

Send agents out on urgent assignment when they're supposed to be in court? Prioritize our cases over yours?" Bowers fumed, no doubt adding more strikes against them in his head. And Aidan knew it. "Byrne's my best agent, and my partner. You're not sidelining him because of a fucking grudge."

"Cam did his job, to a tee," Nic added, lowering his arm. "The artifacts are secure, the AD's flash drives are returned, and *no* lives were lost. Everyone's in custody, our CI is safe, and we have the evidence we need to close this case."

"We'll see if I agree with your assessment, Attorney Price." Turning on his heel, Bowers stormed out, the little ding on the elevator a fitting end to his defeated departure. The collective whoosh of air in the room, all of them releasing their breaths, was audible.

"You're on leave, for a week," Aidan said to Cam.

Cam shrugged. "I figured as much." Standard protocol after undercover assignments. Time to realign and catch up on the email and paperwork. "Thanks for not saying so in front of Bowers."

"Recovery, not suspension. Paid, you earned it," Aidan said. "You too, Hall, unless you need her for the prelim," he added to Nic.

"You got a copy of that flash drive for me?" Nic asked.

Lauren dug around in her jacket pocket, produced another stick, and tossed it to him.

"I'm set, then," Nic said. "I'll call if I have any questions."

"In that case," Lauren said, "I'm gonna go home and sleep for a week. Any objections?" None made, she hurried out, probably thinking they'd change their minds.

Aidan sank down in his chair, looking like he needed to sleep for a week too. "You two good?" He reached for his coffee cup, took a sip, then sputtered a string of Gaelic curses.

Nic bit back a laugh; Cam let his out. He'd seen the string of the tea bag when Jamie had handed Aidan the cup. Seemed Nic was in on the joke too.

"Do I have you to thank for this?" Aidan asked Nic.

"I believe your husband brought that to you."

"I'll tell you how you can make it up to me."

Nic smiled. "How's that?"

Aidan's brown eyes drifted down, to where Bowers's office was two floors below. "Get that asshole's job, and soon. Otherwise, I'm gonna kill him. Then Jamie's gonna kill all of you."

Nic chuckled. "Noted."

Aidan waved them toward the door. "Get the fuck out of here already."

They were still laughing when they reached the stairwell door at the other end of the bullpen. Cam held it open for Nic, following him through. "US Attorney one day, huh?"

Nic tilted his head—an ear up, an ear down—then stepped closer, backing Cam against the wall. "Unlikely, especially as I'm fucking the local ASAC."

That was what Cam wanted to hear. Running his hands up the wrinkled dress shirt, Cam grabbed two handfuls and yanked Nic against him. "Are you now?"

"Was planning to," Nic said with a wink.

Cam's jaw dropped open, exaggerating his genuine shock and amusement. "Did you just wink at me?"

"Lauren says I'm picking up your bad habits."
"Oh, I've got plenty of bad habits for you to pick up."
Like kissing in public stairwells.

Chapter Twenty

Nic swung his truck into the brewery parking lot, the safety lights casting an eerie glow through the low hanging fog. "I'll make this quick, I promise," he said, putting the truck in Park. "Eddie's still gone, so I need to sign a check for a vendor coming in later." He glanced sideways, grinning at Cam in the passenger seat. "Since I don't plan on coming back in today."

"Why's that?"

"I've got something besides paperwork in mind to keep me busy."

"Oh, is that right?" Cam grabbed his collar, yanking him half over the console and into another searing kiss like the one in the stairwell. "What exactly have you got in mind?" he whispered against his lips.

"That whole fucking the local ASAC thing, unless you have an objection."

"No objection here." Cam gave him another quick hit of those lips then shoved Nic back in his seat. "Grab a case of the pilsner while you're at it."

"Thought you were partial to the stout? Only a few cases left."

Slouched sideways in his seat, Cam lolled his head, a

soft smile playing at the corners of his reddened mouth. "I am, but the pilsner is your favorite."

A cluster bomb exploded in Nic's chest, heat pinging all around, expanding, filling his chest and forcing words up his throat he hadn't uttered, much less considered, in almost three decades. He lifted a hand, palming the side of Cam's face, the stubble rough and wonderful against his palm. "Cam, I—"

And then a bomb went off for real, outside the car. An explosion blasted in front of the truck, smoke and fog combining for zero visibility, which made seeing where the gunshots cracking the windshield came from impossible.

Cam didn't have to tell him to hit the deck; they both crouched, heads nearly colliding. Another round of shots and the glass windshield splintered, popped, then rained down over them.

"Who the fuck's shooting at us?" Cam shouted.

Nic had a pretty good idea. He popped open the console between them and withdrew his Beretta. He cocked the weapon and switched off the safety. "Cover me."

"Cover *you*?" Cam protested, readying his own sidearm. "I'm going out there, not you."

"This is my problem," Nic replied, reaching for the door handle.

Cam grabbed his trailing arm. "What fucking problem?"

Another round of shots raced up the hood and through the windowless front, shattering the one behind them.

"Fucking hell," Cam cursed, ducking low again.

"Just cover me, and I'll explain when this is over." He needed to get out there, before the shooter got on top of them. Given the angle of the shots, the sniper was high, so Nic had time, but every second Cam kept him here, was one more second Cam got closer to death.

"Dominic! Let me go instead!"

Nic reached his hand out, through the rain of glass, and palmed Cam's cheek once more. "I can't risk you, not for this."

Hard black eyes clashed with his, but ultimately shuttered. Cam turned his head and kissed Nic's palm, wisely not risking lifting up to kiss over the console. "Go! I'll cover you."

Withdrawing his hand, Nic scooted toward the door, popped the handle, and kicked it open. One last glimpse of Cam, at the face of a man who'd grown to mean more to him than any other in a long time, before Nic slid backward, rolling out of the truck and hiding behind the door. He waited for Cam to start shooting, then raced for the side of the brewery building. Gunfire nipped at his heels, but not as relentlessly as it had struck the car, the return fire from Cam diverting the shooter's focus.

He reached the side of the brewery building, flattening himself against the dark wood. There was a break in the gunfire, followed by the smash of metal across the parking lot, like someone jumping down onto a car hood from someplace high. When the gunfire resumed, it was on the same level as them, aimed right at Cam in the truck.

Mouth dry, skin burning hot, the memory of sand and blood trying to steal his attention, Nic forced it back and scrabbled along the wall, feeling in the dark for the breaker box. His fingers finally hit metal and he busted open the lock with the butt of his pistol, his utility keys inside the main building. Lock clattering to the ground, Nic ripped the door open and grasped the big red handle, levering it up and turning on every light inside and outside the brewery.

Light cut through the early morning dark, and the hail of gunfire ceased. Nic readied for battle, for the shooter and possibly more of Vaughn's men to charge them. Cam did too, scrambling out of the car, weapon raised. But the shadow on the edge of the fog disappeared back into the bank, footsteps fading.

Cam took off after the shooter, and Nic, propelling off the wall, barely caught him. "Boston, no!" He grabbed Cam's wrist and swung him back against the main building wall.

Cam struggled against the hold. "What the fuck, Nic? He's getting away!"

Nic held him tight until the squeal of tires cut through their heavy breaths and the blood whooshing in Nic's ears.

Letting Cam go, Nic slumped next to him, firing arm dangling at his side, as he struggled to catch his breath. "There're shot spotters in the parking lot. I need you to call the cops."

"Yes, let's get them out here. We need to report this."

"No, I need you to call them off," he wheezed out.

Spinning toward him, Cam shoved him back against the wall with a hand to his chest. "What the hell is going on?"

"They weren't trying to kill me."

Cam threw his other arm out toward the ravaged truck. "Those sure as shit look like bullet holes to me."

Under the bright lights, Nic could see how the picture would give Cam that impression. Hell, maybe Mel was right. Maybe these weren't just threats anymore, but if

Cam went full agent-mode on this, he'd discover secrets Nic never wanted him to find out.

Messes he never wanted to discuss again, especially with Cam.

"They were just threatening," he said.

"Threatening what?"

He skirted out from under Cam's hand, turning for the door. "Let's get inside."

Cam grabbed him by the waistband, tugging back. "Nic, what the fuck is going on?"

Nic shook himself loose, stepping over to the main door's keypad. "I'm going to tell you, Boston." He held the door open. "Just, inside, please, in case the shooter changes their mind."

That got through to him. Nic closed and locked the door behind them, passing Cam in the hallway and heading straight for the bar. He laid his gun on the end of the shiny bar top, raised the bar flip, and stepped behind the bar. "Call the cops off, please."

"And tell them what?" Cam crowded into the back bar with him. It was a spacious area, relatively, but with Cam and all of his Agent Byrne persona filling it, the back bar seemed half its usual size.

"Tell them we've got it handled."

"It's not my jurisdiction."

"Tell them who you are and that it's a threat connected to one of our cases. Federal jurisdiction."

"Is it?"

"Jesus Christ, Boston, now is not the time to argue. Please, just do it, for me." Low, manipulative blow, but Nic would play any card he had right now to keep the local cops out of his business.

Another few seconds' stare down, then Cam spun

away, digging out his phone and radioing in. It took some negotiation, but shortly after the first sirens reached Nic's ears, they began to fade away, diverted. He grabbed two pint glasses, filling them with Imperial Stout from the tap, while Cam wrapped up the call. He hung up and wasted no time crowding Nic back into the corner.

"Explain," he demanded.

"My father's having financial issues."

"You two are estranged."

He was a good investigator, having put enough of the story together already, no doubt from the other night and from Nic's silence on the matter.

Nic scooted around him and retrieved the pint glasses, holding one out to Cam. A peace offering that mollified him only slightly. Nic waited for him to take a sip, took one of his own, then said, "Before this week, I hadn't spoken to Curtis Price in twenty-seven years."

"When you came out?"

He nodded. It had been the most horrible week of his life—from graduation, to losing everything that mattered, to his father disowning him. "I walked into the enlistment office the day after I got my high school diploma."

Cam's brow knitted. "What does that have to do with—"

"No matter the relationship," Nic said, cutting him off, "I'm still the son of a supposed real estate mogul."

Not so much knitted now, as racing toward his hairline. "Supposed?"

"Dear ole Dad is up to his eyeballs in debt, and not the legal kind."

Cam drummed a thumb on the back bar near Nic's hip. He was picking up some of Nic's habits too. "Someone wants to be sure they get paid," he correctly surmised.

Nic took a long swallow of his beer, wishing he could burn this mess away in one of his fermenters, suck the waste down the pipes into the sewers where it belonged. "I don't want a cent of his money. They can take all of it."

Cam glanced around. "This place in jeopardy?"

"Not a dime of his went into it, but the loan sharks don't care. They either want to use me as leverage to get Dad to pony up, if there's even any money left, or they want me to make up the difference."

Setting his glass aside, Cam laced his fingers behind his neck and paced the length of the back bar. "Nic, that didn't look like just threats outside."

"I know," he admitted.

"What happens if they eliminate you?" Cam asked, the language technical, distancing.

Kill him, Nic said to himself. Vaughn could do it, make it look like an accident, or a hit. Make it appear connected to one of Nic's cases. He was a high profile prosecutor after all. Without any heirs. It was just a matter of forging some documents to turn Nic's estate over to his father, and in turn to Vaughn. Except doing so could expose the illegal loans and Vaughn's shady dealings. A poorly kept Silicon Valley secret, but a "secret" nonetheless.

"They'd rather keep it quiet," Nic answered. "Make their threats so I pay them and make it all go away quietly."

"I don't like this plan," Cam said, and Nic laughed at the familiar words. "You're a goddamn sitting duck."

"Now you know how I felt."

Cam hid his fuming scowl in his beer glass.

Setting his down, Nic reached out and laid his hand on Cam's side. "And I'm not just a sitting duck. I'm building a case."

"On your own?"

He shook his head. "With Mel's help."

"Mine too now."

He squeezed the other man's side. "I can't ask—"

"You didn't ask." Cam drained the rest of his beer, then slammed the glass down, turning to him. "If I want to build something with you, you need to be around for it."

"Build something?"

"Yeah, Price, building something." He ran a hand over Nic's chest, around his neck, and drew him into a lingering kiss.

That taste, his beer on Cam's lips, was way more addictive than it had any right to be. Nic pulled back, breathless. "This is messier than you signed up for."

"You were the one concerned about the mess."

"Because all this shit…" He gestured at the brewery around them, at the parking lot and shattered glass outside, at the picture from Aidan and Jamie's wedding on the photo wall behind the bar. "Not to mention—"

Cam kissed him quiet, tugging his bottom lip between his teeth and tugging a moan deep from within Nic's throat. When Cam let his lips go again, it was to start on his shirt buttons. "Exactly, not to mention," he said, working the pearl buttons free of their holes, "I want to keep you, *this*, to ourselves for a while. Build it quiet, like we build a case, and when we're sure it's solid, then we present it."

Nic shucked off his shirt, as Cam moved on to his belt and zipper. "I like that case strategy."

"Learned from the best."

"You better start getting busy then."

Cam grinned against his lips. "You set that one up for me."

"Are you gonna hit it?"

Cam dove a hand beneath Nic's waistbands, clutching his ass. "I'll tell you what I'm gonna hit."

Nic groaned again, half at the pun, half at the tongue teasing the sensitive spot at the crook of his neck.

"Keep tossing softballs, Price."

Nic righted his head, mouth at Cam's ear. "Are you going to start running the bases sometime today, Boston?"

"Right over the plate." Cam angled his face in, capturing Nic's mouth again, and that addictive taste eclipsed Nic's worries, for now.

They receded further as Cam trailed a path of kisses down his neck, teased his nipples with slow swipes of his tongue, then dropped to his knees, taking Nic's pants and briefs the rest of the way to floor with him. He nuzzled Nic's crotch, keeping up the torturous licks and nips. "Now, I'd like to learn what it's like to blow my man in his brewery."

Nic wound his hands through the blue-tipped hair, more than on board with that plan. Cam, however, grabbed both his hands and pinned them to the bar, exerting control as he had the other night. Nic was happy to second chair this argument.

"This is not you fucking me. This is me fucking you."

"Christ, the mouth on you…"

Cam looked up, devilish dark eyes twinkling. "Do you want it on you?"

"Fuck, yes."

"Hands on the fucking bar, then" Cam said.

Nic curled his fingers around the lip of the bar, nails digging into wood. He was going to leave dents for sure.

Cam had thought the sight of Nic surrendering—spreading himself over the beach house desk, arms wide, artful back on display, ass out for the taking—was the sexiest thing he'd ever seen.

Had thought maybe Nic standing behind his bar, dress shirt hanging open, pants and briefs around his ankles, blazing blue eyes rolling back as Cam took his dick down his throat might have eclipsed the first vision for sexiest sight ever.

He was wrong. On both counts. So fucking wrong.

Dominic Price, naked astride Cam's hips, reared back on his haunches, skin flushed beneath all that ink and shining with a sheen of sweat in the early morning light filling Cam's bedroom, was by far the hottest thing Cam had ever seen in his thirty-five years on Earth.

Head thrown back, Nic gutted out a groan each time he lowered himself down on Cam's dick. It was the furthest from buttoned-up, cool, calm Attorney Price Cam had ever seen the man, and fuck, to know he'd undone him like that made Cam's dick, clamped in the vice of Nic's ass, even harder.

As if sensing Cam's building orgasm, Nic righted his head, chin falling to his chest like a rag doll. Eyes heavy-lidded, his rugged face was a heady mix of pleasure and pain. "Close, Boston," he grunted.

"Thank fuck." Cam clamped one hand on Nic's thigh, the other on his right hip, over the rippling JAG tattoo and forced Nic to shorten his strokes as Cam powered up. "Jack yourself."

Nic rammed down harder, faster. "Don't need to."

Fuck, hotter still, and good to know for future reference, but tonight… "I wanna see it."

Blue eyes slit open, fiery ice, and when Nic took himself in hand, pumping, Cam stared in greedy lust, his own thrusts becoming frantic.

"That's it, Boston, that's it," Nic panted, until come covered his hand and Cam's torso. His ass clenching around Cam's cock was enough to shoot Cam off with him. Head falling back, eyes fluttering closed, his fingers slipped off Nic's warm, slick skin to the threadbare sheets. He clutched them in his fists, arching his back as he rode the waves and emptied himself into Nic.

When he came back to Earth, and the bed, Nic's long body rested atop his, Nic dotting kisses along his collarbone, gooseflesh rising in their wake. Cam lifted a hand, brushing back the sweat-drenched hair that had fallen into Nic's face. "Remind me again why we circled each other for months."

Nic rested his face on Cam's shoulder, looking relaxed for a change. "Because arguing is half the fun."

Cam kissed his forehead. "I'm too tired to argue tonight." He squinted as a ray of sun snuck around the bedroom curtain. "Or rather, this morning."

"No objection here," Nic mumbled, half asleep already.

"Up, baby, gotta get rid of the condom," Cam said, nudging Nic's hip.

His bedmate grumbled about moving, so Cam moved for him, rolling them onto their sides and carefully slipping out.

"So smart, Agent Byrne." Nic grinned mockingly, face half in the pillow.

Cam slapped his ass for the sass, while a contented, humming Nic wiped his hand on the sheet. He nestled down into the bed, not seeming to care that the sheets were a disaster, even before they'd made a mess of them.

Shaking his head, amused to no end by this side of Nic, Cam cleaned up in the bathroom, then did a quick lap around the house, checking locks and making sure blinds and curtains were drawn against the rising morning sun.

A swoosh by his feet, the *pitter patter* of claws on hardwood, and Bird, whom he'd fed and watered when they'd first gotten in, snuck into the bedroom ahead of him, hopping onto the bed with a *meow*.

Nic startled, but not enough to do more than grumble and attempt to shake the cat off from where he was crawling up his back.

"Fucking Bird."

Cam grabbed the trouble-maker and dropped him back on the floor, shooing him out of the room. "Spoken like a true Lakers fan."

"Wrong end of the state."

"Warriors, then."

Nic buried his head in the pillow, muffling his laughable words. "Worse, Kings."

"Oh, you poor baby." Chuckling, Cam slid back into the bed beside him. "But I understand, being a Red Sox fan wasn't always championships."

"Fuck," Nic groaned, snuggling up to him. "You're gonna be insufferable come October."

"Says the Giants fan."

He got a light snore in answer. Good; Cam didn't want anyone to see the stupid grin on his face. Nic had implied they'd be together for at least the next several months. Cam liked that idea, a lot, assuming, during that time, Nic didn't get caught in the crosshairs of his father's mistakes. Worse still that Nic was in jeopardy for a man who'd disowned him, who'd turned him out for being gay. Cam didn't even know the fucker, but no way he was going to let Nic get hurt because of him, more than he'd already been hurt.

Threats, Nic had argued, but Cam was far from convinced. Someone had tried to gun him down tonight. What was next? Worst-case scenarios ran through his head. Sure, Nic could take care of himself better than most, but depending on how much force was brought to bear against him, he could be injured, killed, kidnapped. He was Curtis's only son, after all. And a successful one in his own right. The loan sharks could try to ransom him or force Nic to deed over his interest in the brewery. In any of those scenarios, Cam didn't see Nic walking out alive.

Cam shouldn't have walked out of last night's scenario or the past week alive either, much less happy and with his psyche intact and the man he'd wanted for months in his bed, but Nic had helped make all that happen. Had anchored him when he'd needed it most. He had to do the same for Nic. Had to make sure Nic stayed anchored to this Earth, with him.

Extending his arm, he snagged his phone off the bedside table where he'd plugged it in. Nic snuffled, pulling him closer, then settled back down, snoring evenly. Cam brought the phone closer and texted Lauren.

Get me everything we have on Curtis Price.

He didn't expect the text right back, assuming Lauren had already passed out. Nic's father? Did something happen? Was there another attempt?

The rest of the pieces fell into place. Tonight wasn't the first time Nic had been targeted. The sniper at the initial botched raid. The car at the foiled South Park meet. The unknown calls and hang-ups.

Another text came in from Lauren. Shit, I might have said too much.

No fucking shit. He was her boss. She should have told him all this before now, if she and Nic had already put it together. Unless…

Nic shifted in his arms, reacting to his sudden tension. He'd probably asked her not to say anything, with how closely he'd played all this to the vest, and with Cam undercover on a dangerous assignment himself. Nic had been protecting him.

Now he had to protect Nic.

Everything, Lauren. Full report when we're back in the office.

On it.

A ray of sunlight snuck through the curtains again, splashing light across Nic's back. The giant tattoo came to life, the intricately carved GS standing out in stark relief. How had he ever missed it on first glance?

His biggest mess, Nic had said. Then tonight, when asked why he'd left home, he'd been holding something back. Cam had let it go, too eager to address the immediate danger, then too eager to get his mouth around Nic's dick. In the light of morning Cam realized Nic had glossed over the exact details of the falling out with his father. Cam sensed it wasn't just his coming out. He also sensed it maybe had something to do with Nic's familiarity with abuse cases and victim support organizations. Was it Nic, or someone else? This GS? Who or what, exactly, had driven him to that enlistment office the day after graduation? His investigator's brain wouldn't let this go now.

He sent Lauren another text. *And see if you can find anyone with the initials GS connected to Nic or Curtis.*

She sent back the thumbs-up emoji, and some of his tension rolled away on a quiet laugh. He darkened the screen and laid the phone back down on the table.

Relaxing into the mattress, he dragged Nic closer, half on top of him, so he could wrap both arms around the other man, holding him tight as he kissed his drying brown and gray curls.

He needed to know everything, if he was going to be ready. This was serious.

Cam wouldn't lose someone else he loved.

* * * * *

To find out about other books by Layla Reyne or to be alerted to sneak peeks and new releases, sign up for her newsletter and join the Layla's Lushes Reader Group on Facebook.

Keep reading for an excerpt from Single Malt *by Layla Reyne, now available at all participating e-retailers.*

Acknowledgments

First and foremost, thank you to all the Agents Irish and Whiskey fans who clamored for this spin-off. I fell in love with Nic and Cam while writing AIW, and I couldn't wait to tell their story. Your enthusiasm went a long way toward making that happen.

Thank you to my agent, Laura Bradford, and to Angela James, Deb Nemeth, and the rest of the Carina Press team for running with me on this idea and for your editorial, design, and marketing support along the way. Working with you all continues to be a pleasure.

And thanks as always to my beta readers, Kristi, Victoria, and Tera, for your invaluable feedback and encouragement.

Chapter One

Tonight was a top-shelf whiskey kind of night.

Cleared by the Bureau to return to work after an eight-month absence. Three-piece suit cleaned, pressed and ready for his first day back. New partner and new assignment waiting for him. Aidan didn't know the identity of either yet, but that didn't matter. He needed something—anything—besides alcohol and playgroups to dull the crushing survivor's guilt.

Pushing aside half-empties in the kitchen cabinet he'd repurposed as a bar, he dug the Macallan 18 out of the back corner and set it on the granite countertop. He'd just grabbed a crystal tumbler out of the adjacent cabinet when the doorbell rang. He pulled out a second glass, not altogether surprised by his late-night visitor. He left the glasses and scotch on the dining room table and crossed the living area to his door.

Checking the peephole, he confirmed his visitor's identity and swung the door open. "I wondered if you'd make the drive down tonight."

Melissa Cruz breezed past him, tossed her oversized Fendi bag on the couch, and toed off her studded Valentino sandals. "Least I could do, seeing as starting tomorrow you'll be making the drive up to San Francisco every day again." The offspring of an African-American ballerina and a towering Cuban refugee-turned-restaurateur, his sister-in-law, and now boss, sashayed on model-long legs across the living room while pulling her thick fall of dark curls into a ponytail. Aidan had never met anyone as graceful, or as deadly.

"Please," he said, closing the door behind her. "I know you're just here to mooch my whiskey."

"And you know I'd rather drink tequila." She pulled the cork out of the tall, slender bottle of scotch and sniffed, wrinkling her nose. "Gabe never could break you of this nasty habit."

Aidan pressed the heel of his hand to his stinging chest and swallowed hard, struggling for words. "Mel," he managed hoarsely.

"You ready for tomorrow?" she asked, obligingly changing the subject. She poured two fingers' worth into each tumbler and held one out to him.

Taking the glass, he fell into the chair across the round wooden table from her. "I don't know, boss lady, am I?"

Mel had been promoted to Special Agent in Charge of the FBI's San Francisco field office two months ago. A well-deserved promotion to a position she'd been gunning for since Academy.

"Your medical and psych evaluations say so, but *Dios sabe*, you're smart enough to fool just about anyone."

He took a swig of his drink, eyeing her over the rim of the glass. "Except you."

"Except me." She pinned him with her dark brown eyes, full of sympathy and concern. "I hurt too, Aidan, same as you."

He drowned his rebuttal in another swallow of scotch. He loved Mel like a sister, and he didn't doubt her pain, but no way was it the same kind of agony he suffered every day. From the hole in his chest where his world used to be, to the pins in his arm that, with every move, reminded him of all he'd lost. She'd lost her brother and a colleague, but Gabe had been his husband, and Tom Crane, his FBI partner for fifteen years.

"If you're not ready, you don't have to come back yet," Mel said. "Or at all for that matter. Between your trust fund and the inheritance from Gabe, you're set."

Aidan tossed back the rest of his whiskey, letting the burn slide down this throat and fill his hollow chest with fleeting warmth. As much as he'd enjoyed spending extra time with his niece and goddaughter, Katie, he'd finished his physical therapy, passed his psych evals, and was eager for the distraction of work. At forty-two, he still had plenty of agent years left in him.

"What've you got for me, SAC Cruz?" he asked, making his stance on work clear.

Mel emptied her drink and turned the glass over on the table. "You're off undercover work and long-term assignments. I want to keep an eye on you awhile longer."

"No argument here."

Gabe, an investment banker who'd worked all hours, hadn't minded his interminable absences. Now, though, with his family still tender after losing Gabe and almost losing him, Aidan didn't intend to disappear for weeks on end in the barrios chasing drug dealers or in grimy mob bars working over informants.

"Good." She tapped her manicured trigger finger against her glass, a tell that meant she was holding something back.

"What else?"

"I don't think it was an accident."

The same words he'd ranted for a month after waking from his two-week coma, only his allegations had been born out of shock and denial. He couldn't cope after learning his husband and partner were dead. Eight months removed from that terrible night, he'd progressed past pain and guilt-induced conspiracy theories, past angry finger-pointing at incompetent local detectives, to accept they'd been in the wrong place at the wrong time. That he hadn't swerved fast enough out of the way of an oncoming SUV.

The entire time, Mel hadn't spoken a word to him about the accident and now she was saying his grief-crazed notions had been right?

"What the hell?" He slammed back from the table, toppling his chair and surging to his feet. He kicked the chair out of the way and paced the narrow strip of hardwood floor between the table and wine racks. "Why are you telling me this now and not eight months ago? I drove myself crazy for weeks, thinking I'd missed some clue or that I should be out there catching the assholes responsible for their deaths. And fuck if I wasn't right."

She let him burn out his anger raging and pacing. Once he'd gathered himself, righted his chair, and sat back down, she rose and went to her bag on the couch. Returning with a small black flash drive and a red-striped restricted personnel file, she pushed the former across the table to him first. "This arrived for me on the day of my promotion."

He picked it up and turned it over in his hand. It was a generic model, something anyone could buy at any office supply store. "What's on it?"

"I don't know."

"You don't know?"

"The files are encrypted. It was delivered to my

home, no return address. I tried opening it on my personal computer, but I can't get past the file directory."

"You didn't have our guys try to crack it?"

"Given the circumstances of its delivery and the attention I received with the promotion, I didn't want to risk it."

"Because you think this—" he held up the flash drive "—has something to do with the accident?"

"Every file on it is dated the day of the crash."

He dropped the jump drive as if he'd been burned. It bounced, end over end, to the center of the table. "So that's my next assignment? Uncover the truth behind the accident?"

"No, that's not your assignment."

He furrowed his brow. "I don't follow."

"This investigation—" she tapped the flash drive with her nail "—is off the books for now. Someone above me shut it down as soon as SFPD ruled it a hit-and-run. Until we know for certain it wasn't, and who and why the investigation was shuttered, we fly under the radar."

He nodded toward the personnel file. "Is that someone you suspect is involved?"

"No." She nudged the folder toward him. "This is your new assignment."

Opening the file, he read as far as the top line, which identified the department the file belonged to, and slammed it shut. "Cyber?" He shoved the folder back at her. "What the fuck?" He reached for the bottle of scotch and poured himself another double. He'd agreed no undercover work, expecting she'd assign him to a local field team. Maybe legal or financial crimes, given his law and business degrees. Cyber had never crossed his mind. Sure, he was technically competent and logged an embarrassing mountain of hours playing "Destiny," but he was no hacker, nor did he know how to track one. "Do you really think Cyber's the best use of my skills?" He glared across the table, willing Mel to change her mind.

"Your skills as an investigator and field agent are the very reason I'm putting you in Cyber. Your partner and mentee has the hacker end of things covered."

"And who are you partnering me with?" He slouched in his chair, downing half his whiskey. A split second later, once her words sank in, he bolted to the edge of his seat. "Wait, did you say 'mentee'? Are you partnering me with a rook? That is the last thing—"

"Calm down. I'm partnering you with Walker."

"The Whiskey kid?"

Mel nodded, pushing the personnel file back in front of him. "Jamie's the best we've got in Cyber. He also shows promise as a field agent, though he hasn't been out there much in his three years since Academy. That's why I need you to mentor and assess him. He's committed to Cyber for two more years, so you'll work cybercrimes cases that take you out in the field."

"You'll never be able to put him undercover. His ugly mug was all over ESPN when he played."

Mel raised a disbelieving brow. "Ugly?"

She had him dead to rights on that lie. Opening the file again and flipping past the cover sheet, Aidan stared down at the younger agent's headshot. Light brown hair—short on the sides, long and wavy on top—piercing blue eyes, high cheekbones, a wide, easy smile. *Ugly* wasn't a word anyone ever used to describe Jameson Walker, dubbed Whiskey by the national sports media given his first and last names. As a married man, though, *ugly* was what Aidan had told himself anytime the sinfully handsome two-time NCAA champion crossed his path.

"Fine." He pushed the file away and threw back the rest of his whiskey. "The kid's never met a reporter or camera that didn't love him, which only reinforces my point. He's blown for UC work. Way too recognizable."

"That doesn't preclude him from all fieldwork." Frustration laced her voice. "He's got potential; you'll bring it out in him."

Aidan didn't want to rile Mel; he'd been on the receiving end of her temper more than once. But he didn't see how a partnership with Walker would work. He had no interest in cybercrimes and no interest in being partnered with someone so goddamn attractive while he was still reeling from the losses of eight months ago.

He scrubbed his hands over his face and into his hair, clenching the blond strands. "*Hermana*, this is a bad idea, for so many reasons."

Standing, she rounded the table and rested a hip next to where he'd propped his elbows. Hands that could snap a man's neck wrapped gently around his wrists, tugging his hands from his hair and holding them in hers. "Trust me, *hermano*. It may not seem like it with your first case back, or the second, or even the third, but I'm giving you everything you need."

"Everything I need for what?"

Her fingers tightened around his. "To solve their murders."

Standing inside the cave door, Aidan tucked the file he carried under his arm and peeked through the server racks. Interior to the thirteenth floor with no view of the outside world, "the cave" was what everyone called the converted boardroom housing Cyber Division. A few other agents sat at their workstations along the back wall but there was no sign of Walker.

Good.

Aidan needed the extra minutes to pull himself together. He'd caught maybe two hours of sleep last night. After Mel left, he'd booted up his personal laptop and plugged in the flash drive. He made it as far as the Finder window's directory of files with the date that made his chest ache, and got no further, though not for lack of trying. Realizing the encryption was beyond his skill level, he'd pinged a couple tech-savvy informants, and when they failed to get him through the wall, he logged into Xbox Live and messaged his "Destiny" buddies, hoping to find a hacker among the gamers. No such luck. By sunup, he was on his youngest sister's doorstep, laptop and doughnuts in hand, offering to get his niece ready for preschool if Grace would take a crack at the encrypted files. As head of IT at Talley Enterprises, she worked magic with computers, but in the two hours she'd given him, she managed only one wave of the wand, cracking a file containing two bank account ledgers Aidan couldn't make heads or tails of.

A voice inside his head, one that sounded an awful lot like his boss and sister-in-law, reminded him the quickest path to solving the riddle of the flash drive was right through those server racks—or should have been. Last night, between bouts of beating his head against the wall, he'd reviewed Jameson Walker's file. BS, with honors, in computer science from North Carolina, top of his crypto doctorate class at MIT, one of the Bureau's top cyber agents in only three years. But Aidan was reticent to trust a thirty-year-old kid he hardly knew.

A kid who'd broken every road course record at Quantico, stripped the test car afterward, rebuilt it overnight, and broke his own record the next day, which was why Aidan had spent the better part of his first day back culling vehicular data from his accident reports and redacting all identifying information. Walker knew how cars moved. Would he see something in the tire tracks the SFPD detectives had missed? Would something in the way Aidan's Tesla had crumpled lead them to the dark SUV that had never been found?

Before he started to spiral into the doubt and guilt that always colored his thoughts about that night, Aidan shook off the memories and straightened his tie. He was nervous enough as it was for a meeting with a man he'd passed in the hallway countless times. It wasn't just the jump drive in his pocket or Walker's good looks making him uneasy. He'd been partnered with Tom Crane right out of Quantico. They'd learned the ropes together and built a solid foundation of trust that kept them at the top of the Bureau's clearance board. He and Tom had been a well-oiled machine for fifteen years. Aidan didn't think he'd ever be so professionally well-matched again—definitely not with a partner twelve years his junior and in a division where he had little experience. He didn't know how to be a mentor. He'd never flown solo or been in one place long enough to take on that role. The pressure of doing so now was a responsibility he hadn't counted on when returning to work.

"No need to get gussied up for me."

Aidan startled at the deep, Southern drawl behind him. Despite the other man's presence around the office and on television, Walker's North Carolina accent always threw him for a loop. Not something heard often in the Bay Area and one of the many reasons sportscast-

ers and every secretary on the floor loved him. More
disturbing, though, was the fact Aidan had been so lost
in thought he hadn't heard Walker approach. Was he
that out of practice or was the other agent that quiet on
his feet, despite his six-foot-five shooting-guard frame?
Banking the question for later, Aidan turned to face his
new partner.

"Don't flatter yourself, Whiskey."

Grinning, Walker leaned his muscled shoulder against
the doorjamb. "You're the one straightening his Windsor
knot and playing with those shiny cufflinks."

Aidan stopped his thumb from absently swiping over
the gold and emerald clovers Gabe had given him on
their wedding day. Tugging his jacket sleeves down, he
gave Walker a discreet once-over, not letting his eyes
linger more than professional courtesy allowed. Dusty,
worn Chucks, battered Levis, a gray Giants jersey hanging open over a snug black tee, revealing a sculpted
torso and cut biceps. It took all of Aidan's considerable
undercover work to hide the spark of desire rocketing
through him. Eight months since his husband's death,
ten years since he'd felt a flicker of interest in another
man besides Gabe, and it was this one—his new partner, his mentee, a straight man by all accounts—who
stoked those embers to life again.

"I'm sorry." Aidan shook off the disturbance. "Did I
miss the casual-day memo?"

"Easy, Irish." Walker removed his baseball cap and
ran a hand through his hair, ruffling the flattened waves.
"Boys and Girls Club outing at AT&T Park this afternoon."

"Irish?"

Walker's blue eyes sparkled like he'd solved an impossible puzzle. "The cufflinks, the brogue in your voice that slips sometimes…" He leaned forward and Aidan fought not to react to the heady tropical scent of White Cristal cologne. "And I've only ever seen eyes that color on natural redheads."

"What color is that?" Aidan asked, putting aside the fact Walker had seen through the disguise he'd worn for three decades.

"Autumn," Walker answered, voice dropping an octave. "Like a pile of fall leaves back home, right after it rains. Dark brown swirled with brick red and flecks of gold."

Coffee with a dash of Goldschlager, Gabe used to say. But damn if Walker's description, spoken in that seductive drawl, didn't send another flare of desire scorching through him.

A flare instantly doused by guilt and propriety, compelling Aidan to snap, "Awfully poetic for a jock."

The sparkle in Walker's eyes died and all affability bled from his face. Shouldering past him through the server racks, Walker lowered himself behind the messiest desk in the mini-bullpen. On either side of two laptops, stacks of files teetered, pens lay uncapped, and empty soda cans rolled. He pushed aside a file heap, paid no mind to the papers he sent flying, and threw his heels up on the desk corner. "I don't think you came here to talk poetry, Agent Talley. What do you need from Cyber?"

Shit.

In his haste to shut down his own traitorous reactions, Aidan had swung too far the opposite direction. Walker was his partner, his mentee, and slinging insults would not earn his trust. Instituting damage control, he circled the desk and hitched a hip up on the opposite corner. "Mel didn't tell you?"

"Mel?"

"SAC Cruz."

Walker shook his head, and Aidan added another bottle of scotch to her IOU tally. "You've got a new partner."

"Who?" He dropped his legs and shot to his feet so fast Aidan barely had time to get out of the way. "Am I getting transferred out of Cyber?"

"No." Other agents were staring. Aidan waved them off and beckoned Walker to sit back down. "We'll be doing a bit of both. Mel wants you assessed for fieldwork."

"*We*?" Walker appeared adorably dumbfounded. "You're working Cyber now? But you and Agent Crane were this office's top field agents."

Aidan ignored the kick to his gut elicited by Walker's mention of his former partner and fell back on arrogance to hide his vulnerability. "You'll be learning from the best then."

"But I'm good with computers."

The hesitation and disappointment in Walker's tone surprised Aidan. Surely a guy his size, one who'd taken his fair share of bumps on the court, wasn't afraid of a little fieldwork. Aidan had also read the medical reports in Walker's file. The injury that cut short his NBA rookie year was no longer an issue. In fact, if Aidan had read the report correctly, it healed before the start of what would have been Walker's second season, if he'd returned. Something about his decision not to and his reluctance to leave the cave now set off Aidan's alarm bells. He'd have to dig into that and determine if it was going to be an issue going forward. For now, though, he had more pressing matters to deal with.

"I hear you're also good with cars." He tossed the accident file on Walker's desk. "These are field reports from a hit-and-run. I want your read on them."

Walker pulled the file toward him and thumbed through its contents. "What are you looking for?"

"The other car, which was never found. Deductions you make about the accident—speed at impact, directionality, etcetera. Any discrepancies between your conclusions and the existing accident reports. I want a new set of eyes on this."

"I've got a few identity theft matters to wrap, and court testimony tomorrow and Friday for a piracy case. I can look at this over the weekend and have a report ready Monday. Will that work?" The coolness was still there in Walker's tone but his eyes had warmed with a detective's hooked curiosity.

Aidan could work with that. He'd been married to a former athlete. Competition and achievement were powerful motivators for people like Gabe and Walker. "Monday it is." He deliberately infused his eyes and words with unconcealed challenge. "Impress me."

Don't miss
Single Malt *by Layla Reyne,*
and the rest of the Agents Irish and Whiskey series,
available wherever Carina Press ebooks are sold.
www.CarinaPress.com

About the Author

Author Layla Reyne was raised in North Carolina and now calls San Francisco home. She enjoys weaving her bicoastal experiences into her stories, along with adrenaline-fueled suspense and heart-pounding romance. When she's not writing stories to excite her readers, she downloads too many books, watches too much television, and cooks too much food with her scientist husband, much to the delight of their smushed-face, leftover-loving dogs. Layla is a member of Romance Writers of America and its Kiss of Death and Rainbow Romance Writers chapters. She was a 2016 RWA® Golden Heart® Finalist in Romantic Suspense.

You can find Layla at www.laylareyne.com, on Twitter, Facebook, Instagram and Pinterest as @laylareyne, and in her reader group on Facebook—Layla's Lushes.